# WHEN
# THESE WALLS
# CRUMBLE

SAHRA PATTERSON

**author**HOUSE®

*AuthorHouse™*
*1663 Liberty Drive*
*Bloomington, IN 47403*
*www.authorhouse.com*
*Phone: 833-262-8899*

*Published by AuthorHouse  03/25/2021*

*ISBN: 978-1-6655-2076-8 (sc)*

*KJV - King James Version*
*Scripture taken from the King James Version of the Bible.*

*"As Iron sharpens iron
So does one man to another"*
**-Proverbs 24:2**

# PROLOGUE

*Nina swerved for the third time to avoid a fallen branch. She was sitting up straight and peering over the wheel to focus through the debris and rain forcibly ascending toward her car. A pillar of lightening darted through the black sky overhead and Nina jerked with fear. This was insane. She had to hurry and this storm was not the friendliest weather to travel in when you're rushing. Her heart felt like it was going to beat out of her chest and she was sure if it weren't for the tormenting winds swaying the car and the pounding rain on the roof, she would be able to hear each beat of it.*

*The scenery outside her windshield was dark, rainy, windy, and eerie. Her focus was off and she kept pressing her brakes but there was nothing there in the darkness. Then before she could stop, she saw them. She felt the hit way before she actually saw the bodies ascend through the air. As the car screeched across the highway, and impacted with a tree, Nina's vision blurrily left her, and total blackness engulfed her senses, as she slipped into unconsciousness, but not before the two faces of the couple she had hit flashed before her eyes again; her mother and father.*

# To New Beginnings

*My God,*
*I thank you for all things. If it weren't for you, what I have and*
*all that I am, would not be. I know that there is so much I have*
*yet to become in your eyes, but I pray that you be patient*
*With me, and while doing so, send me that woman that my heart and soul*
*Desires.*
*Giving you all the glory you are worthy of,*
*-Jeff*

# CHAPTER I

THERE WAS A POINT IN a man's life when work was the only thing that he could control and for Jefferson Edward Smith III that control was defined by the way he expressed his love for drawing, creating, and building. When he was at his drafting table, with his pencil in this hand, he felt like he ruled the world; that it was all his. The fact that it came with power, and money, just sweetened the pot.

He was a 33-year-old black man who was worth more money than some people who had worked for 50 years could even dream of making. But none of that meant that he was arrogant, egotistical, or narcissistic, because though he may have only been 32, he had accumulated wisdom and a work ethic far beyond his years; something that his successful businessman, father had taught him. He may have been a black man rich in wealth and money, but one thing his father had told him to never forget; was that he was still a Black man in America, and no amount of money could change that.

His father had also taught him that success came from working harder than the people you have working for your work. And though spirituality had taken a backseat in his life, he had been taught to still fear God and to live and work by the scripture: *"In all labor there is profit: but the talk of the lips tendeth only to penury."* In other words: work brings profit, but mere talk leads to poverty, so actions do speak louder than words. And it was that same scripture that his father backed his success upon. To whom else could he follow behind, then a man who had built a real estate and construction company from the ground, from nothing to success; then made room to incorporate his son's architecture gift into the company, tripling the yearly clients, dividends, and business overall? His father had taught him quite a lot, and Jeff knew what money did to most people, the way it changed them, made them greedy and hungry for attention and power, but it wasn't in him to live for money, instead he lived to draw.

What Jeff had recently realized was that at some point in a man's life he had to face the reality that he can't survive on money, power, and work alone. He would be the first to agree that money could buy a lot of things, but true love wasn't one of them. There were other things that were necessities such as food, water, sleep, and a good woman to bring stability to it all. Such as the case with fine wine, fine art, and fine buildings, Jeff had a keen eye for fine women as well. But lately he had been lacking the exact fine woman he needed. He needed the type of women who was 97% drama free. He knew from a mother and sister, that there was no such thing as a 100% drama free woman; that's what made them so interesting. Until now, he had desired a woman who he didn't have to worry about dwelling on marriage and seriousness of a relationship, but instead just wanted to have a no strings attached good time. It was never a problem of having a beautiful candidate ready and willing at his call, but the beauties he had encountered were so mundane. He didn't discriminate in anyway; he had dated pretty much women of the rainbow in every shape and size there was. But they never left him feeling a need to precede with anything more than a good meal, fine wine, maybe some music and dancing, and a "Thank you for the date", flower arrangement the next day. Anything else could only lead to drama and misunderstanding when it came to cutting ties.

But lately…. things were different; an intelligent, real, independent, as well as beautiful candidate was a rarity. Those qualifications were rare in the guileless beauties he had wined and dined lately. He hadn't realized how sexy those qualifications were to him, until he came across Nina Jackson in the Westfield Memorial Hospital one day. Words couldn't describe the woman. First sight of her left him with the urge to leave his mouth hanging open but under professional circumstances he had to settled for an internal panting for her; a panting that shot heated sensations to the lower regions of his body. Her tight, curvy, figure was dressed in a powder blue, tailored pantsuit with a crème color blouse that dipped mid-cleavage in the front. The rest of the suit hit every valley and mountain of thickness that his mind could only imagine, was underneath that material. She had class. Her exposing just enough of skin made a man crave to see more. She had a beauty that radiated. No make-up, just pure natural beauty. And even though she wore a disturbed scowl, she was more beautiful than anything he had ever seen. She had these big brown eyes that were place delicately behind reading glasses. Her full lips left nothing else for a man to do, but to imagine nibbling on them right before taking them into his own to taste and determined if they were as sweet as they looked. Her skin was a smooth rich chocolate; so sweet-looking; and it left a yearning on his tongue. Standing there looking at her, with her hair pulled on top of her head in an unsecured twist, and curls tumbling down, he could all but taste her. But yet, it was something different about her. There was a beauty beyond the surface; way deeper than his eye could be cast upon.

Intelligent and beautiful all in one package, now that was a woman worth the venture. All the beautiful buildings in the world that he had seen, and created, didn't hold a candle to this woman. She was a piece of art that he wanted to find out just what went into her. But from the way things got started, she had no intention of letting Jeff E. Smith III, or any other man for that matter, anywhere near her, if it did not involve a professional interest in her job and her work. Jeff knew then he had to dedicate the same time, effort, determination and skill to getting to know her, as he did to doing his job.

# NINA'S BEGINNINGS

*Ok God,*
*It's been 5 years and 6 months. I feel like I've dealt with enough, but*
*Evidently you think differently, since it seems I'm always*
*Talking, and you're never really listening; at least that's what I*
*gather since I'm still facing the same problems, and the same*
*Loneliness. I've decided to make my own changes.*
*I've decided to accept my loneliness. Spend my time being busy*
*So that I won't think about my past or my problems. And I will*
*Take myself seriously, since no one else does.*
*So this will probably be the last time you will hear from me.*
*Thanks for nothing anyway,*
*–Nina*

# CHAPTER II

NINA STOOD IN THE MIRROR wondering if she should keep this dress on. She smoothed the soft material of the black dress down her thighs, then turned to the side and inspected the way the off-the-shoulder collar made her shoulders look. She added a silver heart pendant necklace, and matching bracelet, and the diamond stud earrings that use to belong to her mother. Then she stood back and observed her reflection in the floor length mirror before she racked her hand through the thickness of her hair, trying to control what the combing and brushing hadn't gotten earlier.

"Ugggh", she let out an annoyed sigh! She had changed four times, and none of her dresses seemed to look good enough. She couldn't for the life of her understand why she was making such a big deal about what to wear since this was the fifth date and she was determined not to get too emotionally consumed, too soon. Besides she had given up on love, it just merely did not exist in her world. She had come to the realization a little while back that God didn't intend on everyone in the world having their own Adam or Eve.

Jeff had called her on her way from the Community Center, asking could she join him for dinner at a client's new restaurant. She had agreed, considering she didn't have anything else going on; although he didn't have to know that.

That was 3 hours ago, it was now 7:15, and Jeff was supposed to be there at any minute and she was still wondering if she was presentable enough. She smirked at herself in the mirror as she slipped her feet into a pair of cheetah print and black sling backs. The funny thing is she actually found herself thinking about him often throughout the day.

Considering the rocky start they had gotten off to when they first met. She hadn't even wanted to be in the same room with the arrogant jerk then.....

Nina remembered she was working her usual mornings at the Hospital as a part-time Program Coordinator/Social Worker and Administrator for the Pediatric Ward that consisted of full time hours. All of those titles carried double the work, triple the duties, and she did it all without a complaint. Her morning had been jammed packed with presentations and meetings for an upcoming Children's fair, and the last thing she needed to hear from Carol, the front desk receptionist, was that the big wigs were in the building due to a Board meetings. Of course they would be peeking their heads into everyone's office to "see how things were running" and to "find out if the employees needed to discuss anything"? As if she really needed to see some stuck up, snotty men, dressed in suits, who sat around all day barking out orders to someone else, while they make decisions how to take money away from much needed programs, and add a private golf course onto the Hospital for the donors, board members, and doctors to "recreate". It just reminded Nina of what her father use to say, "Every job has its games you have to play to get what you want, it's not fair, but it's the money that controls everything, so don't hate the players, hate the game." The whole thing made her sick to the stomach.

Nina dropped the reports and files on her desk as she logged onto her laptop. She was deeply engrossed in creating spreadsheets when there was an annoying knock at her door. She let out an aggravated sigh and yelled, "Come in", without taking her eyes off the screen.

"Excuse us," a deep but sensual voice floated from the door.

Annoyed but lulled by the sensual voice, Nina lifted her gaze to three suits in her doorway. Two older white men who stood behind what Nina knew had to be the most beautiful man she had ever seen in this hospital in her two years there. He was about 6'2, mocha brown complexion, with hazel brown looking eyes. He wore a brown pinstriped suit that seemed to blend into his skin. He had a Michael Ealy look about him, but even more gorgeous. He was almost too perfect looking to believe.

He flashed her a to-die for smile that nearly turned her knees to jelly. "I'm Jeff E Smith, part of the Hospital Board. I apologize for interrupting; I can tell you were deeply engrossed with your work. Mr. Jones, Mr. Edwards and I, just wanted to introduce ourselves and insure things are well with the Pediatric Ward Programs."

Nina didn't remember when she stood up, and she had almost forgotten the other two men standing behind him, but she regained her professional stance and extended her hand to all three men. After giving them a brief summary of what was coming up with the programs, she was way happier to see the men go, than she was to see them come. She wiped the memory of the gorgeous Jeff E. Smith from her mind, ensuring herself that those good looks were going to waste on an arrogant suit of personality as him. She'd seen his type before. He was so full of himself, that she wouldn't dare give him the satisfaction of seeing her even take notice of his handsome looks. She was sure other women made up for it.

When she had pulled things together enough to pack up some work to take home; her laptop, her cell, and her briefcase, she readied herself to go grab something for lunch before she was off to the Youth Center. As soon as she opened her office door, Jeff E. Smith himself was beaming that gorgeous smile at her, from where he stood in front of Carol's receptionist desk.

He hoped that the look of annoyance on her face wasn't any indication of what her answer to his question would be.

"*Oh hell*", Nina thought. What had she messed up that quick that he was back? But she noticed his other two sidekicks weren't with him. She mustered up a professional smile as he approached her.

"Ms. Jackson, could I speak with you a moment?"

"Sure would you like to go into my office", she asked hoping he'd decline.

"That isn't necessary; I just wanted to request your presence at lunch with me this afternoon."

He spoke arrogantly, as he stated his invitation. But if he could, she could to. She may not have acquired the Ivy league education and the prep school grammar he did, but her four year degree from state university and her Master's in business administration had taught her how to have a professional conversation even if it was with an arrogant black man, who probably didn't know he was still black.

"Well Mr. Smith, I'm actually on my way to my afternoon job, if it's concerning business, I would prefer we discuss it here."

"Does that mean you don't eat lunch?"

Nina was getting even more annoyed. Just because he owned part of this Hospital didn't give him the right to question her eating habits. She took a mental breath so that her attitude didn't surface, and she maintained her professional decorum.

"My intentions were to grab something on the run and-"

He smoothly cut her off, "Eating and running doesn't make a successful days work. Please join me."

Nina glanced at the clock behind him on the wall. It was 12:15, she wasn't due at the Center until 2 anyway, and the man did have a part in signing her paycheck. She hated playing the politics of the workplace.

When she hadn't answered, he spoke, "You will join me, Ms. Jackson won't you?"

Nina flashed a reconciling smile, "Yes, I will."

She needed to say a quick prayer that she wouldn't go to the restroom and strangle herself before this lunch was over.

---

Nina lifted her linen napkin to dab at the corner of her mouth. So far she had drunk had two glasses of water, a glass of tea and had no appetite for the Greek chicken salad that sat before her. Her mouth felt like a desert, and all the streams of fluids she sent through did no justice. She knew the restroom would be her next venue, for eliminating those fluids, as well as going through with that strangle.

To this point she had filled Mr. Smith in on all the upcoming events of the Pediatric Programs, discussed the cuts in budget as well as staff, and filled him in on how she swung from the Hospital to the Center on a daily basis. His eyes and ears stayed on her every word while the smile never left them or his lips.

He had yet to reveal his agenda for the lunch, but Nina knew when she heard him say meet him at Romero's, a five star Greek restaurant, that this wasn't the average Tuesday afternoon lunch with some social worker form the Community Center on Lloyd street, on a Tuesday afternoon.

"Well I hope I have satisfied your curiosity of what the Pediatric Ward has in store for the upcoming year, Mr. Smith."

"Tremendously, and you did so in a very eloquent way, but would you please call me Jeff?"

Nina hesitated and didn't know if that was a good idea. What she was more afraid of was where this was going? He was basically one of her bosses, and here he was sitting here with this goofy ass smile, not really paying attention to any of her business talk, and now he was asking her to call him by his first name.

He must have detected her fear.

"Please", he repeated again.

"Okay", she said uneasily. Nina relaxed her shoulders from the business tense they had been in for the past 45 minutes, since it seemed their meeting was taking a turn toward more relaxed.

"I didn't request your presence for lunch because I wanted to talk on hospital issues, though you made it very interesting. I'm not even the regular Jefferson E. Smith who normally graces the Hospital Board meetings with his presence. It's usually my father, but since he couldn't make it, the next best thing is what they got, his shadow, Jefferson Edward Smith III."

Nina noticed his smile loosened. It had less business now, as well. She cocked her head slightly and gave him a surprised look.

"Nina, if I may call you that, I requested your presence at lunch because of personal interest? I'm a man who doesn't let opportunity pass by and take every one that I'm confronted with a determination. So after a bit of research to ensure I wasn't disrespecting a husband, I couldn't let this opportunity surpass me. And I would be very grateful if you would join me for dinner tonight so that we can continue to talk?"

Nina was first shocked, then flaming with anger. *How dare this arrogant mofo trick her into coming here with him for lunch, making her believe it concerned her job? And on top of that, what the hell kind of research did he do to find out that she wasn't married? She didn't know what kind of women he used to dealing with but she was not the one to kill over, just because he was a pretty face with heavy pockets. This right here is why men had been her enemy for the past year. They thought all women were only interested in was money and power, and as long as they were liquidating the first of those things out, the woman was suppose to be fluid with the sex. But oh no, this is one man who was about to get a rude awakening.*

She took a deep breath to ease her shaky voice before speaking.

"Mr. Smith, it pains me that I was brought here under false pretense and-".

He cut her off again, "I apologize if that is what you believed, but I never said this was business, you did".

Nina was getting angrier and louder, and him continuously cutting her off was beginning to piss her off even more. But what Jeff was noticing was how much more beautiful she was now than he had noticed before; her round face, big brown eyes, and smooth chocolate complexion was that of a satin doll's. He considered himself a man of class, one who treated a lady, just as she was; like a lady, but he couldn't help but have other fantasizing thoughts of her. Once again his eyes skimmed the swell of her breast that were peeking from the soft silky material of her blouse that she wore with that powder blue pant suit that was tailored to fit every curve and bend of her body. The temptation stirring within him urged him to want to see beyond the layers of the blue material and glimpse the story he was sure that her body could tell him. Her evil stare brought him away from those thoughts as he smiled at the anger upon her face.

"Besides the point, my time is valuable to me and I have much work to do. I must decline your invitation for dinner. Thank you for the lunch, but I must go."

Nina rose, clutching her purse in her hand as she did so. The hell was raging in her blood, because he was still sitting there with that damn smile on his face as if her words weren't affecting him. "And no, you may not call me Nina", she hissed over her shoulder, and then turned on her heels!

She didn't know how fast she was walking, but the breeze that hit her face as she went, was all to welcoming to her heated body. She waited patiently pacing while the valet went to get her car. She assured herself, if Mr. Jeff E. Smith III stepped to her while she waited, she would have no choice but to plant her foot up his narrow, arrogant, ass. Or arse, if that is what he preferred to call it.

Nina laughed at herself in the mirror again, because that seemed like just yesterday, but that was two weeks, 3 dozen of flowers, numerous boxes of chocolates, a whole lot of calmer moments without business ego involved, and numerous apologizes ago, and look at her now; fretting over a dress.

Janette, the one woman Nina trusted her deepest secrets with and who had the honor of being her friend, as well as her very impressionistic boss at the Youth Center, had been constantly teasing her about becoming the new Mistress Smith. Janette brought to her attention all the social columns and media exposure, (that Nina never paid attention to), that carried Jeff's face along side a different pretty, model-looking girl, every weekend. It sent a twinge of uneasiness in the pit of Nina's stomach, but as she told Net, she was just having fun on the 2 year long rebound from Q. This was nothing more, but how she measured up to those beauties he had been with previously, worried her just a tad.

The truth was, when he called, his sensual voice sent chills down her spine. She wasn't nervous talking to him, besides they had talked about everything, but looking at him made her giddy, just as it would any healthy woman who had her eyesight. She knew he was out of her league; he just wanted a change from the beauty queens he normally had on his arm, and if she could have fun and take her mind off her past 2 years while she did it, then by God he'd just be the one to help her. She wasn't going to get all excited about something that wasn't going to last, even though every time they were together Jeff expressed how he loved spending time with her. But Nina took it all in stride, because when this was over she'd have the same confidence she went in with, and things would be fine because she knew from the beginning that this wasn't anything permanent.

Nina had learned that Jeff was a die-hard businessman, who as he had said at lunch that first day, really didn't let an opportunity pass him by. He had been born into money, that his father had built up in a corporation of architecture, construction, and real estate from the ground; big commercial buildings internationally. Jeff had also been born with the same business mind that had made his father the millions that had pushed Smith & Smith Incorporated where it was. His Ivy League education couldn't teach him, what was already in his blood before birth. It was his life, but when he was with Nina, he pushed it to the back burner and put his attention to her. Attention, something that had been neglected to be given to her in her last relationship.

The doorbell rung, bringing Nina from her reminiscing. She walked slowly down the hall trying to get her breathing under control before she opened the door. She paused with her hand on the knob and took a deep breath before opening. Jeff, dressed in black slacks, a peach dress shirt and a black suit coat, stood there smiling that beautiful smile, showing all his pearly whites. His thick eyelashes and thick wavy hair made Nina want to run her fingers across them both.

She smiled, "Hi", and hoped that the nervousness that she felt so foolish about wasn't showing on her face.

"Hello, you look beautiful", he said looking at her from head to toe, then stepping in to kiss her cheek.

Nina made a mental note that this black dress was a winner, as she moved aside and let him in.

"Let me get my purse, and I'll be ready."

She walked to her bedroom to check her hair and the little makeup she wore. As she walked away she felt Jeff's eyes on every part of her body, and oh, it felt so good.

---

Nina turned on the light and dropped her heels at the door as they entered into the sitting area of her house. Jeff closed the door, and they both moved toward sofa in the middle of the room. Jeff sat down on the sofa and Nina stood over him.

"Would you like vanilla ice cream or strawberry", she asked?

"No chocolate?"

"I'm not big on chocolate without nuts."

He snickered, "I'm going to leave that one alone."

Nina smiled, "You know what I mean."

He was so relaxed now. When he had gotten the business call during dinner that he had warned her about before they arrived at the restaurant, his whole stature and demeanor changed. He was serious and rigid almost. But when it was over, he switched back to his cool self.

"Vanilla is fine."

Nina left to go to her small quaint kitchen. The two-bedroom house, with its island kitchen and side dining area, had been all she needed for herself since she had left Quinton 18 months ago. Since then she had made it as much home as she could.

She grabbed the turtle cheesecake, her favorite dessert, out of the fridge and the ice cream from the freezer, and set about dishing the servings out while she thought back on the evening.

Dinner had been great. It was a new Sicilian place, whose establishment had been the product of Jeff's drawings, and the building of Smith & Smith Construction. It was very romantic and the atmosphere itself reeked of class and glamour. Despite the frequent interruptions of the owner, who constantly stopped by to ensure that everything was perfect for them, and other clients that Jeff had to speak to, he had done nothing but let her talk by constantly asking her questions. Wanting to get him solely to herself though, she boldly asked him to come back to her place for dessert. He couldn't say no to the turtle cheesecake. He was definitely a man after her heart. When she returned to the living room Jeff hadn't turned on the TV, but instead was leafing through one of her Essence magazines. Nina thought to herself he probably normally read Forbes and Black Enterprise. When he saw her coming in he put the magazine down, and stood to take the bottle of wine and the glasses from her, while she sat the tray holding the dishes of ice cream and cheesecake on the large oval glass coffee table.

"Would you like some coffee or tea?"

"No, this is fine."

To Nina's surprise when he sat, he stretched his long legs out and sat on the floor. She smiled and joined him. It really amazed her how, right here in her living room was a thirty-three-year old unicorn; a man worth millions in assets, who reeked of the smell of power, and he was sitting on her floor, in her small quaint house. It wasn't the wealth of him that astonished her; after her parents died she had enough of insurance money & inheritance property to live comfortably on a tight monthly budget, without working for anyone. It wasn't the power that amazed her either; besides that was what almost sent her running in the opposite direction. But it was the fact that all that money and power didn't warp him into some snobby, stuck-up, arrogant jerk like she had previously thought he was. He was down to earth and actually humane. That had been a problem to Nina all her life: arrogant people who didn't realize that they were just like everyone else. She never really knew how to handle arrogance, beside just keeping her distance from people who carried the trait and filing them all under 'A' for asshole. Jefferson E. Smith III had proved he wasn't in that class.

They sat, talking about the Center mostly and some of the kids that came through, before long 2 hours had passed and it was close to 11:30. Jeff glanced at his watch. "Another late night; we both have to work tomorrow."

Nina smiled, she didn't mind because after he left it would take her hours to get him out of her mind before she could get to sleep. Just like last night and just like the night before when he had kissed her lips so softly, and left her to fantasize about him throughout the night. The thought of having him here all night skated around her mind. She could probably make some of those fantasies come true. She was 1 year and a half clean from any sexual encounters, and it was almost like hell. But going there with another man right now wouldn't do her any good, or him either.

"Yeah", she had to think twice before she blurted out, 'you can stay.' They had had a few discussions that had lead to the topic of sex indirectly, and Nina knew he was a man who could and had had his pick of lovers. She had let him know that sex was something that she didn't want to get involved with because of the relationship she had been previously involved in; a relationship that sex had become all that was left in the end. She was trying to strengthen herself physically, mentally and spiritually and having sex right now with a man that could just as easily leave her soon, would quickly destroy all the hard work she had put into her self over the last few months. Besides she knew that sex had only gotten her nowhere before. Jeff told her he understood and respected her stand. They both knew with all the attraction between the two of them it would only be a matter of time, but Nina was trying to lengthen the time. She really liked Jeff, but there was no need in setting herself up for the fall that she was trying so hard to avoid.

He helped her clean up and then she walked him to the door. He put his arms around her waist and stared down in her big brown eyes; the warmth of his arms around her engulfed Nina's inner woman. "I have never been this relaxed and had this much fun with any woman on a date before. You make it really easy and calming."

"That is hard for me to believe. You do everything with such charm, talking to a woman should be no problem for you, besides it's not as though they are listening. Your charm has them so captivated, you could say anything, and it wouldn't matter.

"That's the thing. You're not one of those women. Every time we are together, there is a part of me that finds it hard to settle after I leave you. I can't help but constantly think about holding you in my arms, and staring into your beautiful eyes."

Nina smiled and turned her head away.

He gently placed a finger at her chin and turned her eyes to meet his again; eyes that looked like they told stories by their depth. When he spoke his voice was deep and gentle, "I didn't mean to make you uncomfortable."

Nina took a deep breath to calm her self from his touch. "You're not. I've been thinking of you the same way lately."

He licked his lips in that way that gave her goose bumps. Momentarily, Nina felt she could have had an orgasm right then.

"I know where you stand on this intimacy issue, but I would be lying if I said every time I'm with you, I didn't think about making love to you, or that I don't think about being with you often throughout my days. I don't want to push you, as a matter of fact I find it intriguing to have found a woman who isn't throwing herself at me, but rather appreciates herself and what she has to offer without thinking it has to be sex. But there is one thing I would like to know; could you tell me if any of these thoughts have entered your mind at all?"

Nina hesitated. She wanted to say no. She wanted to be the strong one and push him away and tell him that none of what he felt was mutual. She was just having fun to get over another past relationship hurt. None of this meant anything to her; it was just something to pass the time away until something better came along. But she couldn't. She couldn't because despite the fact that he had turned out to be a perfect gentleman, something that almost was non-existent in this new millennium, she was experiencing something inside her that she'd rather die secretly knowing, before she admitted were her emotions getting involved. But she knew he was up too close in her space, not to know that she was lying if she said no. So instead she lifted her gaze to his grey eyes and smiled, "Yes".

"I just wanted to make sure." He leaned over, kissed her passionately; lingering for a moment on her lips, letting the swell of his tongue caress hers; a kiss that sent a rushing heatwave of temptation inside Nina. Before her hands left there resting place around his neck and explored other regions of his body and manhood, he pulled away slowly. Leaving her to breath uneasily, he told her goodnight as he left.

She was mad at him for sending that fire inside her to another level of hot. She was even more scared now, because she knew it was more than lust that was going on. There was something deeper brewing inside of her. A feeling that 18 months before, she had prayed wouldn't return for any man. Just one more pray that seemed to go unanswered.

After Nina watched him go, she cursed at herself as she made her way to her room to take a very, very cold shower.

# CHAPTER III

JEFF PULLED HIS SILVER S-CLASS Benz up to the big tattered building. It had definitely seen it's better years. The crumbling brick of the front looked as though one good shake would bring it to the ground. But being a lover of buildings and architecture he could tell the building and its history were still that of a greater time.

He got out and stood on the curb. There were kids of all ages scattered about the block in front of the building. The entire block, with its old buildings mostly closed and dilapidated; historical churches and worn housing community, seemed to all be from a greater era in history. If his mother had known he was here, she would have scoffed at him being anywhere near this part of town, but that was his mother; even she couldn't appreciate the beauty that still existed here.

He maneuvered his way through a group of small girls playing hopscotch and jumping rope. He nodded and smiled at a group of giggling and blushing teenage girls at the entrance of the building, as he passed them; and escaped inside away from the playing kids and the friendly sounds of wager coming from the game that some older boys played on the basketball court. The walls were collogued with murals of the outside scene he just came in from, and organized flyered-bulletin boards. He took a moment to revel over the bright colored murals. He was so enthralled that he didn't notice the petite, young, lady that was standing beside him smiling until she spoke.

"The older kids here take great pride in the work they put into this, and from the look on your face, it seems they've achieved their mission."

Jeff nodded still enthralled, "It definitely captures the eye."

"Hi, I'm Janette Walker, one of the Center's Directors." She extended her hand to Jeff.

Jeff finally took his gaze away from the masterpiece and took the soft delicate hand that was offered, into his. He could tell from Nina's description that this was the soft, delicate, fiery and bossy, Janette that Nina spoke so highly of. She was about 5'2, light brown complexion, short pixie cut, and a beautiful smile.

"Nice to finally meet you, I'm-"

"Jefferson Edward Smith III", she finished for him with a smile. "Even if Nina had never spoken of you so highly, it would be hard to not recognize you from the publicity your company and family always receives in the media."

He hated it when people noticed the media and tabloids, because whatever the media wrote, preceded any impression he could make when they first meet him.

"I must tell you, all that isn't always true." He smiled at her.

Net smiled back. Well the pictures were definitely an understatement she thought. He was even more beautiful in person. "Nina is in her office, second door on the left. Can I get you something to drink: coffee, water, or tea?"

"No thank you, I'll just go find Ms. Jackson. It was a pleasure to meet you."

"You too." Net reminded herself as he walked down the hall and she watched the stagger in his long bow-legs as he went, that she had to high five Nina later, because she had definitely hit the fine, man jackpot and nobody deserved it more than she did.

Still amazed at its artistic value, he made his way down the mural hallway in the direction Janette had pointed him. Nina was leaning on the front of her desk in front of two delightful little boys who looked to be about twelve or thirteen. Just as beautiful as always, she wore an off one shoulder beige sweater, that seemed to be sculptured for her full breast, and a flurry, knee-length beige and black skirt. Her thick calves and ankles were bare, exposing the same Nestle chocolate skin as that of her bare shoulders; right down to her stiletto sandals and French pedicure toes. She probably was going for the conservative look that morning when she got dressed, but exposing that little bit of skin, left a man's mind to wonder too much as to what else was underneath. She, not even knowing what she did to a man, probably wasn't aware of the fact that the boys in front of her, mouths were hanging open and their eyes were bulging not because they were enthused at what she was saying but because she was blowing their minds. He'd had the same look too many times himself at that age. They definitely would have wet pleasant dreams that night.

Nina glanced up and gave him a surprised smile, and raised her eyebrow suspiciously. He winked at her and took a seat while she finished up. When she was done, the two boys walked pass Jeff with puffed out chest and glared at him as if he was unwanted on their territory and in the presence of their woman. Jeff snickered and turned toward Nina approaching him. She was wearing that big smile that in the beginning he thought he'd never get to see. He rose and kissed her cheek, inhaling her sweet flowery scent.

"Come in", she motioned for him. "What are you doing here; I thought I was meeting you at the restaurant at 7?"

Jeff reached for her hand as she lead him into her office, "Well it was a beautiful day, so I decided to do something I hadn't done in a while; ditch work and enjoy some daylight."

Nina raised her eyebrows, "You, ditch work? You had a canceled meeting, right?"

He smiled, "Yeah." He had plenty to do, but she had been on his mind all day. So he decided to come down and see the Center that consumed so much of her time and that always brought a smile to her face when its name was mentioned. Besides what was a VP of the company if he couldn't ditch work sometimes.

Nina cocked her head to the side and smiled up at him. He was wearing a navy blue suit and a royal blue shirt and tie. He almost looked dreamy, and she knew how corny that was.

She knew Jeff and his Dad worked harder than they would ever ask their employees to. They didn't have to, but they did. That was another thing she had been wrong about when she met him Most people in their positon only talked about money and how to get more of it, every once in a while throwing in politics and how their republican views are running the country. They thought they were all that mattered in the world, and anyone whom wasn't in their class, obviously choose to be poor. They didn't know the half of it. She knew she could be bias in the matter of society and the rich, but she knew for a fact from her work experience that rich people rarely knew what was going on in poverty stricken communities.

Regardless, Jeff wasn't the average suit, though he wore them damn well; he wasn't happy unless he was in there doing the work too. He spent most of his awaken moments in meetings about new projects or in front of his computer or drafting table. Whether it was on the construction site or at his drawing table; he was a hands on kind of man, and she couldn't wait until those hands were on her. She blinked and shook her head to bring herself from her daydream. *What in the world was she thinking?*

"Well, it's almost 5, so I can show you around and then we both can get out of here."

Jeff followed her through each room and corner of the Center, hanging onto her every word. He noticed how she boasted and gave him the grand tour of the building as if it was the White House or Carnegie Hall. He could see nothing but pride of the place in her voice as she spoke, especially when she passed one of the kids who greeted her as "Ms Nina". And he still didn't believe she knew just how beautiful she was.

Her black and brown streaked hair hung straight to her shoulders today with a little flip at the end, and her sense of dress never ceased to amaze him. She was nothing he had ever experienced before. And soon, he planned to show her how much he appreciated her and her beauty.

---

Nina slammed her hand down on her buzzing alarm clocked and moaned. It was 6am, and though she didn't have to be at the Hospital until 8:30, she didn't need to lay there any longer either. She needed her run to help her get a start on the day.

As she laid there a moment, she remembered back on the days her mother use to come into her room, throwing open the curtains and saying, "Get up girl, it's time to thank the Lord for another day." The thought brought a smile to her lips. With that in mind, she jumped from the bed and started to get dress for her run; of course after making her bed, another childhood habit from the Jackson household that was hard to break.

Running was something she had picked up in the past few months. It had started as walking for relaxation, but she was proud to say that she had now worked up to 4 laps around her neighborhood, equaling out to 2 miles. And the day of meetings that she had in store, she would definitely need a clear, relaxed mind. She hated meetings. She loved her job, but the meetings were the worse. But thank God she had a job.

Nina went through the house opening blinds, letting the sunshine in. Then she opened her front door; standing there marveling on how beautiful a day it was. She did have much to be thankful for; a job, a new man friend who was unbelievable, her life, and her health. There was a time when all that seemed it would never be possible for her. She closed her door, and took a deep breath before starting her jog, and said out loud, "Yeah, thank you Lord, for another day."

# CHAPTER IV

It was Friday, and Jeff and Nina had not seen each other in over a week because Jeff had been putting in overtime on unexpected project. He had called her at the Hospital and asked her to come to his place for dinner. He was cooking.

Nina had visited Jeff's mini bachelor style mansion only once previously for a Sunday brunch, right before he took her to an off Broadway show at the Theatre. He had lavished her like a queen, by having roses, and a car and driver to chauffer them so that they could enjoy each other's company on the trip there. Nina had looked in awe as he gave her a mini tour through the 4 bedroom, 3 story. It was beautiful and that was an understatement.

It had almost been two weeks, since they had had that intimacy talk at her place, and Nina knew that things were about to shift into the sexual territory. When they were together, Jeff was attentive to her every move, he was affectionate, and his every touch was sensual to every one of her senses. Every time his hands grazed any part of her skin, or his kiss brushed her face or lips, he sent a fire through her making it hard for her to maintain decorum. When they had spent what seemed like hours kissing at the end of evening, she went to bed trying to extinguish her fire alone. Those nights seemed like hell. And although she had all intentions of going home tonight, she brought a few things in her carry on bag, just in case. A woman could never be unprepared, no matter how much her intentions to go home after dinner were.

When she arrived and rung the bell, Jeff answered dressed, the most relaxed she'd ever seen him. He was wearing lounging gray sweats and a tee shirt. (*She at first thought the man even slept in a suit.*) His feet were stuffed into some type of slip-ons, and he had the phone glued to his ear, *(that much probably never changed)*. She was feeling a little overdressed in the peach cuffed cropped button down shirt and the high-waisted, black slacks she was wearing. It was casual, but yet she would have been more comfortable in some sweats herself.

He didn't cease in talking, but paused long enough to bend down and kiss Nina's lips; just a light brush of his lips, that sent heat jolts all the way down to the tip of her toes. He closed the door and went back to the kitchen, leaving Nina in the huge hallway with its cathedral ceilings, and recessed lighting. She put her bag down beside the foyer table and followed all the sensual aromas to the kitchen.

The kitchen was big enough to be the center of a gourmet restaurant. It was clean, emasculate, and beautiful. Gleaming silver appliances nestled between black granite countertops, white cabinets, and in the mist of all that beautiful furnishing, a beautiful man.

Jeff was standing over a pot stirring. She peaked into pots to see noodles, Alfredo sauce, chicken, shrimp, and mixed vegetable. Nina had told him Italian was her favorite, and he remembered. There was a cheesecake drizzled in chocolate and nuts sitting on the counter of the island and she almost jumped in glee at the sight of it. She heard the strong soulful chords of Fantasia coming from the dining room and followed the music. The long mahogany table was set for two with candles, and flowers. Wine was chilling and salad was waiting. After a moment of bobbing her head to Raheem Devaughn savvy lyrics, Jeff came in.

"Do you like it so far?"

"You did all of this, for me?"

"Of course, I thought I'd make up for canceling on our date, and not being around the last week."

"You, did all of this?" Nina asked again, amazed. Was there anything the man didn't do?

"Okay, you got me. Kay started cooking before she left and advised me as to what to do to bring it all together and threatened me not to burn anything."

Jeff put his arms around Nina's waist, pulling her back against the hardness of his chest and kissed her behind the ear. His warm soft lips were brushing behind her ear lobe and Nina actually felt her knees buckling. The broadness of this body behind her providing support to her back and the heat coming from him was doing a number on her. She stepped forward to the table to get her composure back, before she began to sway into a drunken stupor from the effects of him being so close to her. Jeff slowly let his arms fall from her waist and smiled at her as she turned to face him. He had seen this often in the last couple of weeks; especially since he had shared with her how much he knew he was sexually attracted to her and how it was only a matter of time before he would show her just how much. She had been pulling away from him for weeks now when things got heated, but he was determined not to push her. It had never been an issue before to get a woman into bed, but then Nina wasn't just any woman. He knew that.

"Are you ready to eat?"

"Starved."

He pulled her chair out for her, and pushed her in gracefully, before rounding the table and sitting across from her. They sat, ate, and conversated; each enjoying the others company. After they had eaten, they both sat back, stuffed.

"So what's for dessert", Nina asked, remembering the cheesecake.

"You're not really wanting dessert right now, do you?'

"No, I couldn't eat another thing, just curious."

"Well I have an idea that may help with working off all that food." He rose from his chair and reached for Nina's hand. Nina just looked up at him smiling a moment. "I'm not going to bite you".

She smiled took his hand and stood to join him.

"At least not until you tell me." He said pulling her into his arms with a smile. "Dance with me."

Nina smiled at herself as he took his hand in one of hers and put his arm around her waist. She laid her head against his broad chest and she seemed to melt as they moved slowly to the sounds of Trey Songz.

"You move like this a second nature to you. You never said dancing was a hobby of yours."

"It's not, you just make it easy to dance with, so it must be second nature to you."

"With all the parties my parents use to host, dancing was an essential, but it definitely wasn't one of my favorite pass times." He smiled down at her. A smile Nina thought would make her do anything he wanted her to do.

"I bet there was never a dull moment with your family and all the glamour and glitz."

"Believe me, it's not all it's cracked up to be. Unlike my sister, I hated it. I enjoy quiet and quaint more. Much like I'm enjoying this time spent with you."

"You are such a charmer," she said astonishingly looking up at him, with those big brown eyes that screamed sexy to him.

"You always say that, and I'm not even trying to charm you. I'm truly being sincere with you; you can't believe that?"

"Jeff, you have been titled the 'Most Wanted Bachelor', by *The Charlotte Tribune*. You have a way of charming women by just looking at them and smiling. Even if you never said anything, they would swarm to you for an opportunity to be next to your wallet."

"And are you one of those women?"

"No, your wallet means nothing to me. I'm more concerned about being lied to, rather than being the one who's trying to get next to your wealth."

"Unlike what you believe, I'm not trying to charm you. Yeah, I can be a charmer when called for, which is the business in me to get what I want, but with you, you're not the average woman, nor are you business and I can tell that you don't put up with anyone's bullshit, so I know my dealings with you have to be correct and proper, therefore I'm being very honest with every word I say to you."

Nina studied him for a moment before she answered. He was serious now, his charming smile had left him, and was replaced with the same serious look he wore the day he first asked her to lunch.

"I'm sorry. I've dealt with people who haven't always been truthful in the past, which makes it hard for me to trust people; even if they are being sincere."

"Listen, I back up everything I say, always. If I don't mean it, I won't let it escape my lips. The past couple of months with you have been unbelievable, and I'm not intending to let any of this go."

Nina gave him a smile. He had to be unreal, she thought. He leaned over and kissed her lips slowly and passionately. Nina got that hot feeling again. This time she was determined to not let this moment be spoiled by her past insecurities of men. She lifted her hands to his shoulders and lost herself in his kiss. They had stopped dancing now, but the rhythm of the music was pulsating through their bodies, passionately while he was touching her slowly. Both of their bodies welding together from the heat they created. Without warning he quickly, pulled away and sighed.

He dropped the gaze of his hazel eyes, and looked into hers with a smile.

"I don't have to tell you what's on my mind right now, I'm sure you already know."

Nina wanted to high tail it and run, but at the same time her heart was beating in her throat, and giddiness was running circles around her stomach. "I want you to tell me", Nina smiled up at him.

"It should be very obvious that I want t make love to you."

Nina just smiled at him and tried to lick away the burning heat he had left on her lips as she turned her gaze away.

He was hoping that he wasn't hanging himself with his next question. "So is there any chance of that happening tonight?"

Nina smile uncomfortably. She started staring at some African statue on his wall that looked like something she had seen on a National Geographic show. There were a million and one things going on inside her head. A gorgeous man, who never had to ask any woman to sleep with him, was standing here and expressing to her how much he wanted to make love to her. It wasn't that she was afraid of the actual act, it's just she didn't want to become a notch on his sexual belt of honor. She was no dummy. She knew what the public said about his sexual reputation. Despite her efforts to be done with men on a physical level until she got herself together spiritually, the truth was the drought she was in was truly getting old.

"Jeff, I don't know."

"Nina, I'm not pushing you."

"I know, I just don't want tonight to happen, and it screws up the way things have been going lately. Everything has been going so well up until now."

"How would things change?" He was staring directly into her eyes and his eyes were now transparent in the candlelight. She wasn't sure what color they were now. *Why did he have to keep looking at her that way with those devil eyes of his? They made her loose about as much control as his touch did.*

"They could change as soon as you realize that all you really wanted was to have sex with me and you stop being the person you are now. Much like it is with most men, when they get what they want."

"Nina listen", his voice took on his serious business tone again. "If you don't want to make love tonight that is fine, I'm not upset. But the attraction is still going to be there, and whether its tonight or two months from now, we both know how we feel about each other, and I'll be frank with you, the past couple of months have meant something very special to me as well; something that I don't want to end.

Nina just stared at him. She didn't know whether to take him seriously or not? She remembered the time when she would have, (not meaning she did), slept with a guy on her second date, and here she was two months into this so-called relationship, and this guy was a dream come true and she was still hesitating even though her body was aching for him. She didn't want to act on her sexual frustration right now. That was the thing though, she was determined not to get hurt this time the way Quinton had hurt her so many times. It never failed, anyone who she loved, always ended up hurting her. She had blamed her parents for doing the same for so long, until she finally realized it wasn't their fault. *What could possibly go wrong from here if she did sleep with him?* It had been nice so far, and she had waited longer than usual. Not that she was the promiscuous type, but she was a 29–years old, grown woman who could count her lovers on one hand, minus two fingers. It's just she was very timid about sex and love. She always put her heart into both of them too much. But if he never called her after tonight, at least she could say she had slept with the product of a millionaire. But from the way things had gone since the day they had met, she knew Jeff would have been out from day one if that was the only thing he had been about. She had definitely treated the man in a way that would have made him run if that were the case. He was different, she hadn't figured out yet what made him that way, but he was. And frankly for the moment he had proved himself.

While she was battling in her mind, Jeff decided maybe he was putting to much pressure on the issue. He pulled his arms from her waist and turned to the table to clean up. He wasn't upset, but there was this unexplainable feeling inside him and it wasn't just a lust for her, but at the moment the best thing he could do is busy himself.

"I better get this stuff cleaned up", he said looking a little disturbed.

Nina grabbed his elbow, "Jeff, wait."

He turned to her, giving her a questioning look.

"How about we leave the cleaning up for later, and go upstairs now? I do want you to make love to me." Her heart was beating so loud in her head that she hoped the words didn't come out shaky. The words had escaped before she had a chance to retract them.

Jeff found himself stumped for a moment. He had never found himself having this conversation about whether he was going to have sex with a woman before. But then again, he had never went the extra mile to send all of his help away and prepare dinner himself for a woman, nor had he ever felt this way about any other women before. Normally women were going out of their way at his expense, not him at theirs. But right now, he felt out of control, something he never was with a woman or anything for that matter. His normally orchestrated actions and words were suave and right on point, but right now he almost didn't know what to do with his hands, or what to say. She was phenomenal and rapidly making him loose control.

"Are you sure you want this? I mean I don't want to take something from you that you will regret later, or despise me for".

She gave him that smile that made rain clouds disappear. "I'm positive."

Jeff took her hand softly and pulled her toward him again, kissing her gently. He rubbed his cheek against hers and whispered in her ear, "Nina, don't do this for me, do it because it's what you want. If you want things to be different, we can wait until another time."

"Jeff, I want to", she said before leaning in and wrapping her moist soft lips around his. When she pulled away from a very passionate kiss, he brought her hands to his lips and kissed them.

While holding one of her hands and leading the way through the taupe colored walls of his corridor, passing paintings Nina didn't know the names of, but had seen in art history books, and art galleries beneath the high cathedral ceilings, up the spiral stairs and to his master bedroom suite. Nina remembered the room from the tour. It was obvious he had someone decorate for him and he wasn't there all the time, because everything always was in place and clean, and in Nina's experience, men aren't that organized. But then again, he had people who devoted themselves to keeping his things that way, because it was their job.

Nina had fell in love with the room the first time he had shown her. The smell of pine and ginger filled the air. The dark wood furnishings sat cascade in a room that was ¾ floor to ceiling windows, overlooking the pool and small garden out back, and then the city of Charlotte, beyond that. On the wall opposite the double French patio doors that lead out to the balcony, was a fireplace, sitting area, a desk, and entertainment center. Outfitted in beiges and crèmes, it reeked of lux, but yet comfort at the same time. The bathroom was another room in itself with its separate shower, tub, and Jacuzzi. Nina thought she could live in this room alone, just give her a kitchen, she would be set. Hell the first level of her house could almost fit into this one room.

It amazed Nina how in the mist of all this luxury, Jeff appeared to be no different from any other man she had dated. And by just watching him walk down the street on an average day, (without the presence of one of his Italian suits, or his BMW), you'd never know he was walking money. He didn't put on the airs that many snobbish rich people did. It was only when he spoke that you could tell there was prep school, elegant pedigree and expensive education in his genes.

Nina stood in front of the towering king size bed that stood a foot off the floor, and whose covering had been turned down already, revealing ivory satin sheets, while Jeff let her hand go and moved to put on some music, and dimmed the lights. He was going out of his way to make sure she was comfortable; but right now the butterflies in her stomach were making her crazy like a high school girl on her first date. He came back to her smiling. His body's silhouette in the dim light made Nina assure herself that the way her body was aching right now definitely meant she was game for this.

Jeff pulled her into his arms, keeping his eyes locked on her. He rubbed the center of her back softly, and then bent down to kiss her with all the passion that had been building in him. Nina hands automatically began to roam. Before long he had discarded her shirt and her bra to the floor and Nina had unknowingly and caught up in the moment, taken his shirt off. It didn't take long, before Jeff was in rare from, showering kisses all over her and tasting every inch of her skin, but yet he did so in a sensual and slow pace. And then he brought his attention away from her breast long enough to look into her eyes.

"Are you sure you're okay with this", he asked?

Nina nodded and smiled at him, "yeah."

He smiled back at her and eased her onto the bed. Both fully naked now, bodies creating fire between them. The only thing that mattered to Nina as he affectionately loved on her was that her almost 2 year celibacy was coming to an end, and she hoped that this was worthwhile. She was going here again. *Why was she going here again? 2 years and she had purged the desire to be sexually involved with a man out of her mind. She had avoided lustful stares from various men, objected to sexual request, and had opted out of any dates that would even tempt her to end the night in a horizontal position because she was horny.* But what was really worrying her right now, was she had decided to do this not because of sexual need, but because she was truly feeling him emotionally. But *What if he wasn't getting any satisfaction out of this for himself? What if he was thinking that this would definitely be the last time he went there with her? What if …oh hell, it didn't matter, because the man was driving her literally up his wall right now as he softly kissed her inner thigh trailing his path to the center of her womanhood?* She was truly on the verge of tears of happiness. She was trying so hard to hold her screams and moans in, that she hadn't realized how she was clenching. He kissed her softly a few times, and then looked in her eyes again, something Nina wasn't use to.

"Are you okay? You were tensing up, like something was wrong."

Nina bit her top lip, she felt herself shaking with passion trying to hold in her orgasmic screams and it was hard for her to catch her breath. "No, I just wanted everything to be perfect, I didn't know you were going there, I'd rather had been freshly waxed and-"

Jeff interrupted her with a laugh. For a minute Nina felt like the butt of a private joke. When he saw the look of sarcasm on her face, he knew he had to explain. "Baby, it couldn't be any more perfect than I had imagined."

Nina softened her expression and relaxed a little. The way he was so frank and up front made her giddy and hungry for him even more. And then there was the XL Magnum that was voluntarily retrieved and put in place without the slightest indication from her. She exhaled, *Oh my.*

---

Nina laid upon Jeff's chest, naked and tangled among the sheets, listening to his quiet breathing. The May breeze coming in through the balcony door, was leaving warm whips across her bare skin. She could hear the waterfall of the fountain from outside. Still a little shocked from the lovemaking escapade she had just been on, she could see the outline of city lights of Charlotte, 10 miles away from his balcony doors. Looking out over that city, at that moment, after all the events that had taken place from the evening, gave her such a high, mind-boggling feeling. She felt like she was almost floating. This was definitely her nirvana; just so unbelievable.

It was unbelievable that this man could have so much going on for himself, but yet still single. There had to be a flaw somewhere, and Nina was afraid when she found it, it would be a huge one. So she had to be careful as to how involved she got with him. *What was she thinking, she was already too involved with him? She had just had a whole lot of sex with the man. Uggghh!*

She tried to maneuver and see what time the clock on his table read, without waking him. She was sure it was almost 11:30. When she got a glimpse, it read 11:57. It was even later than she thought, she needed to go.

Jeff stirred, rubbing his hands across Nina's bare back, while moaning. Nina looked up to see his eyes still closed. He kissed her forehead, and Nina placed a soft kiss on his chest. He smiled and opened his eyes slowly.

"How long have you been watching me sleep?"

"Not too long", she smiled.

"Don't tell me you don't sleep either", he smiled at her?

"Not much, but that's not why I'm awake now. It's getting late and I think I should go."

"You don't really think that I'm going to let you leave here at this time of night?"

"Jeff it's just-."

He cut her off.

"What kind of man do you think I am? Despite what you hear about me in the media, I'm not some womanizing animal. And though you may have heard this before, it wasn't coming from me. Nina tonight, I made love to a beautiful woman, whose beauty shows not only on the outside, but the inside as well. I know you have some hang-ups from a previous relationship that you are still bitter about, but I want to be around for a minute. And if that means I have to wait until you are ready to move forward, I have time. But don't push me away, and don't make yourself believe that I am the enemy. Let me be here for you, especially tonight. So please stay?"

Nina looked at him a moment in silence.

"If you want I'll sleep in the guest room and let you sleep here. I mean, a lot of good it will do since we've already had a lot of sex, in a lot of damn different positons; but hey, if it'll make you feel better, I'll go", he said with a sly smile.

Nina smiled. "Is this how you get all of your women friends to stay, with that speech?"

"All other women wouldn't still be here right now."

Nina didn't know exactly what that meant. "Okay, I'll stay tonight."

"How about the whole weekend?"

"Jeff!"

"It didn't hurt to ask. Besides what's keeping you from doing so?"

"Nothing, I just think it is best-"

"See there you go thinking again. You think way too much in moments like this."

Nina smirked, "excuse me?"

"You could stay, and we could do this all weekend." He said as he pulled her down for her lips to meet his. Nina didn't mind staying right here, in his strong arms all night, or all weekend for that matter, but she didn't want to go against all of her own principles so soon. This moment needed to be savored. As for the future, she'd have to play all that by ear.

Nina rolled over and squinted at the early sunlight bursting through the window. She opened her eyes slowly, and focused them enough to see Jeff standing in the door of the bathroom smiling at her, naked in all his glory. He had no shame in walking around like that, and why should he, Nina thought; his body was all too beautiful to hide.

"Morning", he said coming to her slowly.

"Good morning", Nina said back as he bent down to kiss her lips. She turned her head making his impact hit her on the cheek.

"What's that all about?"

"I haven't brushed my teeth", she said turning away from him.

He smiled at her. "Do you know how beautiful you are in the morning?"

Nina looked over at herself in the full-length mirror. Her hair was disheveled and she didn't look the way she would have preferred right now here with him. She suddenly wished she'd gotten up first so she could have freshened up, but after Jeff working her out into the early hours of the morning, she had gotten some much needed sleep in because she was exhausted.

"Jeff I look terrible", she said patting and brushing her hair down

"You're beautiful", he kissed her lips before she could move away again.

Nina managed to pull away and slide off the opposite side of the bed before he could grab her. She stood up pulling the sheet with her to cover herself.

"What's wrong now", he asked looking up at her?

"Nothing, I just want to get washed up, and be fresh before we go at it again." She had made it by him and was standing in the bathroom doorway, looking back at him.

Jeff was coming toward her, his broad shoulders square. "You're a damn perfectionist, do you know that."

"Look at the pot calling the kettle black. So hate me."

"I could never do that." He said looking down at her wrapped in his sheet. "I saw everything you have last night and I look forward to seeing it again. What's with the sheet?'

"What's with all the questions?"

"You act as though you have something to hide."

"Maybe I'm not that carefree with walking around naked in front of you."

She stated matter-of-factly.

"You're beautiful."

"You don't have to keep saying that."

"It's obvious that I do because it seems like a shock to you as if no one has told you that before. You should not let what negative things someone in the past has lead you to believe about yourself." He pulled the sheet from her hands.

Nina sighed as the cool air hit her. She wasn't a shame of her body; not totally anyway. She had some areas she felt could be more tone and less jiggle but who didn't. What she really was skeptical about, was Jeff seeing something that would make him realized she wasn't the perfect, tall, skinny, size 6, model type of women he was use to being with. She had big bones, curvy mounds, plus the thickness of Ruth Jackson's strong genes; a carbon copy of her mother's full hips, and thick thighs, strong calves, and full 38D cup breast.

She wasn't fat; besides she worked at her flat stomach, toned legs and firm thighs She was thick, but firm; "the perfect 10", Q use to say; which she knew got her a lot of looks from most men, but Jeff wasn't most men. He was the type who you saw in the social column each week with a different Beyonce looking, chic on his arm. There is no way he had even been in contact with a woman who had even seen the things she had done before and the scars and road maps her body wore showed it.

And then there was her tattoo; right in the center of her lower back. She was sure Jeff hadn't got a good look at it the night before. Quinton had been fascinated by spiders. So in her crazy state of mind, thinking the two of them would remain together, she had got the spider, crawling up the stem of a rose. Now she wished she'd never been so naive to do such a thing.

As for the scar, the darkened, raised, nine-inch mark was located just above her pelvis on her left side. In the dim light the night before he would have never seen it, but now they were standing in the brightness of the morning sun, there was no way he'd miss it. She hadn't been with a man since Q, and she knew it was going to be painstakingly horrid trying to explain the scar without details. She really wasn't in the mood for this type of conversation this morning.

Jeff dropped the sheet where they stood. Nina instantly raised her hands to cover the scar, but Jeff had already seen it. He took one of her hands in each of his and slowly moved them away, and then put his arms around her waist, pulling her warm body against his. He didn't ask about the scar. From the way she reacted to its exposure, he figured she really wouldn't want to discuss it. He rubbed her back while squeezing her as he caught a glimpse of her tattoo in the mirror; with a chuckled he whispered in her ear, "Nice tattoo."

"Thanks", Nina said exhaling in his strong hold. He did wonders for the self-esteem. When he let her go and kissed her forehead, Nina wanted to attach herself to him and make him screw her brains out right there on the bathroom floor.

He walked pass her, turned the shower on, and then turned back to her. "Do you care to join me?"

Nina tried not to be too eager, as she made her way to the shower and got in first. This man was blowing her mind.

# CHAPTER V

"**Y**OU GOT SOME DIDN'T YOU?**" Net closed Nina's office door behind her as she sat in front of her desk watching the glow all around Nina's head. "The fact that you didn't call me to tell me before now is questionable, but we'll talk about that later. You are glowing all over of the place. You slept with Jeff Edward Smith III?"

"Net, would you hold it down? A kid may come through here." Net was talking a mile a minute, but Nina was about to burst with excitement herself. Aside from her Auntie Laurie and Uncle George, Janette was all the family and or friend she had left since Q, and the only one she confined in. Though Janette was older than she by 3 years, was married, going on 2 years, with no kids, she was the best girl sister friend, Nina could ever have asked for. After the things she went through after her parent's death, most of her female acquaintances, (if they could even be considered that), merely spoke and kept a distance. Which was fine with Nina, she hadn't wanted to explain anything to anybody.

Jeanette was pretty, small and petite on the outside, but boisterous and strong enough to take on any monster at heart. She was the top professional boss, one-minute and could flip it into girlfriend from the hood mode when needed in a flash.

"My girl." Janette put up her hand to high five Nina.

Nina smiled and gave her the high five she was expecting. "You know you are not right?

"So, tell me, is millionaire dollar dick, better than middle class dick?"

Nina gasped at her, "Net!"

"Girl, I'm just being real. It's no one here but the two of us and you know how we do; so was it?" She crossed her short designer pant leg, and bounced her 4 inch heel sandaled foot while waiting on Nina to entertain her.

Nina sat down and stared at her friend for a second. The whole weekend had been incredible, but scary at the same time. She began to share with Net how her weekend went; giving all the right details, and leaving the sentiments out.

"So by Sunday morning I wanted to show him I knew how to do more than just screw, smile, and enjoy his generous bedside hospitality, so I got up early; starving from the overnight workout, and went to the kitchen to cook him breakfast. Here I am bent over in his fully stocked refrigerator in nothing but some boy shorts and a tank shirt; stuffing my face with grapes and holding cheese, turkey sausage, and eggs in my arms when I heard someone coming through the back kitchen entrance."

Janette giggled, "Who was it, his wife?"

Nina rolled her eyes, "No, it was Katherine, his housekeeper; I guess you could say?" She was very friendly, but Nina was extremely embarrassed. She felt like his mom had caught her. When Jeff had told her about Katherine, she was expecting an older lady who stopped by once a week to make sure everything was still in order from the cleaner's last visit. She was not expecting the beautiful woman who had stood in Jeff's kitchen that morning. Katherine was a saucey woman in her late 50's, with highlighted auburn hair that hung in double barrel curls to her shoulders. She had a very pretty face and beautiful bright eyes that made her look so familiar to Nina. Nina couldn't remember where, but she seemed like someone Nina had met before. She had one of those smiles that calmed and soothed whomever the receiver was. She put off a warm aura of comfort. She knew who Nina was and she talked to her like she'd known her for years. By the time Jeff had come in, she had taken the food from Nina against her wishes, and was cooking breakfast.

When Jeff came in, he lit up like a kid at the sight of her. It didn't take Nina long to see that aside from the fact that she was dressed relaxed but elegant, she was more than just a housekeeper to him. She couldn't put her finger on it, but something was different about their relationship.

"Honey, don't you feel the least bit of embarrassment. I've learned to accept whatever around Jay here. He's grown. He's also a very handsome man, and I'm just happy to see him with an equally beautiful young woman", she smiled at Jeff. She turned back to Nina, "You go put something on so you don't freeze and breakfast should be done when you come back down."

Nina returned her warm smile, "Thanks". Jeff took her hand and gave it a squeeze as she passed him.

He watched Nina leave the room and then turned to Kay and smiled. Kay smiled back and gave him a wink.

"You really like her don't you", she asked?

"Why do you ask that?"

"You cooked for her, at least I did; its two days later, she's still here, you told me about her and I still got to meet her."

Jeff smiled because she was right about the majority of that, "You've meet my dates before."

"No I haven't, you tell me you have a date, and that's the end of it. You never have them cone here and you never have cooked for them. Their names never surface again."

"She's different, Kay."

"You don't have to tell me that, the child was down here about to cook you breakfast. None of those other fast, anorexic, women you have dated, probably never even ate breakfast, let alone know how to cook it." Kay said all this with a flip of her hand in the air.

Jeff laughed with her.

Kay nodded after quieting her laugh. "I like her. I haven't seen you this relaxed around anyone but me in a long time; I think she's good for you."

"Come on, don't start this settle down talk again."

"I'm not. I also won't stand here and tell you what you already know about building a relationship with her before getting in to deep physically. But she's good for you. I see that already and I know how hard you go at something that is really worth your attention and affection." She paused while he took in the truth she spoke. "Now get out of here and go get ready for breakfast." She shooed at him.

Jeff came over and stood by her at the stove. He towered over her by feet and inches. He put his hands on her shoulders, pulled her close, and then kissed her forehead. No one would ever know what this little woman meant to him. She was real, almost more real than Mother. She knew and could at times control Jeff Smith like no one else could. With her, all his business control meant nothing. She was a rare gem; much like he was finding out the one upstairs was as well.

"Ni, I'm glad to see you smiling, seriously. I hadn't seen you happy about a man since Q."

"Don't mention him, and this is just having fun, it's nothing serious. Besides I didn't want to go down this road again, but here I am".

"What do you mean?"

"Net, I was trying not to do this. I was trying not to get in this type of situation with another man. I slept with him; like all weekend; over and over again. Can you imagine what he probably thinking of me now?"

"I'm not trying to make you feel better about what you did, but think about something: you two have been going strong at this dating thing for almost 3 months, and you are just now going there with him? And he stuck around this long? I think he may be around for some time."

"I guess", Nina said staring at her hands. What really had her so scared and uptight was the way she had been feeling. Net was right, when she finally got home last night, he called and they spent an hour on the phone just talking as if they hadn't been with each other all weekend. So it wasn't like sex was all they knew how to do. That had been the case with Quinton.

"Well, hey, you said you were at least having fun. Getting back to the first, Q stopped by this morning."

"Did he bring his new family", Nina asked sarcastically, not looking up at Net but instead busying herself by shuffling papers on her desk?

Janette ignored her sarcasm. "No he didn't. He said he was around and just wanted to stop in but he acted as though he was disappointed to see only me." Net hesitated before she went on. "He asked about you."

"That's nice. I've got a Parent Conference at 3:00, do you think you could handled the Girls Pow-Wow for about 15 minutes for me, until I'm done?'

Net knew Nina was done with that conversation and got up to leave.

She was also happy to see her friend had moved on to much better things. "Sure."

"Thanks, Net." Nina watched as she opened the door and her professional statute took control the moment her Jimmy Choo's stepped over the threshold. Q was not someone she was ready to give any real thought to. Too many wounds were still fresh and the scars not yet healed.

"Hello Ms. Johnson. Would you please have a seat?"

Nina gestured to the chair in front of her desk and closed the door and then took her own seat. She could tell by the attitude she'd already been given by Angela Johnson when she walked in that this meeting was not going to be a pleasant one. But after the woman heard the great things she had to say about her daughter Cassandra, she was hoping it would take a turn for the best.

Angela Johnson was what you could call… a lot. Nina knew from experience of working with people that you couldn't judge them by their circumstances or their outward appearance. But Angela's attitude told her story> She was the same age as Nina, and a single mother of two, but her face wore the lines of hard life & partying; tired from poverty and lonesome for love. Given different circumstances, and a smile, she could be a beautiful young woman. But at the present she was happy and content to settle for where she was; bad attitude and all.

Angela stood about 5'8, choco-brown complexion, round face with slightly slanted brown eyes. She wore little make-up and her hair was in micro-braids, and pulled into a ponytail. She was dressed in a pair of skin-tight, ripped black jeans, and a halter shirt that tied around her neck.

"Can we hurry up and you just tell me what this girl has done now?" She waved her colorful long nails in the air as she talked.

Nina took a deep breath to maintain her own professionalism.

"I understand you may have had to accommodate this meeting by leaving work, and rearranging your schedule, but I appreciate your time, and will try to make this as quickly as possible."

"I don't work, I just need to get home, some people do have kids you know?"

Nina winced at the sarcasm. She didn't know Angela on a personal level, but she knew the circle of females that she hung with. Most had kids at the Center and almost all were frequent goers of Q's club. She knew for sure one of Angela's friends held Q's attention sexually at one time or another. She just couldn't be sure if it was while they had been together. So, Nina was sure this sarcasm was a direct result of her association with Quinton. She thought all the rumors that had circulated after she had left Q had died down by now, but she guessed some people had nothing to do but to continue talking about old news. And now wasn't the time for her to get pissed about it. She had to remember her interest her was 12-year old, Cassandra.

"Well, I wanted to talk to you about Cassandra. She's not in trouble or anything; this is actually the total opposite. At the end of each school year, the Center begins to prepare for Enrichment Programs for the summer which teaches some of the kid's skills as well as give the opportunity to enjoy activities that they may not normally have the opportunity to enjoy. There are several local churches that get involve and supply the funding, supplies and transportation for these activities. Since there isn't always enough of room for all the kids, we have to make decisions as to who gets to go into the Program. Because Cassandra has been very active this year in helping other kids in tutoring, exceptional grades and overall behavior and progress, I wanted to make sure she benefits from the Program this summer. I believe it would help Cassandra tremendously with some skills for the future, while at the same time she can enjoy picnics, amusement parks, and getting to know other kids in the area. We just have to have your permission and fill out some paperwork. We need to know by the end of next week. Do you think maybe you'd let Cassandra participate?"

Angela smacked her mouth, and looked very uninterested.

"I don't know, I'll have to think about it. Sandra is s'pose to help with her baby brother through the summer. I do need personal time to myself and when she's out of school I expect her to watch him. So I'll think about it. If that's all, I need to go." She was gathering her purse, and starting to get up.

Nina was fuming with anger. Here she was going to ruin an opportunity like this for her child. Cassandra was just a child, who deserved to have a summer of fun, like children do. Angela had just said she didn't work, but yet she wants the child to be around so she can leave the responsibility of another child to her.

"Ms. Johnson maybe you don't understand the importance behind someone at Cassandra's age getting involved with activities as well as spending time with pupils her age; it could help shape her future and help her to gain knowledge for things that may influence what she does for the rest of her life."

"I heard you the first time and like I said, Cassandra is suppose to be there for her lil brother. I said I would think about it."

Nina slowly breathed in and out, and then counted mentally to ten. "Okay." She stood up. "You do that, think about it strongly, and if you have any questions feel free to contact me", she said handing the folder of paperwork to her.

Angela snatched the folder and turned to the door, and then doubled back with a look of disgust on her face as if something suddenly hit her. "I don't know what you think of these kids down here, but they do have responsibilities at home. You come here with your fancy clothes, your fancy car, your fancy education and the influence of your fancy, rich new boyfriend and think you can tell someone else how to raise their kids and what is best for them? Well I can tell you one thing, I was Cassandra's mama before you got here, and I'll be her mama way after you're gone. And if I think she needs to be in your Program I'll let you know. Otherwise you do your job and stay out of the business of parenthood until you get some damn kids that you can call your own."

Shock was the first thing that overcame Nina. It wasn't the fact that Angela was talking to her this way; she had been in this job long enough to know that many of the parents thought she was a snob. Another case of what she liked to call 'same race hate'. It was nothing new to her. What they didn't see was that she was just like them in a different circumstance trying to help someone out of the circumstance they were in. But now not only was this woman downing her for trying to help her child, she knew too much of her personal business. It was none of her business who she was dating. It had nothing to do with the matter at hand. She had already insulted Nina on the issue of Q and kids, now this? Nina had had enough.

She struck her hand on hip, finger in the air, ready-to-fire-off pose.

"For your information Ms. Johnson, I-"

Nina stopped mid sentence. Her gaze landed on the innocent face of Cassandra waiting outside the door behind her mother. The sweet, innocent girl who had confided in Nina about the life she lived that carried way too many responsibilities for a twelve year old girl, and the same little girl who had told her she wished she would one day be free like her. There was no way Nina could let her see her lose control. Influence and positivism was what Nina had to remind herself she was an example to a lot of these young girls. Instead of firing off, Nina dropped both of her hands to her side and changed her expression.

She cleared her throat. "Ms Johnson, thank you for your time. And it would mean a great deal if you would just look over the information I gave you about the Program and let me know if you have any questions."

Angela gave her an annoyed look, and then turned on her heels.

'Come on girl", she said as she passed Cassandra.

"Bye, Ms. Nina", Cassandra said in a soft voice.

"Bye-bye, Cassandra. I'll see you tomorrow." Nina forced a smile and watched as she tagged behind her evil mother. If the woman could spend half as much time being concerned with her daughter as she was in being in other people's business she could be a better mother for sure.

---

Nina hung her work clothes in the closet, then stood back and massaged her temples. It had been a horrific day. As if Cassandra's mother wasn't enough of a headache, she then had to deal with 15-year old Jaime from her afterschool class, telling her she thought she was pregnant.

Once a week Nina coordinated the teen-girls Pow-wow, a session where the girls could get together and talk about anything. It gave them the opportunity to have someone who cared listen, (Nina), and to get to know and help other girls their age with the struggles of teenage life. She thought it was important for them to take time to get to know each other, and unify, instead of hate each other for what they may appear to be on the outside, and not getting to really know each other; much like teenage girls do and grown women for that matter too. Nina's goal was to get them all to understand their importance to have a seat at the same table. Uplift each other and empower one another. Most of the times Nina observed and listened to the girls talk until they asked her for her opinion or she needed to clear some issue up for them. She personally looked forward to the sessions every week, and though the girls complained about the way Nina nagged them, and made them think sometimes, they had proven they enjoyed it too because they returned every week after.

They had just gone over their list called, "If This World Was Mine", that Nina had asked them to prepare the week before. She had gotten the idea from an E. Lynn Harris book she had read. Nina had learned that the kids at the Center accepted what life and circumstance gave them; it didn't mean they were happy with it, but they knew that was what they had to deal with. They could deal better than some adults could at times. Sometimes they put aside their dreams and wishes because they believed that their situations couldn't change. So she gave them the assignment to see what their dreams and wishes really were in life, without them realizing what she was trying to find out, although she knew they were hip to her. They really enjoyed it, even though at first they had complained about they weren't suppose to have homework assignments from the Center. Nevertheless, every girl had come back with her list.

After Nina had let the girls go, Jaime had lingered behind. She never came directly up to Nina, but Nina knew she needed something, and slowed the process of wiping the whiteboard down to give her time to get up her nerves. When she turned around the young girl's normally tough demeanor was broken, and what replaced it was a look of fear. She really was a pretty girl, but her potty mouth and hardcore attitude overpowered how beautiful she was and how softcore she truly was on the inside. Nina knew she had to play it cool to get her to talk and feel comfortable, so she didn't want to sound too eager when she spoke.

"What's up Jamie?"

"Nothing. I, um, was wondering if I could talk to you a sec?"

Nina looked down at the papers on her desk, and then realized she needed to give Jamie eye contact to let her realize know she was paying attention. "Sure, what's up?"

Jamie fidgeted, bouncing her weight from one foot to the other. When she spoke her tone was almost a whisper. "It's about pregnancy."

*Oh hell!* Nina wanted to run from the room, but knew that Jamie had to really trust her if she came to her about this. She moved to close the door, and gestured to Jamie to have a seat at the table, and then sat beside her.

"Okay, what about it?"

Jamie started staring at her hands and wringing them again. Nina noticed she was almost shaking. Nina placed a consoling hand on top of hers to make her stop. She was afraid the young girl would jerk away; most of these kids didn't like to be touched. It wasn't something they got often, but Nina felt the girl's nerves calmed under her hand.

"Jamie, you can tell me anything that's on your mind. Whatever you say stays right here in this room with us."

Jamie bit the corner of her lip, and then raised her gaze to Nina. "I might be pregnant."

Nina's head was whirling while she searched in it for the right thing to say. "You don't know for sure?"

"No." She dropped her gaze from Nina, and stared at the floor.

"I'm assuming you had unprotected sex?" It was no surprise these young girls were sexually active. Nina knew most of the young girls there were having more sex than she got. But the fact that they were having unprotected sex was the issue. If they thought they were grown enough to do it, they needed to realize the consequences, and take responsibility for all actions taken.

"Nina, it wasn't planned. We were unprepared. It just happened."

Nina felt her head becoming cloudy with a headache.

"That's no excuse Jamie. If you were unprepared that was all the more reason why you should have waited." Nina felt herself getting louder. She took a deep breath and closed her eye for a second, then reopened them, determined to handle this in a better way. "Okay, does he know that you may be pregnant?"

"No, I'm just two weeks late with my period. But if I am, I'll just do what I have to do, I don't need his ass." Nina detected the anger that rose in her voice.

"You two aren't together?"

Jamie rolled her eyes. "No, he's with some other bitch now."

Nina knew that whoever this boy was he wasn't someone Jamie expected to be around, which would make Jamie a single parent, alone, struggling. She wished she could grab the young girl and shake the knowledge that no one had ever told her, into her head.

"I think what you need to do first is to just find out if you are? Then if you are, we'll deal with what comes next. Until then, I'm going to give you the number to the clinic-"

"I don't want to go to no clinic, Nina, too many people trying to be up in my business."

Nina wanted to tell her, she was too young to have any business, because if she had any she would have taken care of her business and had some protection, but decided not to. She raised her hand to her now throbbing temples. "Okay, how are you getting home?" Nina glanced at her watch. She knew the Center's van had left by now.

Jamie shrugged her shoulders in a nonchalant way. "It's just a few blocks away, I'll walk."

She knew she was going beyond her duty here, but at the moment, the girl needed some guidance. "Do you mind if I take you home?"

Jamie looked startled.

"I just want to talk to you a little more, and stop by the drug store to pick you something up on the way, okay?"

Nina watched as a smile spread across the girl's face as she realized what Nina was talking about; she relaxed a little, and then nodded.

"That way it will be a little more discreet. We'll start there, and maybe you can get some sleep tonight knowing one way or the other, alright?

"Alright." Jamie was smiling a relieved smile, but Nina didn't think she should be happy so soon.

Nina got up to pack up her briefcase before they headed out. And she knew she'd sleep a little better knowing as well.

And now in the privacy of her home, she was so glad this day was over. She had left her cell phone # for Jamie to call her when she found out. Before Nina had got home, which was only 20 minutes away, Jamie had called and told her she was in the clear. The girl was literally laughing and screaming on the other end. Nina made her promise she'd go to the clinic and get some free testing, as well as literature about sexually transmitted diseases and samples of contraceptive, before this happened again. Jamie promised she would. As Nina had hung up, she thanked God for saving one from the cycle.

All she wanted to do now was cook dinner and wait on Jeff to arrive. It would be nice to be with him; just his presence; him being there would make all of today's headaches disappear.

Just as she was sliding the chicken into the oven, her telephone rung. She glanced at her microwave clock, it was 6:05. It had to be her Auntie Laurie. It was due time for her every three day phone call. Without looking at the caller ID, she answered, "Hello".

"Hi Beautiful."

Nina's heart skipped a beat at the sensual voice on the other end.

"Hello, handsome. How are you?"

"I would be doing better, if I was there with you."

"So why aren't you?"

"That's sort of the problem."

Nina was silent. She knew what was coming.

"One of the CAD guys haven't finished enough of the plans for his deadline tomorrow, and we're running into some code problems. So I need to make sure this is going to come together right before I can leave here tonight."

Nina didn't say anything.

"Sweetie, are you there?"

"Yeah."

Jeff knew she was not happy. It was obvious in her tone, or lack of it, since she wasn't saying much. "I would come over after, but it may be late."

Nina finally found her voice. "That's okay. Just give me a call later, okay?"

"I sure will."

Nina hung up the phone and sighed; another lonely night.

She reached into her wine rack for a bottle. She read the label. It looked like Merlot would have to keep her company, and give her that fuzzy warm feeling tonight since Jeff wouldn't be.

# CHAPTER VI

Nina thumbed through an architect magazine in the lobby of Jeff's office. Cynthia, his assistant, said he was meeting with his father and some others about a project in Florida. Jeff had told Cynthia to tell Nina when she arrived to please wait; he'd be out shortly. Nina had been waiting for about 15 minutes when the door to Jeff's office opened. He, his father and two older gentlemen stepped out, still talking. Jeff escorted his father and the two men to the elevator then turned to Nina. He looked overly tired to Nina.

But even the lack of sleep he had had the past two days, didn't blur his vision enough that he couldn't enjoy the sight of the beautiful woman that waited there for him. She wore a yellow, midi shirt dress that showed just a bit of skin through a cut out in the center of the back. A pair of nude stiletto sandals, matching bag, a gold pendant necklace and good studs as accessories completed her look. Her cropped bob-like mane was hanging straight and pulled back behind her ears. She smiled at him as he approached, and all he could think was sunshine; and he wanted to kick himself for what he was about to do.

"Nina I apologize."

That sparkling smile was killing him, "That's okay", she said.

He took her in his arms into a tight hug and took a long whiff of her perfume before he let her go. She smelled subtly of sweetness. "You are not going to be smiling like that when I share the news I have with you."

"You have to cancel lunch, don't you?" Her smile faded a little.

"Yeah, but that's not the worse part. Because of the meeting I just had, I have to leave for Miami this evening. There is a construction site that is making quiet a mess of the designed project and I've got to go down and straighten some things out before a phase deadline on Monday."

Nina's heart sanked. He had just got back in town two days ago, and here he was leaving again. Prior to that he had canceled dinner and the one night they had gotten together, he was so tired that Nina had forced him to go home to get some sleep. She might as well be having a long distance relationship, because out of those two days since he had been back, this lunch was the first opportunity they had to see each other, and now that was cancelled.

Jeff detected her disappointment, "Look, I'm sorry. I know we were suppose to be spending some time together this weekend."

Nina tried to smile, "Really Jeff, it is okay." Ruth Jackson had taught her well in the department of being a lady instead of making scenes in public places. Although she had steered away from her ladylike qualities in the past and showed her true colors, she had progressed, and now she wouldn't give Jeff the cussing that was sitting on the tip of her tongue. Besides, there was no real reason why she was so upset, but deep down there was something going on with her emotions that she didn't quite want to surface right now. It was too soon, and she didn't want to feel the way they were making her feel.

Oh, but Jeff saw a fire flicker of anger in her eyes. "Nina, I can tell you are upset. I have an idea; why don't you come with me? You can miss one day of work tomorrow, can't you? I'll arrange for my charter to fly us back Sunday night in time for you to be back at work on Monday."

Nina widened her eyes. Being upset went jumping out the 4-story building and splattered on the sidewalk, downstairs. "Are you serious?"

"You don't want to go?"

Nina glanced over at Cynthia, who was looking at them smiling. She winked at Nina. "Of course, I do. I just thought you had a lot of work to do, and you wouldn't want me there in the way."

"Would I have asked you if I didn't want you to go? So what is it going to be?"

Nina lifted her eyebrows in shock, "Sure." She knew if she didn't hurry up and say yes, her consciences would change her mind, and she'd say no.

"Okay. Cynthia see about getting us a private charter to Miami." He

turned back to Nina, "I hate to leave you, but I've got to do some things before we go. I'll have someone pick you up around 6 to take you to the airport." He turned to Cynthia, "could you get a car also ...?"

Cynthia cut him off with a wave of her hand, "I got it, I got it." He turned back to Nina and lowered his lips to her hand, and then left her standing in the lobby, still in a daze. She turned to Cynthia, "Did that just really happen?"

Cynthia beamed at her, "I believe so. And the smart thing to do would be to go. I have been working for Jeff for 5 years now, and I have never seen him do something like this"

Nina finally was able to move herself from the quicksand that had seemed to be holding her feet. She thanked Cynthia, and set out to call Net, and pack. She was going to Miami, with the he had asked her, because he wanted to be with her. Unbelievable.

---

Nina glanced over at Jeff's laptop. There were a lot of buildings, lines, and graphs that she couldn't make any sense of, and from the way Jeff was staring at them, they didn't make much sense to him either. He had been that way since they had boarded on the luxurious little plane. When he said charter plane, she'd thought a dust crop plane, or even one of those propeller planes, but this was a small version of her house in the air. She could have really marveled in it and enjoyed it more, if Jeff had been able to be thorough in showing her about, but instead he had pointed at the restroom and the kitchen area when they had gotten on, and started setting up his laptop and making calls. She was left to roam and it was only half as exciting.

The nice pilot she had met when they had boarded was announcing that they would be landing at Miami Airport in 15 minutes. Nina had sat beside Jeff attempting to read a book, while he was busy on his phone and drawing on his laptop. They hadn't said much since they had taken off and Nina was anxious to spend the time with him.

After their luggage had been put in the car that was waiting for them, Nina relaxed in the soft leather seats. Jeff reached over and took one of her hands in his and rubbed it softly. Nina almost leaped out of her skin at his touch. He just didn't know how he made her feel, and she didn't think telling him would be healthy for her, or at least not her emotions right now. In the last couple years she had faced quite a few demons, not just in her closet, but also in other peoples: mainly Quinton's. Although she and Quinton's relationship had been over way before she left, she still at the moment didn't want to feel the way she felt for Jeff.

Nina was caught up by the touch of his warm hand and her thoughts of bliss when the car phone rung. *Is there anywhere they couldn't find him,* she thought? She sighed and looked at the busy streets of Miami whiz by, while Jeff let out a string of orders to someone. After about 5 minutes, Jeff hit the Bluetooth disconnect button.

"I'm going to go by the hotel and get you settled in our room, then I have to get to a dinner meeting. You can have Room Service bring you some dinner up. I shouldn't be gone long."

Nina swallowed back the bitterness that wanted to surface in her reply, "Okay". She was trying hard not to let him see that she was upset.

"Thanks for understanding." He squeezed her thigh softly, but this times that feeling he previously gave her before didn't return.

She gave him a smile and turned back to looking out of the window. *"He's a business man, Nina keep that in mind",* she told herself. *But so was Q.*

<hr />

Here she was, in a five star hotel, on the beautiful beach of Miami, surrounded by night life partying, with a man who was gorgeous to die for; it's 10:30pm on a Thursday night, and what was she doing? In bed, alone, watching reruns of Girlfriends on a 60-inch flat screen. She could have done that in her own bed in her own home. Jeff hadn't gotten back yet. He had called to make sure she had eaten, and was okay. He said he was out at the site. The clients wanted corrections to the mess that had been made started on immediately. So he had to meet with the forum and some of the workers right away. He was planning to be in by 10, but here it was 30 minutes after 10, and no Jeff.

When Nina had called room service to order only some pasta and wine, the receptionist seemed surprised and had stated, "Is that all Ms.

Jackson", as if she herself, couldn't believe this woman would require their 5 star, award winning chef to prepare a measly bowl of pasta and pair it with a cheap bottle of wine? But Nina didn't feel like lobster and champagne, she had barely touched the pasta she ordered. Her overwhelming frustration had taken away any appetite she had had.

She started surfing through the channels for something exciting to watch. This reminded her too much of those nights she was alone waiting for Quinton. But with Quinton, there was no telling where or whom he was with. But with Jeff, she knew he was working. And he wouldn't have had her come if they weren't going to get to spend any time at all together.

She turned to look into the sitting area in the next room, as she heard the door opening and her heart skipped a beat; he was finally in. Nina propped herself on the pillow and glanced over at the wall mirror with the help of the dim T. V. light, and tried to make sure she was decent. Jeff dropped his bags and came into the open French doors of the bedroom, toward Nina.

"Hi." She said as he came near.

He collapsed on the bed beside Nina, burying his head in her lap. He moaned loudly. "I am so tired." Nina placed a hand on his head, rubbing softly. He rose up and looked at her. "I'm sorry about not being here."

'It's okay."

"No, it's not. These construction foreman my father has hired act as though they don't know how to do the work and I know they do. It's like they're having this sudden brain lapse. I'm standing there with these guys telling them what they already know. And they're looking at me like I'm speaking Greek. Finally about 30 minutes ago, the light bulb comes on in their heads, and they finally get it. All that talking when I could have been here with you, catching up on what I've been missing." He lifted the covers up, and left a trail of kisses softly on the inside of her thigh.

Nina smiled down at him, and rubbed his head. "Why don't you go take a shower, and come on to bed?"

He slowly pulled himself up, and Nina watched him as he striped, and went to the bathroom. She then hurriedly got up and pulled from her carrying bag, a set of massage oils and lotions. The least she thought she could do is make him feel relaxed; besides if she didn't, some other woman would welcome the chance to run her hands over that gorgeous body, or do anything else he wanted them to do.

# CHAPTER VII

"**S**O WHILE YOU WERE LIVING the big life in Miami, some of us were here working", Net said sarcastically, rolling her eyes to the ceiling.

Nina smiled and bumped Net's hip. Net busted into laughter along with Nina. "Girl, you know I'm not mad. It wasn't anything I couldn't handle. I'm just glad you got away, finally."

"It really was a lot of fun. Very relaxing."

"Relaxing, whatever. I know you two probably never even left the hotel room. The last thing you did was relaxed."

Nina collapsed in the chair in front of Net's desk and began to recalculate all that happened on her trip, which hadn't been much. It had been more than relaxing. No work, no obligations, and no man. She was left with great amounts of free time to rest and indulge herself.

Jeff had ended up spending 85% of the time on site. It was annoying, but Nina had to remind herself that is why he had went there, to work She had just been asked along.

Jeff had taken her to breakfast that Friday morning, and then had rushed off to get back to the site. He had tried to keep her occupied by having a car at her disposal to take her to a near-by spa and then shopping on him. Since Nina hardly ever got to pamper herself at the spa, she welcomed the opportunity. But when all the pampering was over, and she made it to the first boutique, she knew this was not her type of shopping. She saw one dress that cost her monthly mortgage. There was no way she could charge something to him, that she couldn't pay for herself, or at least wouldn't pay that price for. She and Net had discovered a while back, the magnificent world of outlet stores. They could wear the designer clothes for a fraction of the cost. And even then, some things Nina still refused to buy. Nina had splurged and bought herself a bracelet and some lingerie that was on sale, whose price still had her hesitant.

She decided to go back to the Hotel. She thought Jeff may finish early and they could go back out together. Fat chance. She had thought about a quick work out or taking a few laps in the pool, but decided against it. She didn't want to mess up her pores or her hairdo so soon after leaving the spa, at least not with working out or swimming, but if Jeff came in that would be a different story. Until then, she'd settled in with reading one of the books she had picked up at the bookstore.

Around seven, she decided to wait no longer. She was not going to sit in that room alone any longer. She dressed in a DKNY royal blue halter dress that tied around her neck, and a pair of sandaled heels in the same color. She was going downstairs to the Jazz Club, at least she'd be out of this room. Just as she was approaching the door to go out, Jeff opened and came in.

His suit coat was thrown across his shoulder, his shirt was open, sleeves rolled up, revealing his white tank t-shirt, and his tie hung loosely around his neck. Nina knew from one look that he had worked just as hard as anyone else at that site.

"Hey, Sexy. You look nice, are you slipping out on me", he asked dropping his briefcase?

"Hey you. I was just going downstairs to listen to some Jazz."

Dropping his things in a chair, hecame closer, stopped about 2 ft from her, then leaned over and kissed her cheek. Nina tried to pull him closer by grabbing both ends of his tie, but he stopped her.

"No, I need to shower."

"You look really tired; how did your day go", Nina asked as he began to strip of his clothes?

"Very tiresome, but I think we got a lot accomplished. How was your day? Did you go shopping?"

He was standing in the bathroom doorway, bare chest with his pants undone. Nina glimpsed the chord of muscles running into a strong V right down to his pelvic area. *Damn he was sexy.*

"I did enjoy the spa, but I didn't do too much shopping."

"Why not, I told you to enjoy yourself."

"I just didn't feel right spending all that money at your expense. The spa was enough I really enjoyed it. Thanks".

Jeff smiled, and then shook his head. The woman was the most modest, most independent woman he had ever come in contact with. "What am I going to do with you?"

"How about another back rub when you get out of the shower?"

"I thought you were going downstairs."

"That was only because I was bored; I'd rather be here with you." Nina gave him a wink.

"Thanks." Jeff went into the bathroom, smiling. That woman was really having an effect on him.

"You're really falling for him aren't you?" Net asked her still glowing friend.

Nina blushed, "What are you talking about?" Her gut feelings were saying yes, but admitting it, even to Janette right now, was out of the question. She was still too much in denial.

"I'm talking about the fact that you went away with him. To other women that little act may mean nothing, but to you that is a code of ethics. When you go there with a guy that means you really are falling for him."

Nina just stared at her friend. Net knew without Nina even saying anything what was going on inside of her.

"Come on Ni, I'm your girl. I know that when you take along your edible body oils, that is what you do."

"I never said my oils were edible." Nina said surprisingly.

"Zip it girl, I was with you when you bought them. You're falling for him."

"That is ridiculous. I told you I was just having fun. Temporarily. No big deal", Nina was backing toward the door for an escape.

Janette beamed at Nina. "Okay, but don't mess up things around here. I know how love can make you crazy", she laughed.

Nina licked her tongue out as she went. To think, her being in love again was ridiculous, and being in love with a man like Jeff E Smith III, that was ABSURB!

Jeff sat back in his chair and watched as his father closed his office door and approached his desk. He wore his always-stern business look on his face.

"Hello, Father. I thought you were going to be out of the office all day today."

"Well, there is something I wanted to talk to you privately about. And since lately all your time outside of the office is being consumed with a certain beautiful young lady, I figured the only way I could have a non-business conversation with my son is in our actual business."

Jeff smiled at the reference to Nina, but knew his father's stern look meant something was to his liking. "Well what's bothering you?"

"Not necessarily bothering me, but has me concerned. What's going on with you son?"

Jeff was confused for a moment," What do you mean?"

"Son, you took this young woman on a business trip with you, and you used the company's plane to bring her back home early."

Jeff could tell his father was a little bothered by this. "Well I didn't know it would bother you so much. Had I known it would cause a problem I would have just made us reservations on a commercial flight back."

"Come on son, be serious. You know the plane is not what I'm concerned about."

"Well Dad, I asked her along because I wanted to spend some time with her. I've been breaking quite a few dates with her lately because of work."

"You're getting serious about this young woman aren't you?

Jeff didn't like where this was going. It would be different if he was 17 again and was having this conversation with his father, or even if his father didn't have that grime look on his face. And even though his dad said this was non-business related when he came in, Jeff knew better. This was ALL about business.

Jeff pushed his chair back, and put his hands in his pockets as he walked over to his window. "Dad I'm not a horny teenage boy anymore."

"I know that."

"Neither am I a college junior who can't determine what is more important: getting my degree or getting the girl down the hall into bed?"

"Son, I'm well aware of your age."

"Then why are we having this conversation? I know my priorities and I know how to handle my business. Are you not happy with the business I've been producing lately?"

"Son, I'm very proud of everything you are doing around here. But I want it to stay that way. It just seems like you use to be more focused on the business when you were dating around. You weren't getting so serious about one particular woman."

"So you think it's okay for me to be with a different women every night as long as my head stays in the business, versus me being with one woman who may get my mind off track?" Jeff signed and chuckled, "I thought I'd never hear the day that my father was an advocate of being a womanizer."

"Jeff, you know that's not what I'm saying."

"What is it then, Dad? I mean that is what it sounds like you are trying to say. Is that what you did when it came to all the times you spent away from us when I was young? Were you with different women other than my mother? Is that what it takes to keep your head in the business and to become successful?" Jeff knew he had gone too far.

His father stood motionless; in shock. All this that was going on with Jeff was so uncalled for. They hadn't stood off like this since he was in college. This anger that was coming from his son was stemming from something else; it was obvious.

"Nina seems to be a very sweet young lady; I just don't want her to get hurt in the sense of you not spending enough time with her."

Jeff sucked up his animosity towards his father and tried to mellow out before speaking again. "Dad, I want a life. Something that doesn't require making money, or sitting in front of a drawing board or a computer screen, or standing on a construction site every minute of my damn life. Don't get me wrong, I love all that. But I also want more happiness. And yes, lately I've been finding that with Nina."

"Son, I just want you to realize that women have power, and that power can ruin you or make you. I just want you to stay on a successful track Jeff, that's all, okay?"

Jeff stared at his father a moment. The man was intelligent and successful on every level, but he had no clue as to the fact that he had sacrificed his happiness as well as his families' for so many years to obtain that success. He loved his father, but didn't want to become so successful that he lose his own sense of what a life outside of business was.

He took his hands out of his pockets and held them up in surrender. "Okay, Dad. I understand that. Once again, I will not make you unhappy, nor will I upset the success that this business has established."

His father could hear the sarcasm in his son's voice. It was almost as if his son couldn't stand him anymore. He wanted to say more, but decided he wouldn't push the issue. "I do love you son."

"I know Dad, and I love you too.

His father took a deep breath and turned to leave, but then turned back to his son. "I appreciate all the hard work on that clean-up in Miami."

"You're welcome."

"I'll see you later."

Jeff blew out some steam and collapsed in his chair. He loved his father, but he wish the man could understand that he could only be himself; he couldn't become someone he was never born to be.

# CHAPTER VIII

N INA OPENED THE GLASS DOORS of the Center to be greeted by an atmosphere of quite. It was 2 o'clock, the time of day when there was still quite before the storm; or at least before the kids came in. This was the moment of the day Nina waited for. These few transitional moments gave her the opportunity to settle from the morning she had at the Hospital, switch gears, and get ready for an afternoon of tutoring, conferences, and the non-stop interactions of energetic youth. The youth were the best part of her day.

It wasn't that she considered herself old. It was just that so many people had given up on the younger generation, but she looked at them as an opportunity for change, an opportunity for something new. Yeah most of the kids that came thru the Center, came in with a label of trouble makers, but they had only been typed that because no one wanted to take the time to pay attention and teach them something, letting them know that there were options to everything in life.

So when she had meet Jeanette 6 years earlier through some acquaintances, and Jeanette told her of what the Center was trying to do, Nina was happy to be a part of it. Nina really felt she had a purpose there. It was a beginning for a new Season in her life, as well the start of a beautiful friendship with Jeanette.

She walked through the hall, speaking to individuals who were at their desk and looked up as she passed. As soon as she got into her own office and put her bag down on her desk, Jeanette came racing in behind her, and it was written all over her face, the look of disgust. Nina knew she was not in for a girlfriend talk right now. Janette was in boss mode, and Nina was pretty sure one of their star youth were at the core of whatever the problem would be.

Jeanette closed Nina's door in one quick move, and then turned to Nina, eyes blazing.

"Nina, please tell me you did not take Jamie Clark to buy a pregnancy test."

Nina exhaled, before she collapsed into her chair. She didn't know what she was expecting Net to say, but she had been expecting the worst from the way Net came in. This was a relief; she could handle this. "Well, it was a little more to it then just taking her to get a pregnancy test. She came to me scared and confused."

Jeanette remained standing. Her short petite arms were poised, and her hands were on her hips.

"Nina, don't take this lightly. This morning when I got here, John Engle from the State office was on my voice mail ranting about Jamie Clark's mother calling the State Department all day yesterday to report the Center, because we had employees who were providing sexual advice to her underage teenager without her permission."

"What!" Nina didn't give Jeanette any time to keep going. She was on her feet now, with her hands on her hips. "You mean she took out the time to make phone calls to tell on me, but she couldn't take the time to make sure her daughter would use a condom, to keep her from getting pregnant, now did she?"

"Come on Nina, this is serious. Engle is talking about calling a hearing."

"What is the big deal? She came to me confused, thinking she was pregnant, and she needed to know."

"Why didn't you tell her to go to the clinic?"

"I did, but she was upset about people being in her business. Look Net, I didn't do anything wrong. I was just trying to keep another baby from being found in a dumpster or to at least give the girl some peace by knowing and not waiting. Now you know if I had told her to go to the clinic and left it at that, she still wouldn't know to this day. After finding out, she assured me she would go to the clinic to be tested again, as well as get info about birth control. After checking up on her, I found out she did go. The issue here is, shouldn't Tonya Clark be glad her daughter is protected now, as well as more informed?"

Jeanette sighed and collapsed in the chair across from Nina's desk.

"You know that to Tonya Clark it's not even the fact that you helped Jamie, it's the fact of who you are."

Nina sat down too. She knew exactly what Net was referring to. Tonya Clark was a hating nuisance from the past. When Nina first started at the Center, she of course thought she could change the world of all these kids by just being nice to the parents in conferences, and letting them know options that were available to make things easier for them. Tonya Clark schooled her real quick on the fact that not everyone needed her "goody-two shoe, ass to come in and wave the broom she flew in on to make things better for them, because frankly she was happy being an unemployed 26-year old with three kids by three different fathers, in so many words. She was the first lesson that Nina got, that taught her that Change isn't always perceptive or universal. "Net, she really took out the time to cause trouble like this for me?"

"I'm afraid so. I know you are a wonderful person, you would never do anything to harm anyone, and you are so empathetic and compassionate about what you do: you're just trying to help others, but not everyone else sees you that way. It's a mentality that you and I will never be able to understand, because as much as we try to make others believe we are just like them, they will never believe we are."

Nina looked down at her desk. It disgusted her the way people put too much time and energy in holding grudges, especially when there was no known reason behind it. "How did Tonya find out anyway?"

"Jamie asked the lady at the clinic could she be tested for STD's and get an HIV test."

Nina brightened with a smile as she looked up at Net. "That's my girl." She felt all she had been telling the girls in the sessions was paying off.

Net smiled, she knew how important the little things were when a child actually listened to something you told them. It made her proud also. "Well, you have to have parental consent, and Jamie took the paper home to Tonya to sign, mentioning your name in the process, and it's all down hill from there."

"Shouldn't she be happy for her daughter?"

"Yeah, but what Engle is saying is that you overstepped your boundaries and not just gave her the info, but acted on providing methods for her."

"So, I'm not suppose to care, that's what he's saying right?"

Net was quite for a moment. She knew the emotions that her friend was dealing with. She too could feel the pain of her past. "Look Ni, I know sometimes it's hard not to care for these kids, but to State they just want us to make the resources available, and leave it up to the parents."

"Right, up to parents who either don't care, or don't know themselves. State complains about there being too many teenage mothers in the system that they provide, but when we go the extra mile to make sure they have what they need so that they may not become a recipient in that system, we've overstepped their boundaries. The fact that we saved someone from becoming another case isn't important. They don't care one way or another. So what am I up against, with Engle?"

Net looked at her friend with compassion. "Well the worse is still to come. Tonya told Engle she was going to the papers about this, and we're not sure if that was just a threat, but in case she does, Engle said they might have to call a hearing just for precautions. That could mean rumors for both here and the Hospital for you."

"You have got to be kidding. It's not like I took her to get an abortion or something."

"Nina, I know, but the press blows things up. For now Engle just wants you to write a statement to him, to keep on file of your side of the story."

"Fine." The whole situation was absorbed to Nina.

As Net rose and patted Nina's hand, Nina leaned back in her chair and stared out the old push out windows. A few moments earlier she was on cloud 9, now she had descended somewhere around 2; things changed fast.

Nina inhaled the wonderful aroma of cologne and man as Jeff tightened his arms around her and she laid her head against his chest. He had come into her bedroom where she sat on her bed with her laptop, and she had leaped into his arms without a word. She needed to be in his arms.

After holding her for a few moments, she looked up into his face.

He leaned forward and kissed her lips softly. He didn't let her go, but just stood there; holding her close to him and looking down at her.

"I'd ask the real reason for all this, but at the moment I just want to keep believing it's because you're so happy to see me."

She gave him a slight smile, "I'm always happy to see you."

He smiled back, "But?"

She pulled away and sighed. "I needed your arms around me. I've had a day from that level before you get to hell; if there is such a place."

Jeff started unbuttoning his shirt and undressing as Nina went back to her place on the bed. "What happened today?"

Nina watched him carefully undress as she told Jeff of the Jamie incident. When she told him about the pregnancy test, he froze. Standing in front of her in just his boxers he turned to look at her. "Babe, tell me you didn't."

"Not you too?" She shook her head and held up her hand when she realized that Jeff was about to trip.

"Nina if this woman is that desperate to make trouble for you, she could actually succeed if she went to the media. Babe, I know what it's like when media gets a hold of something, they run with it and it escalates into way more, and what they make of it can cause problems, for both the Center and the Hospital because of your association with the kids."

Nina didn't want to hear all this again. She had ran all the negative aspects of her past that could be found out if the media got involved and got their hands on the right information. For the second time that day she was getting annoyed. "What kind of problems Jeff? Is this going to smear your precious family name?"

He could tell by the disdain in her voice she was getting upset. "That's not what I meant. All I'm saying is things could get worse when both the media and the State are involved."

"Okay." Nina personally was tired of this conversation. She began to pack up her laptop and get ready to get into bed. It was only 9:30, and though she had waited for Jeff to get in from his dinner meeting, she suddenly didn't want to talk to him anymore.

Jeff knew she was inflexible. And he knew when she got into a mood, she locked up and shut down; so he didn't press the conversation any further, but instead went about undressing, and then left the room until she cooled off a little. Normally he would not deal with this nonsense from any woman; he'd just get his things and leave but she had some type of pull on him, and he wanted to be there with her. It had been on his mind what his father had told him about falling for her, as well as the conversation about loving so hard, that Kay had mentioned. He was really beginning to see the truth in it all.

At 12am, they laid beside each other silently; not touching; neither of them asleep. Nina had pretended to be sleep when Jeff finally came to bed around11:30. The room was silent and the tension was so thick, it placed a suffocating fog in the darkness. When Nina couldn't take it any longer, she sat straight up in the darkness and turned to Jeff. He didn't move, but she knew he was awake.

"Jeff", she whispered softly.

A moment passed before he sighed and answered, in a low and short tone, "Yeah"?

"Are you sleeping?"

"It depends, are you going to be angry at me some more?"

"No."

"Then no, I can't sleep knowing you're upset with me. Never had been before now, and tonight isn't any different."

Without saying anything, Nina raised the covers enough so that she could slide over on top of him. She softly laid upon him, inching down so that her head rested on his chest. Without a word from him, he automatically wrapped his arms around her.

"I'm sorry", she whispered.

He rubbed her back slowly in circles in response to her. He didn't say anythng, but she knew from his actions he accepted her apology.

They drifted off to sleep.

# CHAPTER IX

## REPEATING PATTERNS AND GOING IN CIRCLES

T HE NEXT COUPLE WEEKS WENT by in a blur. Jeff was out of town a lot, but he never went without leaving something for Nina to marinate on while he was a way, making her long for his return. Nina knew she was strung on the physical sexual attraction, but from the sounds of it, so was Jeff.

He had just got back from a business trip to Oklahoma with his dad, whom Nina had the opportunity of meeting at the office one day, while waiting on Jeff for lunch. Mr. Smith was a charmer, much like his son, but Nina could tell that when he talked business, he meant business. From the impression Nina got, he seemed to be fond of her.

Upon Jeff's arrival back in town, Nina had prepared a special night for the two of them. She cooked a huge candlelight dinner, bought a special bottle of wine, had stopped at Victoria's Secret and bought a special type of dessert in black, lace. Jeff had called her that morning and told her he would be catching na afternoon flight home. Of course he wanted to go by the office check on what was going on and meet with his dad, but he definitely was longing to see her. Nina feeling quiet happy at his words, also didn't hesitate to think about the pattern they had fallen in. Since the first time they had made love, there hadn't been too many times that they were actually together that they hadn't followed suit. Nina had started thinking that their relationship was only being based on sex?

They had spent a lot of time together going to the theater, dining out, and spending hours debating politics and international news, but at the end of the night they found themselves in either his or her bed. She knew their relationship had substance, but at times the little voice in the back of her mind sometimes had her thinking he only stayed around for the sex that she was so freely giving up. She herself felt something more, something deeper coming on; feelings that reminded her of traveling down an all too familiar road. The road she didn't want to take; at least not now. But she was doing all she could to suppress those feelings. After all they had been seeing each other for over four months now. Her relationship with Quinton reminded her that love always seemed to be one sided; her side being the one that was doing all the loving.

Nina heard a loud, hurried knock at her front door that brought her out of her thoughts. She rushed to the door peeking through the hole before opening it.

He smiled at her, "Hello Beautiful?" He stepped in, dropped his bag, and swooped Nina up in his arms.

"Jeff, I missed you." She said hugging him.

They stood there in the door holding each other for a moment. Nina finally let him go. He bent down and kissed her lips. "Damn, I missed you so much." He kissed her again and let her back down on her feet. "I've been thinking about you all day. I couldn't wait until I got here." He planted another kiss on her before letting her go and picking up his things from the doorway to move inside

Nina noticed how tired he looked

"Something smells good", he said. "Are you cooking?"

"Yeah, baked, herb-butter salmon, red potatoes, and asparagus." She said following him to a loveseat in her living room.

"Yummy". After he had been eating a bunch of exotic things in fancy restaurants all week. He couldn't recall any other woman he had dated even knowing how to cook, and making him excited to have a home cooked meal.

He grabbed her before she had the chance to sit down, pulling her to him. "It smells about as good as you look. Why don't we skip dinner, and go straight to bed?"

"Jeff, I worked hard on dinner. I want us to sit down, have dinner, and talk. We have all weekend for all that."

He smacked his lips. "Speaking of weekend, my parent's annual garden party is tomorrow."

"And you wait until now, the day before, to tell me? I've never met your mom! What am I supposed to do about my hair and nails, and then what am I supposed to wear?"

He rolled his eyes. "See there you go, your hair and nails are fine, and as for what to wear, I personally think you should go naked."

Nina pinched his arm.

He laughed as he grabbed the spot she pinched in pain, "Babe, it's not a big deal. You can wear anything, no one there will be as beautiful as you."

Nina smiled and leaned forward to kiss him. "Why do I fall for this with you?"

He smiled, "Because you know I mean it".

# CHAPTER X

## BACK DOWN LOVING HIM LANE

"*J*EFF, *I LOVE YOU!*" NINA slide down the side of her bathtub into a fetal position and cradled her head in her hands. Those words were bouncing around in her head now, screaming in her ears. How could she be so stupid as to blurt that out in the moment of passion? The man had that much erotic, control over her that she was now blurting out crazy things, like I Love You, in the heat of the moment.

'This is crazy', Nina thought to herself. 'There is no way I could love him. I was just caught up in the moment. Among the other things he had me moaning, that was one of them. He probably didn't even hear me. What am I thinking, of course he heard me, I was screaming so loud, my neighbors, heard me.

Didn't I learn anything from my relationship with Quinton? I thought I took care of that wall. I had been so good at building up walls in my life. Wall, where people couldn't see the hurt and pain on the inside. Walls that helped me maintain an independent, determined, strong, image. I built a wall up to hide the hurt of my parent's death, so no one could see me cry. It was the wall that I built, so that people didn't know I cried myself to sleep at night because I felt so alone.

It was walls that I facade myself behind so that the emotional and physical abuse I see on a daily basis to kids who can't change their situation, wouldn't break me down making me unable to perform my job. And it is a wall that I had built, so that I would never hurt the way I hurt, for another man after leaving Q. It was all emotional, and now I'm sitting on my bathroom floor, fretting over me destroying my own wall, because of some nonsense I blurted *out during sex; Sex that I shouldn't be having anyway. There is no way I could be in love with him, it wasn't like this was going to go anywhere. He wasn't into that and Janette could be no more wrong to think she was falling for him. Maybe if she kept quite about it, he wouldn't mention any of it.*

Nina jumped, as she heard a light knock on the door. "Are you okay", Jeff asked from the other side. "You've been in there for a while now."

"*Hell*", Nina muttered to herself. She stood up, took a deep breath and put up her infamous smiling wall before opening the door.

Jeff noticed her eyes were glassy and her smile looked forced. She had jumped from bed and rushed to the bathroom before he had even rolled over. The way she was carrying on during their lovemaking, he thought it had been as good for her as it had for him, but now she was hiding out in her bathroom.

"Are you okay", he asked taking her hand?

"Yeah."

"You bolted from the bed, and you've been in there quite some time. I didn't hurt you or anything, did I?"

"No, I'm fine. Really." Nina was turning her head away; she couldn't even look him in the eyes. He had to know; she was sure of it.

He lifted her chin with his finger so that she was looking at him. "You sure?"

Nina gave him a genuine smile this time. If he didn't mention her previous outburst, then maybe that was good. "I'm sure."

He pulled her into his arms, pushing her robe off her shoulders and to the floor as she came, "Come back to bed with me then."

---

# CHAPTER XI
## OLD FRIENDS, NEW TRICKS

NINA TRIED TO KEEP A smile on her face, as she passed the clusters of people. Rich and elegant was an understatement for this party. She was glad she had chosen the right attire for the event. She had decided to wear a siege and tan, maxi wrap sundress that flowed around her, giving a low key peek of her left thigh as she walked, through the split fabric opening. She had added a pair of stiletto sandals and a matching clutch. Her hair was pulled back in a sleek bun that knotted at the nap her neck. She had added pair of tear drop earrings and a natural dust of eye shadow, mascara, and brown gloss to her lips. At least she didn't feel underdressed.

It was obvious that these people were only the elite; Nina could tell that when they drove up the drive and there was a caravan of Jaguars, Mercedes, Teslas, and BMWs, lining the entrance. She even remembered passing at least one Roles and one Bentley. Jeff had introduced her to so many people she couldn't remember the names. The Mayor was there, some other politicians, a lot of lawyers, and CEOs of this and that company, and out-of-towner's from ATL, Boston, and Md; the list went on and on. So many people to watch she had almost forgotten about the fiasco from the night before. She had been so nervous around Jeff all morning, thinking that he'd bring it up at any moment. He hadn't, but she didn't know if it was too soon to call it safe.

With all the people who were excited to see Jeff after such a long time, and wanted to talk to him, he kept his arm around either her wait or his hand in the center of her back, never leaving her side. Then the big moment came.

Jeff stirred her toward his dad and a very daunting and domineering woman dressed very elegantly in a peach pants suit by some designer that screamed elegance. She had an air about her that showed she was not a woman to cross in the wrong way. Mr. Smith held out his arms to embrace Nina.

"Nina, you look as lovely as ever", he said placing a peck on her cheek.

"Good to see you, Mr. Smith." She said hugging him.

"Nina, this is my mother, mother meet Nina."

Nina extended her hand, "Nice to finally meet you Mrs. Smith."

His mother was so pretty, but the expression on her face wasn't one of a tender, soft spoken woman. She stood for a long moment staring at Nina; taking her in from head to toe with one look. Then she finally took Nina's fingers, only, in her hand in a Diane Carroll way, and then quickly released them.

"The same." She said without a smile. "Jeff and Edward tell me you work with youth programs at the Hospital and Community Center downtown."

"Yes ma'am. I'm the Director of Pediatric Programs at the Hospital, and Program Coordinator at the Community Youth Center"

"I believe my Woman's Organization was at one of your young woman seminars that you spoke at."

Nina suddenly remembered, Jeanette had told her when she found out Nina was dating Jeff that his mother's very Elite Woman's Organization had attended one of their seminars as sponsors. Nina couldn't remember then, all she remembered was being pulled in every direction that day since she was the coordinator and the speaker. She was very nervous about speaking to the group about her experience in school and what it had taken to get through. She had never spoken openly, especially not to a bunch of strangers about her past life as a dancer and living through the lost of her parents. She was doing all she could that day to maintain a state of calmness. But now seeing her, Nina remembered that Mrs. Smith had commended her for speaking about her life that was a motivation to others. She wondered did Mrs. Smith remember that.

"Yes, ma'am, I remember that."

She nodded her head then turned away as though she was bored with talking to her. "Jeff, darling, guess who is here?" Without waiting for Jeff to answer, she continued in the way that both Jeff and her husband were use to her doing. "Stephanie, the Joseph's daughter that you dated a few times. You know she has just been made partner at her law firm? Come, let us go speak."

"Mother, I'm sure I'll get to her before the day is over."

"Okay, well Edward, honey, let us go greet." She said taking his arm, as they walked away. Mr. Smith gave Nina a sympathetic smile and nod, as he gave his wife his arm.

That little gesture gave Nina's heart wrench with pain. It was that moment she felt a desperate longing and missing of her own parents. She reminded herself that now wasn't the time to experience an emotional state. She sighed heavily and turned to Jeff, "She hates me."

"Nina, you just met her. My mother is always peculiar about people until she gets to know them. She doesn't hate you."

"Okay," Nina said, but she knew that from the way that woman just looked at her and the way she remembered her whole Women's Group looking at people snobbishly at the seminar, that she didn't believe Nina belong with her son. And if Mrs. Smith remembered the things Nina had spoken about, she would definitely not appreciate her being with her son.

Nina tried to forget about last night's episode as they sipped wine, ate, and listened to the live jazz band. Jeff introduced her to more people, and Nina tried to maintain her lady like behavior when a group of giggly females surrounded Jeff, as they laughed about old times. Jeff was good at escaping and taking Nina by the arm to get away. It wasn't long before Mr. Smith wanted to introduce Jeff to some business associates.

"I'll be right back," Jeff promised.

"Okay, I'm just going to go to the restroom."

Nina made her way through the crowd of people to the inside. As she rounded the corner to where Jeff had told her the bathroom was she heard one of women from the giggle group talking with Jeff's sister, and Mrs. Smith.

...."You know Jeff hasn't changed. He's the same way he was when he was small. Always bringing some stray home that he thinks can just fit in. I've tried to tell him he's from a different world; he can't mix with just anything or anyone. I mean did you see her; she doesn't even look like she belongs here. And for the life of my son, I at least hope if he's intimate with that woman that he is taking every precaution necessary. I've heard she's been around and has a reputation..."

Nina stiffen first then forgot about the bathroom and quickly made her way back outside. Just as she went, Jeff was coming toward her. She couldn't hide the ager or the unfallen tears pooling in her eyes. "Jeff I know you want to be here, but I've got to go."

He took her by the arms, "Nina what's wrong?"

"Jeff, I've just got to go. If you want to stay, go ahead, I'll call a car."

"Nina wait, just tell me what happened."

"I don't want to talk about it now. I just want to leave."

"Okay, let me let my parents know I'm leaving."

"I'll be at the car." As she turned to leave, she spotted the evil witch of a mother. Nina dropped her head and hastily walked toward the car. She never planned to come back to this place again.

---

Nina took the Kleenex Jeff handed her and dabbed at the corners of her eyes. She knew it was only a matter of time before he was going to ask again what had happened. They made it to her place in silence and got inside without a word. Nina went to her bedroom, and Jeff was on her heels.

"Do you care to let me know what happened now? You were fine before I left, then when I return 5 minutes later all emotional and angry. I've never seen you like that before". He had only saw her get emotional enough to be moved to tears once when something had reminded her of her parents. This was definitely a different uncontrolled Nina from what he was use to seeing.

Nina tried to ignore him, and continued rummaging through her dresser drawer. Jeff took her by the elbow. "Nina would you talk to me?"

"Jeff, I just got upset about something I heard, it's not a big deal."

"Okay, you're crying like someone hurt you, but it's no big deal. Nina what was said and who said?" He was getting angry now.

"I heard something that made me realized that maybe we aren't meant for each other."

"What? Nina what are you talking about?" He looked at her confused.

She sighed realizing he wasn't going to let this go unless she tell him something. "Someone said I didn't belong there, and that you should stop bringing in strays,"

"Who the hell said some shit like that?"

Nina sighed, and looked him in his eyes. She couldn't tell him that his mother was the evil witch behind it all. "It doesn't matter who said it."

"Who Nina?"

Nina sighed and gave in; she knew if she didn't this conversation would never be over. "Your mother."

He shook his head in confusion. "Who was she talking to?"

"Your sister, and one of your old girlfriends. I mean maybe they are right."

"So you think that, that's how I feel also?"

"No, but–"

"But nothing Nina, I thought you of all people could understand the real me. I'll see you when I get back. I'm going to have a word with my mother and sister."

"Jeff, don't make a big deal about this."

"Nina, save it." He went out the door and Nina collapsed on the bed as she heard his car reave out of her driveway. It was cute that he was taking up for her, but she definitely didn't want to cross his mother again after Jeff finished talking with her.

---

Nina tucked her legs back under her after peeking through the blinds to see Jeff coming up the driveway. She took a deep breath and tried to relax, as she looked back at the TV. She wasn't sure she was ready for the outcome of what his mother had to say. After all it had been about two hours, and she was sure Jeff had learned some things, she had yet to tell him.

Jeff came into the living room, laid his keys on the end table and stood just staring at Nina. He looked disturbed and bothered.

"So, how did it go with your mother?" She wouldn't make direct eye contact with him, but kept her eyes on her book.

He started speaking in a slow and low tone "You want to know how it went? Nina, my mother gave me some information that I should have known about already because we have been together for almost 5 months now, and you and I have talked about, just about everything there is; at least I thought we had. So, can you imagine how I felt, going to bless my mother and sister out about coming at you the way they did, when my mother gives me this information, that you never shared with me?"

Nina looked up at him surprisingly, "Jeff, what information? What are you talking about?"

Nina knew what was coming. She sat on the edge of the sofa and waited. She had tried to keep this from him as long as she could.

"Nina, I'm standing there telling them that what they think of you isn't important, because I love you, and my mother then asks me, did I know you were a stripper? Here I am trying to pretend I already knew this as well as hide the anger that you never told me before."

Nina was shocked. First because he had just said he loved her, and then at the fact that Jeff was so upset about this news. She swallowed her smile, and decided she'd gloat about the first later. "Jeff I told you I had done some things I wasn't proud of; I didn't think I had to be so specific about what. And for your mother's information I wasn't a stripper; I was a dancer. Jeff, I'm sorry I didn't tell you before. My junior year in college my dad was laid off from his job, the only income coming in was my mothers. Instead of being a burden with my tuition, I wanted to help out, but it was taking all of my part-time job money to survive and eat. A friend told me she danced as a second job, and she made good money. She was getting ready to quite her daytime job. She got me a gig, I started making fast money, and I was able to help my parents out as well as pay for my remaining year in college with no problems. When

I graduated from college, I left that behind as well. My parents never knew what my "new job" was, and it's not something I willingly shared."

She took a breath to let that sink in. "When your mother's organization came to a youth seminar for teenage girls, I was giving a motivational speech about changing your life and making a difference and I told about my experiences in college and how I struggled to make it through while dancing. When I was done telling my story, your mother thought I had done a wonderful job making something for myself, even though the odds were against me. She also told me she thought my life experiences could be a motivation to others. At least she liked me until I came home with her son as the stray. Then I was the loose girl that she hoped her son was 'taking precautions and protecting himself with because she heard I had reputation." Nina said this using her fingers as quotes. "Jeff I'm not proud of it, but I did what I had to do for my family as well as to get where I am today. And for that I am not ashamed. But if you want nothing else to do with me, I'll understand."

"Nina the fact that you danced isn't what I'm upset about. It's the fact that you didn't trust me enough to believe that you could tell me and that I wasn't going to trip about it. I thought we could tell each other anything. And like I told my mother Nina, I love you, and I'm not about to let the best thing that's ever happened to me slip away because of something like this."

Nina gave him a smile. He was obviously feeling what she had been feeling for the past few weeks as well. She had found herself at the door of where she hadn't planned on ever being again. She had been mentally tormenting herself because, she wasn't sure if it was real love she was approaching, but she knew it was something huge; unexplainable. It had to be love.

"So, is there any other public knowledge that I don't know?" He was standing there in front of her with a more sincere look now than the scowl he wore when he first came in.

"No", she smiled and thought about the other things she could tell but at the moment she knew should continue to keep to herself. "You heard me last night didn't you"?

He let out a deep chuckle, "Of course I heard you. I think the whole city of Charlotte heard you. But today those words have been all that have been on my mind, and I know it's because I feel the same way about you. I've felt this way for some time now."

"Jeff, this is all happening so fast though. I'm still-"

He cut her off, "dealing with your past relationship scars…yada, yada, yada; I know. But if you don't mention that, I won't either. Deal?"

She smiled. *What was she getting herself into?* Love was what she had buried in a grave a while ago and built a wall on top of it, and now she was going back to knock the wall down and dig it up. "Deal".

Okay despite her efforts to not be here, she was. But she was still in control. This was as far as it would go. She was promising herself.

# CHAPTER XII

NINA PICKED UP SPEED AS she rounded the corner and caught sight of Jeff's car in the driveway. There was a burgundy BMW parked at his curb. As Nina slowed her speed to enter the drive and do her cool-down stretches, she wondered if it was one of his clients bringing something by for him, but noticed the tags were a rental. After a quick stretch, Nina went in. She had intended on going straight upstairs to shower, but when she heard a dainty woman's laugh coming from the sitting room she had a change of mind, and detoured with quickness. She knew her appearance wasn't exactly presentable with her biker shorts, sports bra, and vest jacket that she wore. Her hair was pulled back in a ponytail, and she was a tad bit sweaty, but she had to know whom this woman was.

Jeff was leaning in the archway of his living room. His hands were in the pockets of his linen pants, and his white t-shirt was hanging loosely on the outside. His wavy, coyly hair was un-brushed and disheveled, and his eyes were bloodshot and puffy from lack of a full night of sleep. But yet, to Nina he was a picture of perfection. When he saw Nina approaching, he smiled and reached out to her.

"Babe, come here, I have someone for you to meet."

Nina came closer, and looked into the living room at what had to be a supermodel perched perfectly on his sofa. The woman looked like she had stepped off the cover of Wall Street magazine, dressed in an executive fuchsia business suit that molded the body of a Playboy bunny. A perfect size 6, with shoulder,-length, straight jet-black hair. Root grown or root sewn, Nina wasn't sure, but damn it was beautiful. She looked like she could have been damn near intimidating to men and women.

Nina flashed her a grand smile, just as she would anyone else in the boardroom, matching her stare for stare, even if she was in her sweaty running clothes.

"Nina this is Alicia Stanz, an old friend from Chicago. Alicia, this is Nina."

Nina extended her hand and took Alicia's long slender manicured fingers, as she reminded herself she needed to make her own nail appointment.

"Nice to meet you."

"You too."

"Alicia works for one of the top advertising agencies in Chicago and she's here in Charlotte on business and decided to stop by and visit. She wanted us to get together for dinner. Are you free tonight?"

"I have tutoring tonight, Sweetie", Nina said, looking adoringly up at Jeff.

"I forgot", Jeff said. "My baby never seems to cease in helping others".

Nina knew they probably sounded like some sappy hallmark couple with all the sweet-talking they were doing to each other. She knew her own motives behind it, but Jeff was being a little sappier with the sweet talk then normally himself.

"Why don't you two go ahead", Nina said.

"Are you sure", Jeff asked surprised? He wasn't actually up for an evening with the dramatics of Alicia. And he was almost sure he had picked up on the unspoken battle between Nina and Alicia that women were so well at doing with their looks and body language. He did not want to set up a trap for himself that he would end up caught in later with Nina.

"Yeah." She smiled at him.

Jeff was hesitant, "Okay, if that's alright with you?" He looked at her questioningly still.

"Sure. Look I got to get showered for work. It was nice meeting you, Alicia."

"You too, Nesse."

Nina cringed as she turned to walk away because she knew the witch deliberately said her name wrong on purpose. She turned to Jeff, stood on her tiptoes and kissed him long and hard. If this witch could play games, so could she. Jeff smiled at her dramatics.

"I'll see you upstairs." She knew he picked up on her mischief because he was smiling so hard at her.

Now let the witch think she had a chance with her man. Whatever her intentions were when she came they better get redirected, because Jeff was someone else's territory now.

---

Nina flipped on the bedside lamp and Jeff spurned around to look at her, while in the process of taking off his clothes.

"Did I wake you", he asked?

"I wasn't sleep", she said getting up and following him to the bathroom. She stood in the doorway watching him in front of the sink.

"So, how was dinner", she asked catching a whiff of the strong perfume she had followed to the living room just that morning? She had been thinking about the stupidity behind her sending her man on a date with another woman; one that especially looked the way that one did. But then she had told herself, it was no big deal. They were old friends and she didn't know what she was doing anyway in this so-called relationship she and Jeff had going.

"It was good, I wish you had been there." He said, but never looked at her and reached for his toothbrush.

Nina reached over and shut the running water off. Jeff looked down at her, as she slid into the small space between him and the counter and placed her hands on his chest. "I've been waiting for you to get in."

Jeff leaned forward and kissed her softly on the lips once. "I want to shower first."

"Why", she had asked before she had realized it? She was suddenly thinking too much on past experience with Quinton who stayed out late, and also had to shower before he came near her, mainly because of his little escapades with other women while he was out. She had the sudden urge to give Jeff the sex check.

"It's just been a long day and I want to shower first", he said looking down at her, wondering if the vibes he had got from her that morning already had showed up to trap him now.

Without saying a word, Nina unzipped his pants, thrust her hand into his shorts and caressed him, then brought her hand down the length of his now growing penis. Jeff jumped at her unexpected gesture. Nina removed her hand and brought her fingers to her nose. She only smelled his manly aroma. She pulled him by the shirt down to her lips and kissed him. "I love you." She then let him go.

"What was that all about", he asked looking after her confused as she went to the bed?

"Just wanted to make sure you loved me too."

Jeff stood puzzled for a moment then went back to brushing his teeth. But Nina knew no traces of fresh soap or of a woman's scent on his manhood, meant he didn't sleep with that helfer Alicia.

When Jeff finally came to bed, he was still curious as to what she had done "I wanted to make sure your buddy Alicia didn't succeed in getting you back in her bed."

"I see, so I passed right?"

"Your balls are still attached, aren't they?" she asked.

"Yes, and I am thankful for that", Jeff laughed. For her not to want to move too fast, her jealousy was cute. After her not caring that he had went, he was thinking she didn't care at all. He pulled her over into his arms. "What do you mean back in her bed?"

Nina cocked her head to one side and looked at Jeff in a come-on-be-real look. "Jeff, I know she's more than just an old friend. There is no way you could just have been friends with her, or any other woman, that beautiful, for that matter."

He laughed.

"All I know is when I appeared this morning, there was a very irritated she-wolf in your living room, and she definitely didn't like you inviting me along for dinner. It was very obvious that she wasn't just stopping by to see if you wanted to talk about old times. She wanted to get some stroking like old times also. Am I right or wrong?"

Jeff chuckled, "You are in rare form tonight. Have you been drinking?"

Nina raised her eyebrow and looked at him questioningly again. "What?"

"Did she or did she not try to get you in bed with her tonight?"

Jeff chuckled again, because he'd never seen her like this before. Pissed off and jealous was starting to look sexy on her though.

"Jeff tell me did that witch try in anyway to sleep with you tonight?" Nina was really trying to avoid the attitude she could get in these situations and calling her an outright bitch, but Jeff was taking this as a game, enjoying her anger.

Jeff smiled again, "Babe you're really serious about this aren't you?"

"Hell yeah, I'm serious. Are you trying to hide something?"

"No, I mean if you want to know, of course I can tell you everything that happened."

"Yes, I would like to know everything." She had folded her arms across her chest now and was waiting anxiously.

Jeff leaned back on the headboard and saw the look of impatience in Nina's eyes. She was dead serious. So he decided he had to tell her or he would not get any sleep so he began to recollect the events of the evening.

"Okay, we went to dinner, in which we talked a lot about old times; we had drinks in the bar at her hotel, and I walked her to her room. I hugged her and then came home to you." He was reaching for her waist, but Nina hit his hands away.

Jeff figured that wouldn't do it, but thought it didn't hurt to try. He rolled his eyes and began to tell her what happened.

He had walked Alicia to her room and had turned down her invitation for the second time to come in.

"Jay, you're really serious about this Nesa?"

"It's Nina, and I wished you put as much effort in saying her name right, as you do in going out of your way to say it wrong."

"And touché about her too." She gave him a smile. "She's just not your type, Jay"

"And I suppose you know my type, huh?" He put his hands in his pocket and leaned on the wall opposite her door.

"I just mean she's so regular. I thought you wanted someone successful on your level. She's a social worker for goodness sake, Jay."

"And she's a damn good one." He was feed up with Alicia for one night. "Lish, I love Nina, and despite what you think, she's more than "just" a social worker and anything but ordinary. I have never felt the way about any woman the way I feel about her. Not even when I was with you."

Alicia gave him a sly grin, and then stepped closer to him. So close their bodies were touching. Her perfume was intoxicating and he would have been lying if he said being that close to her wasn't having an effect on his glands. Besides he was a man, and he had no control mentally of what his manhood did when turned on by the contact with a beautiful woman's body.

Alicia placed her hands on his chest, leaned in and rubbed her cheek softly against his. Then she took his earlobe between her teeth and pulled; making Jeff flinch slightly. She whispered in his ear, softly and seductively, "Jay, I know you want me as much as I want you right now, the growth in your pants proves it."

He hesitated a moment, actually thinking about the result of going into her room and screwing her, before he went home to Nina. But then he placed a hand on each of her arms, and gently pushed her away. Alicia was a very sexy woman, but after living with her, and almost making the mistake of marrying her, he knew he didn't want her back in his life and sleeping with her would only bring the drama filled woman in front of him back with a vengeance; not counting the problems he would have with Nina.

"In case you don't remember the growth in my pants was always an instantaneous reaction. So, if you would go on into your room and get settled in, I'll be on my way. It was good seeing you again, I hope you have a safe trip back."

He leaned forward, placed a kiss on her cheek, and stood back. Alicia knew that gesture meant nothing; it was just a gentleman of a thing that Jeff did to any women. She finally gave him a disappointed smile. Stepped forward, put her arms around him, and hugged him.

"You, too Jay. It was really good seeing you." Then she went in, leaving him in the hall.

Jeff finished without giving Nina all the sexual details and holding his hands up in the air. "That was all", he said.

"That was it?" Nina was sitting up on her pillow.

"If you're asking if I slept with her, no? Yes, she made numerous efforts to get me to be with her, but I was more concerned with what I had waiting for me at home. Against what you believe, I do know how to say no to other beautiful woman, I just don't know how to say no to you. "He pulled her over into his arms again and kissed her.

Nina thought maybe she was making too much of this, but for some reason, it bothered her more than she wanted to let on.

---

Nina wiggled trying to move the weight of Jeff to one side, so that she could see the clock. It was 6:38am, and his personal cell phone was ringing for the second time.

"Jeff, your phone", she said pushing him softly.

"Get it", he mumbled after moaning, without budging in the least bit.

Nina sighed not knowing what she was going to say considering it look like he had not intentions to talk to anyone at this hour. She decided the proper thing to do, would be to answer since whomever it was had called twice. She struggled to reach out to retrieve the phone from the bedside table.

"Hello."

"Hi, Niece; isn't it, could I speak to Jeff please?"

Nina took a moment to gather her emotions and manner before she spoke to the women on the other end. What the hell did this hussy want now?

"My name is Nina, and Jeff is sleep right now."

"Oh honey, I apologize. I'm terrible with names. But anyway, my flight leaves in a few, and I wanted to know what Jay would like for me to do with his plane ticket for next weekend."

"Excuse me." Nina was wondering if she was awake and hearing correctly.

"Oh, Jay didn't tell you? He has some business in Chicago next week, so he's staying out there to spend some time with me afterward."

Nina just held the phone. She was sure if she applied the smallest bit of pressure, it would crumble in her hands; her blood was boiling with anger.

"So, could I speak with him", Alicia asked again?

Nina shoved Jeff off of her violently, making him jump awake in shock.

"What the hell is going on", he asked confused and rubbing the sleep from his eyes?

The last thing Nina wanted to do was to get pissed at this whole situation but she was already there. She was getting way too upset with the drama surrounding this women and Jeff. This is what she didn't want to happen. She got up from the bed and threw the phone down beside him. "Talk to your freaking girlfriend." She was halfway to the bathroom and Jeff was looking from her to the phone beside him, confused.

He finally picked it up. "Yeah..... Lish it's really too early in the morning for this shit. I told you last night I wasn't coming to Chicago for that.... Why would I want you to buy me a ticket, I can fly there myself if I wanted to, and I'm not. She's more than just a friend.... I doubt it.... It was good seeing you too. Bye." He pressed the end call button and dropped the phone beside him. *Women!*

Nina heard him take a deep breath, before he knocked softly on the door. "Nina, babe, could you come out here, please?"

Nina stared at the door. She felt a sudden nausea feeling coming over her. She was making herself sick over this man. Jeff knocked on the door again.

"Sweetie, please come on."

Nina opened the door slowly and stared at Jeff angrily. He was leaning his head on the doorframe with his eyes half shut. He rubbed his eyes again, trying to focus before he looked at her. He had to hold in his smile, for before him stood the most beautiful black goddess, with the most gorgeous eyes that were at the moment blazing at him. "Babe don't be upset."

"Don't be upset?! Jeff you were planning to go to Chicago to be with that hussy!"

He rubbed his head, hoping he could rub away some of the stress. What he really wanted right now was a cigar to help blow some of this early morning steam off that was now bringing on a headache. "Babe I wasn't going to Chicago, I didn't plan anything." He grunted and grabbed his head again. "It's too early for this shit. Look sweetie, come;

sit down." He started moving toward the bed, and then turned to see Nina hadn't moved. "Please", he pleaded.

Nina sighed, rolled her eyes, and then went to sit on the bed. Jeff followed her and sat beside her.

"Babe, last night I was talking to Lish about an upcoming meeting with some contacts we have in Chicago concerning a new building. It's something my father is handling, but she wanted me to come out and spend the time with her. I told her it wasn't going to happen, but she's just persistent. You've got to understand Lish is that type of person when she wants something, she digs her heels in and won't give up when told no. She's on her way back to Chicago, and shouldn't be bothering us anymore."

Nina was still silent. She had gotten herself all upset about this, and at the moment she felt a little embarrassed. And she of all people knew how women could be when it came to playing games with men.

She hadn't answered yet, Jeff took her hand. "Nina, come on, talk to me."

She sighed, "Alright." If he was lying he definitely could do it well with such an honest face, but she doubt he was. The problem was she felt like she was fallen so in love with him that it was starting to control her. She was jumping to conclusions and taking things way too seriously.

Jeff pulled her close to him and hugged her tight. He was glad that was over. As he stood there holding her in his arms, he whispered in her hair, "You know tonight is when we are suppose to have dinner at my parents?"

Nina pulled away from him to look up at his face. "Jeff, your parents hate me", she whined.

"Nina you know that isn't true. I've talked to my mother about her behavior and she should be on her best behavior. As for my Father, you know he adores you, as much as I do. Besides they asked us to come."

"No, they asked you to come, you just said you were bringing me."

"If you care about me in the least, you'll go", he gave her a pitiful little look.

She smiled at him, and ran her hands over his head, and brought them to rest at the back of his neck. "Okay, you big baby."

"Could you also wear that blue little dress you wore in Miami", he grinned.

"Jeff, that dress is not appropriate for dinner with your parents. If I wore that, your mother would have a field day with me."

"My father and I would love it." He laughed. She punched him in the chest and laughed also. It felt good, to feel good with someone else again.

Nina shifted the baby blue, scuba off-the shoulder skater dress, making sure it hung just right. Jeff looked over and saw her fidgeting. He reached over, put his arm around her waist, pulled her close and kissed her on her cheek.

"You look great."

She gave him an uneasy smile and whispered a "thanks", as his father opened the door.

"Hey you two", Mr. Smith stood handsomely smiling in the grand doorway. Jeff softly pushed Nina in the center of her back, since it seemed she wasn't going to move.

"Well this is a surprise, my father answering the door."

"Well why should bother I others to open a door I'm standing next to. You two come on in." He placed his hands on Nina's shoulders, holding her at a distance and looking her over, "You're just as beautiful as always."

Nina beamed, "Thanks, Mr. Smith, how are you?"

"Couldn't be any more wonderful, with such a beautiful woman in my presence", he said charmingly.

Nina noticed he had such a warm aura about him and the same good looks and suave charm that were mimicked in Jeff got it from. It made her wonder how he could be married to a woman like Jeff's mother, and still remain so calm and maintain such a warm personality. She just thanked God that Mrs. Smith's personality hadn't rubbed off on Jeff. He must have taken from Mr. Smith's side of the family.

Jeff was engaging in business talk, leaving Nina to marvel over the impeccable art pieces in the parlor where they stood. She peeked not obviously into every corner of the room. There were no signs of the evil mother anywhere.

"Is that my dear son?" Mrs. Smith came from the library.

Nina's heart plummeted. There goes the idea of her not being there. The woman nearly floated into the room, looking like a picture of designer created royalty, dressed in a radiant, royal blue, biased-cut, high low dolmen sleeve sheath dress that hit asymmetrically at her knees and hung lower in the back. She walked on a pair of black barely there sandaled heels directly to Jeff and gracefully hugged and kissed his cheek, then kept her arm around Jeff's waist as she then turned to Nina, "How are you this evening?" It was evident in her voice that the greeting was forced out with the false impression of the smile she applied to it.

Nina bite her tongue at the sarcasm in her voice, "I'm fine Mrs. Smith. Hope you are doing well?"

"Yes"

Jeff winked at Nina, and gave her smile for bearing it and being polite.

"Sweetheart, have I got a surprise for you", she said stirring Jeff away a little, pleased with her own self?

"Mother, what could that be?"

Mrs. Smith smiled then turned toward the library entrance that she had come through and motioned for someone to come. Through the door, dressed in a red, one shouldered cocktail dress, was the devil witch herself, Alicia.

Nina glared, "not this bitch again", she mumbled under her breath, but still loud enough that Jeff heard it. Jeff had stopped smiling now; Mr. Smith was shaking his head at his wife's behavior, but Alicia and Mrs. Smith were standing there with big ass grins on their faces.

"Alicia called and said she was in town, so I just had to invite her over for dinner."

"Hi, Jay." Alicia stepped closer and leaned in and kissed Jeff's cheek."

Jeff wouldn't take his eyes off of Nina. Nina was standing now with her weight on one leg, while bouncing the other unconsciously, trying to maintain her anger. She wanted to attack the witch right there, then take her and beat his mother with her, but reconsidered.

"Well why don't we go into the dining room, dinner has to be ready." Mrs. Smith caught her husband's hand and tried to ignore his scolding her about setting up something that obviously shouldn't have been done. She was still smiling at her own set up, leaving the three of them behind in the parlor.

Jeff tried to maintain a low tone, "What the hell are you doing here; you were suppose to leave this morning?"

"I decided to spend an extra day and visit my two favorite people, Mom and Dad." She turned to Nina. "How are you Nessey?"

Nina decided she was not going to make a scene in Jeff's parent's house. She rolled her eyes at Alicia and turned toward Jeff.

"Sweetie, we can go if you like." Fury was pooling deep in Jeff's eyes.

"No, we were invited to dinner, and that is what we are going to do, have dinner. I'm fine." She took his hand, glared at Alicia and took her man into the dining room. This witch was not going to get the best of her.

Thirty minutes later, she was pushing her prime rib and vegetables around her plate trying not to make eye contact with anyone, since no one was interested in her anyway. Alicia and Mrs. Smith were constantly consuming the conversations about shopping trips to Europe and other places. Every once in while, between conversations with his Dad, Jeff would reach over and squeeze her hand under the table. She'd glance over at him' smiled, and turned back to her food, praying these two heifers would shut the hell up soon.

Right before Donae, the pretty servant with the Jamaican accent, that Jeff playfully flirted with, came to pick up the dinner plates, the conversation turned to reminiscing about old times. Jeff was holding Nina's hand under the table when things seemed to go in the worse direction.

"Jeff, do you remember the Church down the street from our condo we lived in Chicago; the one we were planning the wedding at when we were engaged; well they are tearing it down?"

Jeff suddenly released Nina's hand, and dropped his fork from his other hand. Nina did the same, and locked her stare on him. All eyes seemed to be fixed on her. Jeff wanted to say something, but for the first time he was at a lost of the right words to say at this moment; all charm had gone out the door at this time.

Nina pushed her chair back and rose. "Excuse me." She didn't know where she was going, but she had to free herself from the compressing walls of the dining room. When she reached the parlor, she heard footsteps behind her on the marble floors. She didn't know where she was headed; everything was very blurry. She stopped while wringing her hands, and tried to control herself as she started to pace. Jeff grabbed her elbow.

"Babe, let me explain why I didn't tell you." He was talking softly, but it was making Nina even angrier how he could be so calm about something like this.

She jerked her arm free and put her hand up to stop him, "Jeff don't: right now I just want to go home, to be alone."

"But Babe, we're not done. Let's just finish dinner, and then we can go back to my place and talk about this."

"Jeff, your mother invited another woman here for you and she knew I was going to be here. I have been an unwanted guest the whole evening, and I also find out that not only did you use to live with this other woman, but you were engaged to her and you have never, ever mentioned any of this to me. Despite the conversations that you may have had with your mother, it is no secret that she hates me and that's not going to change. You can stay and finish dinner with your ex, but I'm leaving. I'll call a car. Please do apologize for my early departure." She felt herself getting angrier and louder by the minute. She had her hand on the doorknob before Jeff could speak.

"Nina, just wait; please." He sighed and went back to the dining room.

"Thanks for dinner, but we're leaving."

"But Jeff, you have a guest", his mother said.

"Katherine, let the man go", Mr. Smith spoke up.

"Frankly mother, I have seen enough of Alicia for a life time." Alicia looked hurt, as her pasty smile left her lips. "Alicia have a nice trip. Father, I'll see you later, and mother we definitely will be talking about this soon. Goodnight."

Nina waited by the car in the spiral driveway. She had to get out of that house. It contained too many people that didn't care too much for her and neither did she for them. She swore every time she came here, it was bad.

When they were in the car, Jeff looked over at her. "Sweetheart if we could just talk about this, you would understand why–"

"Jeff, just please take me home." Her voice was shaky and she was trying to refrain from bursting with anger, or into tears.

He sighed and ran his hand over his face, trying to rub the urge for a cigar and a shot of anything strong he could get his hands on, to clear his mind.

The twenty-five minutes drive to her place was silent, not even the radio played. But Nina felt the closer she got home, the more pressure was lifted from her. By the time Jeff's Mercedes pulled in front of her house, she would be at total peace: where she belonged. Out of the presence of people who didn't believe she was good enough to belong in their circle.

When he pulled into her drive he turned to her, "Do you really want me to leave?"

"Yes." She opened the door before Jeff had the chance to protest, and rushed inside her house. She closed the door behind her and bailed for her sofa. She closed her eyes to control her emotions, and when she opened them again, her gaze fell on her mother and father's picture over her mantel, and her heart started that aching feeling. She didn't need to feel one of these episodes on top of everything else right now; but she missed them so much. She pulled her knees up to her chest and wrapped her arms around them as the tears began to fall. Before she knew it, her eyes were leaking and her wall had crumbled as the tears washed away every brick she had built up.

---

Nina couldn't believe she was dialing the number that she thought she'd never dial again. Her fingers were shaky and her head was still throbbing. A shower and a glass of wine hadn't helped very much, but it did seem to relax her a minor bit. She had let her cell phone ring until Jeff's earlier calls just rolled over to her voicemail. She needed to talk to someone and since Janette was visiting family in Atlanta with Warren, that ruled her out, even though she knew Net wouldn't have minded if she had called. So now she was resorting to the one other person she had confided in the past. Quinton.

She tightened her grip on the phone as she waited out the rings.

She was just about to hang up, thinking it had been a bad idea anyway, when his deep voice answered.

"Yeah, this is Q."

Nina took a deep breath, "Hi Quinton."

"Ne, is that you?"

She hadn't talked to Q in over 8 months and she wasn't sure if he was going to warm up to the idea of her calling him, but the only way she could find out is to be straight forward about it.

"Yeah. I need to talk to you, could you come over?"

"Right now?" He sounded extremely surprised.

"Are you doing something that's more important?" Nina knew that wouldn't make a difference, but she heard the giggles of a female, that confirmed what she thought was going on.

He chuckled, because no one knew him better than Nina. "Alright. Text me your address and I'll be there in a few."

As she sat waiting, her mind wondered to Jeff and Alicia. No wonder the witch thought she could just waltz back in and get back with him. What angered her more was that Jeff was always telling her to talk to him about anything and confide in him, when he couldn't even share his own past with her? What else had he kept from her? This is partly her fault. She knew as soon as she started showing some emotions, that's when the truth came out. She was just grateful she hadn't shared all her own issues to him yet; as double sided as that seemed.

The doorbell rung at the same time the phone rung. She peeked through her blinds to see Quinton's navy Lincoln SUV sitting in the driveway. "Just a minute", she yelled, grabbing the phone to look at the caller ID. It was Jeff. Nina laid the phone down, and went for the door. *Let him talk to voicemail again.* She opened the door to the tall, dark breath of fresh air that Quinton was. He had caused her numerous problems in the past, but he was still a friend, and she knew that as much as he did. Their problems would never change that. He stood in her doorway; 6'2, gorgeous, bald, all chocolate man, dressed in black slacks and a siege green shirt. The smell of him made her close her eyes, and inhale the aurora of all of him.

"Baby girl."

"Hello Quinton."

He took her into his arms and squeezed her long and hard, while bending down to burying his face in her neck, where he softly kissed her. "I missed you so much." He whispered and held on to her a little longer before releasing her.

Nina sighed, slowly pushed away and quickly moved aside to let him in and closed the door, thinking this may not have been a good idea after all. He smiled, then walked passed her. "You're still the same; always have to be in control all the time."

Nina followed him to her living room and ignored his comment. "You got here quick. Either the female you were with wasn't important, or you two were almost done when I called."

He smiled at her as she sat beside him on the sofa, "What female; what are you talking about?"

"Quinton, don't try to play me. You forget who you're talking to. It's me; I know what you sound like when you're being pleasured. I use to be the one pleasuring you."

He smiled and placed one of his huge warm hands on her leg. "You know there is no one more important than you are. When you call, I come."

Nina rolled her eyes to the ceiling. Being charming and smooth talking were two of Quinton's most attractive qualities when it came to women. Add his deep, raspy, Barry White baritone voice, and he could get any women to do whatever he wanted

He moved his hand from her thigh to her cheek, "I really missed you."

"Well, I missed you too Q, but tonight I really just need a friend to talk to you." She took his hand from her face and patted it with her own, before placing it in his lap.

"So, what has the rich boyfriend done?"

"What do you mean", Nina asked, reaching for her third glass of wine?

"You've obviously been in love lately. I haven't heard from you in a minute, but everyone else has seen you and your new boyfriend out and about. Then suddenly, you call me one night after 11pm, and it's not a booty call. Out of all the people you could have called, you called your ex-boyfriend, turned reliable best friend. And that wasn't by my choice."

While Charlotte was a big enough city, once you had been there a while, circles intermingled and someone who knows someone, also knew you. Word got around. So while Nina had not personally seen or talked to Quinton, he was probably up to date on quite a bit of information on her, by his huge circle of friends. Nina put her glass down. She was beginning to feel a bit warm. She thought maybe she better lay off of the wine. "I just needed to talk."

Quinton's expression hardened and seriousness overcame him. He knew that look on her face. He had come home to it too many times before, when she had lapsed into an emotional state over her parents. "You had one of your days didn't you?"

Nina started rubbing her hands together as a distraction. "Yeah, and then things with Jeff didn't help."

"What, did you finally realize that you don't belong with his snobby ass?

"Jeff isn't like that." Nina felt a need to defend him.

"Then why isn't he here instead of me?"

Nina dropped her gaze to her hands. He had a point. He sat up and reached for her hands.

"Ne, I don't mean to hurt you when I say this, but this dude isn't going to know how to appreciate you because he has nothing in common with you. He's not going to know how to treat you; look at you now."

"And I suppose you staying out all night and having a baby with another woman, is knowing how to appreciate and treat me?"

"Oh shit, I did deserved that." He sat back and ran his hand across his head.

They sat there in silence for a minute. The telephone ringing interrupted. Nina reached for the phone on the coffee table, and saw Jeff's number pop up. She definitely couldn't talk to him with Quinton here. She knew he wouldn't leave a message, so she'd try to call him back later, since she felt like he had waited long enough. To her surprise as well as embarrassment, she accidently hit the speaker button instead of the end button. When Nina didn't say anything, Jeff started talking.

"Sweetheart, say something, please. I know you're upset about what happened, but we need to talk about this. I never meant to hurt you..."
Nina grabbed the phone and hit the end button immediately. She stared

at the phone and wouldn't look at Quinton, because she knew what was coming.

"Okay, what the hell did Mr. Rich Boy do?"

Nina sighed and rolled her eyes, "Quinton please, don't start."

"What do you mean don't start? Did he hit you? How is it that he hurt you?"

"Quinton, please."

"Well tell me, did he put his hands on you? You know that shit is unacceptable. I may have caused you a lot of problems in the past, but putting my hands on you was something I never did, and I won't sit around and let someone else do it either."

Same old controlling Quinton. "Quinton, he didn't touch me."

"Then what did he do?"

"It's not a big deal. His mother isn't very fond of me, so she invited another woman to dinner, and she knew I would be there. The woman was a little more than just an old friend also. You know my luck, it's always another woman."

Quinton knew that dig was just as much at him, as it was at this Jeff guy. "I can tell, that this really does have you upset. You in love with him?"

Nina hesitated a moment, then slowly nodded her head. Until this moment, she hadn't had to admit to anyone but Jeff and Janette that she loved Jeff; loved being around him, loved being with him, and until now, she had kept from herself the notion of being IN love, because she knew what being IN love got her. She had just been saying she loved him. But now, she had to admit that the reason this whole episode had upset her so much was because she was truly IN love with Jeff; there was a big difference.

"So, do you care about him?" Quinton asked again.

"Yeah, I do."

"More than you cared about me."

"I still care about you, Quinton, that won't ever change."

"Well, is it more?"

Nina smiled, "Almost." She punched him in the arm playfully.

Quinton smiled at her, "Lucky mofo. I hope he doesn't mess up like I did."

Nina noticed his expression was becoming softer now, she dropped her stare to her hands again and remained quiet.

"You know sometimes, I wonder if I could pinpoint the very moment that things started going wrong in our relationship and rewind time back to a minute before that very moment to change it. I ask myself often if so, we would still be together now.

Nina gave Q a half smile. "There were so many moments Q. We probably shouldn't have even moved in with each other. We were great friends, but when we started living together and trying to push ourselves to be what we thought others felt we should be, is when things went south."

"You are probably right. We had a lot of great times though."

"Yes, we did" she smiled.

"There is so much I miss with you."

"Like what", Nina asked looking up into his eyes since he had them now set directly on her at that moment.

"Making love to you."

Nina started wringing her hands. The wine among other things was having a whirlwind effect on her head. "Quinton, you make it seem like you haven't been with anyone else since me, and I know that is the farthest thing from the truth."

"No, but you know no one could ever make love with me the way you did. Ne, you know we were great together. We had our problems, but we could always fix that with a little lovemaking. Let me help you take your mind off of all the bad of the night and remember a better time, when it was just you and me." He put emphasis on the final words, by leaning in and kissing her neck softly.

She realized that she was slowly losing control, something she didn't like to do. But he was right, when they made love, things happened. The sex being so great was one of the main reasons it took her so long to leave him. Every time he screwed up, he'd win her over with his charm and lovemaking. It was a catch twenty-two. It kept her there, but it was also the reason for the problems with other women. They knew as well as she did, how good Quinton was in bed and what his charming finesse could do to a woman or make a woman do. Which is where the drama began. She was just happy that she had been smart and made him wrap it up 98% of the time. The other 2% was her reasons for STD testing every 6 months now that they were over.

It was no secret that Quinton was a ladies man, for his profession was one that carried that trait as a requirement. Quinton was a hustler, he owned a list of warehouse in downtown for local entrepreneurs. He was also Co-owner of a small real estate office and a ritzy nightclub. His partner Santasha; was a beautiful, smart, petite magician at real estate business deals. She often doted on Nina & Q's relationship and praised then for being an inspiration for her own relationship goals. And Nina had been fooled by that. It wasn't until she had moved in with him, and months later of her piecing info together did she finally find out Santasha wanted to be more than a business partner. Nina had set boundaries for Q and expressed why he as the other person in their relationship, should dedicate keeping his business relationship with Santasha, business only, because she wasn't in a relationship with Santasha and she didn't' expect Santasha to give a damn about making sure Q stayed faithful. Q agreed, since he swore he never saw anything beyond business with Santasha anyway. And in the end, Nina found that Santasha wasn't the threat or issue at all.

Quinton wasn't a stereotype in any way. He was both sharp and sophisticated despite where he started and came from. He took pride in selecting his clothes and enjoying the finer things that one indulges in. Such was the case with his nightclub, only the best, no-nonsense. So along with the large crowds and liquid cash, came women of every color, shape, and size. But Quinton had promised Nina she would always be the one he came home to. The one he wanted to give everything to, the one he said he loved, the one he wanted to have his children, and the one he said he one day wanted to spend the rest of his life with. Well one day never came.

For two years, Nina was what Quinton wanted her to be. She rarely went out herself even to his club. She worked and stayed at home. Cooking for him, his friends and anyone else that he happened to bring home, at whatever time he decided to come in. She hosted his parties and was the wifey that he wanted her to be, even though he stayed out late, went on trips away without her, and made un-kept promises to marry her over and over. She had temporarily destroyed her relationship with her Auntie Laurie and Uncle George; the only family she had left because of their disapproval of him. She had even dealt with the other nagging women and all their drama. The threatening notes on her windshield, the phone calls, and the text messages from unknown numbers that included explicit videos and pictures. All of it she had dealt with, because out of all the drama he caused, he had been there for her, and she had torn down her walls of vulnerability with him; letting him be her hold all for everything. Until one day there was a surprise at the front door. It was then that her level of tolerance had been reached.

The quality time he never spent with her was obvious then. There was nothing she didn't do for him. But, yet he went out and got something she couldn't give him in the three years that they had been together. And it took her taking herself out of the situation for her to realize how much she was messing up her life with him.

But right now he was here again. His husky voice in her ear and his strong, warm hands cupping her breast sending jolts of heat in between her legs. The feeling, taking her back to those days they'd make love on the kitchen counter, or on top of his truck, or when he came home late, lifted off of herbs and party; wanting to be loved right by her.

Nina was loosing herself more and more: her mind in a whirlwind from all the wine she had drunk. She was moaning his name, cupping his head in her hands, and only wanting to think about the two of them. Taking pleasure at her quivering and sighing beneath him. He kissed her lips, and then playfully bit her neck.

He whispered in her ear. "Damn, I missed you so much."

As Quinton's manhood pressed against her inner thigh, Nina pulled his shirt over his head to reveal those dark brown muscles that she use to love to kiss so much. She caught sight of the so-called sign of love that he had tattooed on his right chest, for her. It used to read her nickname 'Ne', entwined with a vine. She sat up to get a closer look at his arm. Now it read, "Nequan " and the vine had been blemished away and replaced with a date. Nina pushed him away from where he was showering attention on her breast.

"Quinton, no, I don't want to do this."

Quinton, startled, looked at her puzzled. "What do you mean, you were just all into it?"

Nina pushed him up, pulled her shirt back on, and got up. She raised her hands to her now pounding head. She concentrated on her breathing, trying to get herself back together.

"Ne, we were about to make love, what's wrong?"

"Quinton, aside from the fact that I'm involved with someone else, what is wrong, is that." She was pointing at his arm where the tattoo was.

He looked down at his arm. "Ne, that's my son's name. I know you're not angry with me for changing it. You were the one who left me, and even with all the begging I did for you to come back, you told me it would never happen. So, I put his name there."

"Quinton, it's not the tattoo that bothers me. It's being reminded that that is what broke us up. Quinton I can't go back to hurting in the morning after we make love the night before, because you'll be gone, again. All it would have been is a lay for old times."

"Nina, I want things to be different this time. I want to fix and make everything right that I messed up before. I want us back."

"Quinton, we can't and you know that." She was standing across the room, hugging herself and shaking her head.

He hesitated a moment while staring at her. He finally gave into the battle that he wasn't winning and said, "I see. It's this arrogant, rich, mofo that you are crazy about now. His family treats you like shit, but yet you still want to be with him. How many times do I have to tell you he doesn't deserve you? You don't belong with them."

Nina sat down and put her head in her hands. Quinton always told the truth with her, even when he could benefit no good from it. She felt the tears swelling in her eyes and she didn't want to cry about this in front of Quinton, but it was too late, and she wiped at her tears.

Quinton shook his head, and then let out a huge sigh. "Damn, Nina don't do this." He hated to see her cry. He pulled her up and held her in his arms until her hard sobs became shallow. "I didn't mean to hit you when you were already down, but I just want you to see my side. Stop this damn crying, please!"

Nina smiled and wiped at her eyes, as his warm hands lingered at her shoulders.

"You really want to work things out with this jerk, don't you?"

She smiled uneasily, and then nodded.

Quinton sighed and let her go. "Okay. You know I've tried to always give you what you wanted, and sometimes I was a jackass when I didn't. But if this is what you want, okay. Just know I love you still, and if this jerk screws up in any way, let me know. I will handle him."

Nina laughed, she knew Q didn't have a violent bone in his body.

The moment grew silent. "Nina, I'm being real now. I'm talking to you as a friend. Don't let these people destroy the person you are. You're every bit as intelligent, beautiful, and smart as they are, and if they can't see that and accept you the way you are, it's their lost. I want you to know, a good boyfriend I may not be, but you've always got me for a true friend." He brushed his lips at the top of her head, lingering there for a moment, before releasing his arms from around her shoulders.

"Thanks."

"I better go. I don't think I can stay in this house with you much longer and be able to contain myself." When he got to the door he turned to her. "You know how to find me, if you need me. I'll always drop everything for you."

Nina watched as he went to his truck, answering his phone that started ringing as soon as he turned it on. He nodded at her one last time, before pulling away. And as he did she was thankful to have a friend that she could depend on to listen like Q, but at the same time she was happy that that part of her life was over. She was even proud of herself. Someone's prayers had saved her from that.

Nina went in and thought about calling Jeff, but she wasn't ready yet; maybe by the morning.

# CHAPTER XIII

## CROSSING DIFFERENT BRIDGES AND HALF FALLEN WALLS

NINA LEANED ON JEFF'S DOORBELL, waiting for him to answer. She knew he was there because he had left his car in the circle drive in front of the house instead of in the garage. He finally opened the door, with both surprise and relief on his face. From the look of his red eyes and rugged facial hair, it didn't look like he had had the most peaceful night of sleep. He was dressed in a t-shirt and a pair of sweat pants. More clothes than he ever slept in. The soft stubble against his jaw line made him look even sexier in his rough appearance.

"Did I come at a bad time", she asked?

"No, of course not, come in." He stepped aside letting her into the spacious hallway. "How are you?" She looked like she had slept peacefully as bright and radiant as she could be in a pair of jeans, black stiletto sandals and an off the shoulder, dolman sleeve, white blouse. She smelled sweet, hair freshly curled, and just enough eyeliner, mascara, lip liner and gloss properly applied to make her chocolate skin glow beautifully. He did not have to know she didn't get any sleep either, and she had spent an hour in front of her mirror making sure she was perfect before coming over.

"Better." She was on her way into his living room as he followed her. Just as she reached the entranceway to the living room, she heard the hall bathroom door open and the sound of heels on Jeff's hardwood floors

"Jay?" Alicia rounded the corner. "Oh, hi Nina." She snapped her

fingers and pointed to Nina while smiling at herself for getting it right this time.

Nina stood frozen in shock. It took her a moment to find her voice. "I see I did come at a bad time. I'll be going." It was that moment the guilt she had been feeling for even asking Q to come over, left her completely. She was moving back up the hall toward the front door when Jeff grabbed her by the elbow.

"No, Nina don't. We need to talk."

"Why Jeff? I'm sure anything you need to talk about you and Alicia can handle. Besides she has way more in common with you." She tried to jerk her arm away, but Jeff's strength overpowered her.

"Nina, this isn't what it looks like."

"I'm sure it isn't. You supposedly were so worried about me last night that you had to have her here to console you, huh?"

"Nina, that isn't what happened." He released her elbow, and raised his hands to his temples and began to massage to calm himself. He took a deep breath, dropped his hands and turned to Alicia. "Would you help me out here?"

Alicia smiled that conniving smile, rolled her eyes at Jeff and turned to Nina. "Nina, I came here this morning to see if I had another chance to basically try to get back with Jeff. Jeff has painstakingly assured me, repeatedly, that there is no chance of any of that ever happening. When you arrived, I was just waiting for my car service, so that I could leave. I do owe you an apology for trying to cause so many troubles. It's just sometimes it takes a woman the long way around to realize that she once had the best man there ever was, and by then it's too late. I do see that Jay is happier now than I could ever have made him. I wish you two the best of luck. I think I hear my car. It was nice meeting you Nina, and good seeing you again Jeff. Goodbye."

They both stood in silence a moment after she had went out the door. Jeff finally turned to Nina, "So?"

"So what? That still doesn't explain why you didn't tell me you were engaged to her."

'Nina, what if I would have? You know just like I do, that it would only have caused unnecessary drama. You know how you were the other night when I came home from dinner with her; I figured telling you that

I was engaged to her would have only added gas to the flame. Alicia and I were engaged 4 years ago. I thought she was the one because my parents and family liked her. But after living with her I realized she was phony, conniving, and everything I didn't want. But most of all, I found out I didn't love her. I was trying to make everyone else happy. But now I know that I'm in love, and no one else can change that, okay?"

He moved in closer to her and placed his fingers at her chin and turned her head so that her eyes met his. Her eyes hide something; the same something that he saw so many times before. It was like a shield that blocked away a story. Nina turned away from him and shifted so that her back was to him. *Here she goes again? The place she had promised she wouldn't be at another time. Giving into a man again. Becoming vulnerable once more because the crumbling of her built up protection that she had previously built; the one she was now letting fall in ruins, because of love.*

Jeff came closer again, and gently massaged her shoulders. He leaned in and kissed her softly on the nape of her neck. Nina closed her eyes, and restrained from exhaling loudly. He rubbed his hands up and down her upper arms, before leaving a trail of moist kisses along the back of her neck.

When she spoke her voice was soft, calm, and low. "Jeff, I can't keep dealing with your mother like this. All I keep thinking about is, if it's really worth going round for round with her like this? She's always going to be there doing what she can to keep us apart."

"I would like to think that you believe I am very worth it", he laughed. He then turned her around so that she was facing him. "Look, when we make love, do you consider yourself making love to a man?"

Nina arched her brow at him in confusion, "what?"

"Do you think of me as a man when we are making love?"

"Of course I do."

"When you and I are together any other time, like now, do you consider me a man?"

Not knowing where he was going with this, she nodded confusingly. "Yes."

"And you should, because I am a grown man. A grown ass man whose mother can't and won't dictate my love life. Let my mother be, eventually she's going to have to come to grips with herself, because I'm not letting you go anywhere."

He brushed his lips to the top of her head, and swept her in his arms to hold her. She rested her head upon his warm hard chest and closed her eyes again. The image in her mind was that of a half fallen wall.

But to Jeff he believed that though his mother may be playing a major part in the reasoning of what was wrong with her, he knew it wasn't the only reason. There was something more there, and as time went on his intentions was to find out what it was?

# CHAPTER XIV

J EFF MANEUVERED HIS WAY THROUGH the crowd, with a beer in his hand, a cigar in his mouth and a smile on his face for the beautiful woman who sat across waiting for him on the lawn chair; perched perfectly on the edge with her beautiful brown legs crossed. When he reached her he sat beside her and kissed her smiling lips. He thought to himself this is what made life worth living.

"Are you having fun", he asked?

She softly placed her hand on top of the one that held his beer. "As long as you're here with me."

She had never seen him this relaxed. When he said he wanted her to go with him to see some old college friends, she thought it would be some snotty country club setting where everyone would put on airs and talk about stock and money. She wasn't in the mood to talk politics with a bunch of people who she's sure she probably didn't share the same views with. She knew from her own everyday job and reality, they didn't know half of what was really going on in the same world that they so lavishly controlled with their money. But when Jeff told her to dress confrontable and a pair of sneakers may not be a bad idea; she was extremely surprised when they had arrived. She wasn't expecting a real backyard barbeque.

After introducing her to his frat brother/ best friend, David: his wife Kim and their 7-year-old son, and Jeff's godson, Kyle; he had turned into a Jeff she had never seen. Business was far from his current state of mind. He had reverted into what Nina could imagine him being before he became the Vice President of a multi-million dollar company and it looked good on him. He was dancing with little girls, and singing to the old women; being the charmer he was, but relaxed.

"You're really having fun aren't you", she asked nudging his shoulder?

"I really am. Coming out here to David and Kim's is like the only time I can put aside the business and stress and be myself. It's the most relaxed I ever am; it's just too bad I never get to come that often."

"And here I was thinking that I made you the most relaxed when I do that thing you like for me to do."

He looked down at her and smiled, "No, that makes me the most happiest."

The now thinning crowd of people in the spacious back yard, and the lyrics of Donna Summers Last dance from the DJ, was signs of the party coming to an end. Jeff lifted his gaze to the beautiful three-story house that stood before him. An architect's dream house. A house that had a little bit of every architecture structure he had ever used in any of his designs. Houses were rarely the project at hand for him, but he had to say so himself, this one was some of his finest work; something he rarely got to do. He had given the design his best because he wanted his two friends to have the best.

David and Kim were something he hadn't realized until now, that he wanted to be. They had been together since college, and back then, Jeff didn't take females seriously. Females were a past time between classes; more like a hobby. He had been happy being the bachelor, the godfather, and the friend who wasn't settling down because he had his whole life in front of him. But now that whole idea seemed out dated. Not that he was trying to get married and have 10 kids right away his business was too demanding right now. But still having a Kyle to call his own son, and a Kim to go home to and to bed every night with, wouldn't be so bad either.

"Hope you two are having fun."

Jeff was brought out of his thoughts.

Nina looked up into the face of Jeff's 6'2 friend, David. He was dark, chocolate, and handsome. Together, Nina knew they had broken quite a few hearts in the past.

"I'm getting ready to run the rest of these black folks off, since they have eaten all of my food. Then Jay, you and I can hit the tables for a game of pool. Feel free to join us, Nina."

"No, I think I'll let you to handle that and I'll go help Kim clean up. Where is she?"

"She's in the kitchen, trying to rearrange all that her Auntie has misplaced."

"I'll go help her, you guys have fun."

Jeff kissed her again before she walked to the house with the remaining people.

"She's beautiful man." David watched the light that danced in Jeff's eyes, as she left.

"I know, isn't she?" Jeff was still staring after her.

"So, what's the M-O on her?"

Jeff snapped his neck to turn and meet his friend's gaze, "What do you mean?"

"She is not Jeff Edward Smith III, usual kind of woman. So what is the motive, man?"

"What the hell is that supposed to mean? I don't have a type." Jeff was smiling at his friend.

"Come on man, besides the set of twins in college you encountered very briefly, you have never dated anyone who's been that cool. Every woman I've seen you with lately has been, shallow, conceited, and next to unbearable. This woman is beautiful, down to earth, and Kim actually likes her, and that's saying a lot."

"Man, that's crazy."

"Shall I mention Lish?"

"Please don't mention Lish. The memory of her is still fresh in my mind from her visit this week."

"What? She was here in Charlotte?"

"Yes", Jeff said annoyed, taking another gulp from his drink.

"We'll get back to that in a sec. As for the woman at hand, the very beautiful black woman I might add, what's up? You're grinning from ear to ear, and literally dancing around. What has she done to you?"

Jeff let out a sigh and a chuckle. "Made me a happy man, that's all. You know I love all women in general. But Nina is different; that's all I can say."

David grinned, "Jay the Casanova is truly falling in love. I never thought it would happen, but I see it in your eyes man."

Jeff smiled more to himself than to his friend.

"And you're not even going to deny it?"

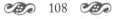

"I'm afraid I can't."

"Well it looks good on you man. Let's grab some beers and hit the game room."

Jeff followed his friend, still smiling at himself. It actually felt good too. Maybe love had lifted that weight that had been on him all these years.

---

Nina found Kim leaning on her front door with her back against it, eyes closed. When she opened them she smiled at Nina.

"Girl, I have never been so happy to see my family leave. Don't get me wrong; I love them, but too much of them can drive you crazy. Then my little cousin wants me to keep her little brat while she goes out to party tonight."

Nina just smiled, not getting a chance to get a word in anyway. The only family she had that she stayed in touch with was her Auntie Laurie and Uncle George from her mother's side, who lived in St. Louis. Her father had been an only child, and all her grandparents had passed away. Aside from her Auntie Laurie and Uncle George, that was it for family. But they definitely had filled her parent's shoes when they had died. The distance between them, didn't take away from the love that Nina knew they had for her.

Up until now, the only family gatherings she had been to were those with Quinton's family. And there was no way they made her feel as part of the family. They thought of her as a goody-two-shoe, and too proper for the likes of Quinton anyway.

Kim was making her way across the spacious marble floor of the foyer. She was about 5'7, with a caramel brown complexion. Her yet black hair was chopped into a short spike style. She was tall and curvy. Her sense of dress was one that Nina could appreciate with a boho style. Unlike the vibes Nina got from other females, Kim was very welcoming.

Nina followed her into the kitchen. Kim was a very fast walker, and talking the whole time as they went. Just as they were entering the mahogany wood cabinet, lined kitchen there came a crash from upstairs.

Kim clenched her fist, and let out a huge sigh before she screamed.

"Kyle if you and John break anything, I'm coming up there and I'm whooping your butts."

"Okay", a union of voices replied.

Kim looked back at Nina, "Do you see what I'll be dealing with tonight? Have a seat while I clean up this kitchen that my Auntie claimed she already cleaned."

"I can help."

"Girl, I like you even more than I did when I met you earlier."

Nina took the towel Kim handed her and started drying dishes to put away

"Well all I can say is I haven't seen Jay this happy in a very long time. You got him smiling and dancing. We haven't seen him in ages because he works too much. The co-owner of a multi-million dollar company and he works harder than the people in the mailroom, and you would never know he would one day own the place. But anyway I don't know what you're doing, but keep it up girl! And let me be the first to say, don't let that mother of his run you off."

Nina laughed; yeah she was definitely going to like Kim.

Nina and Kim busted into another fit of laughter as Jeff and David came into the sitting room. After they had finished cleaning up the kitchen, they grabbed a bottle of wine, slices of the carrot cake that were left and sat back, listening to some music, and laughing about old stories of David and Jeff's college days.

"You two are having too much fun without us", David said landing on the sofa beside Kim. He laid on his back, finding a place in her lap for his head.

Jeff sat down beside Nina, placing a kiss on Nina's cheek. David and Kim exchanged glances and smiles.

"Kim was just telling me some old college stories about you and David."

Jeff stopped drinking his beer in mid-air and looked at Kim then at Nina. "Don't believe anything this woman tells you."

"Too late she knows it all. Kim laughed. "I do mean all."

David laughed too. Jeff looked at Nina. Nina smiled. "I'm still going to keep you." She nudged his arm and leaned up to place what she intended to be a soft peck on his lips, but Jeff was quick and caught her mouth with his own in a much more intense kiss, before letting her go.

"Hey, save some of that for later", David laughed.

"In that case, we will be leaving now." Jeff pretended to get up, pulling Nina with him.

"Why don't you two stay? It's late; besides you both have been drinking. You can make that drive in the morning after some breakfast."

"I don't know, Nina is a screamer, and she may keep everyone up all night. Is that okay with you?" Jeff turned to her and asked.

Nina thought why not? "Yeah."

"Great, I'll go grab something for you to sleep in and show you the guest room" Kim said getting up.

Jeff smiled and winked at Nina as he said, "Alright, but she won't be needing anything to sleep in."

Nina pulled her shirt over her head to find Jeff sitting on the side of the bed staring at her. His shirt hung open, exposing that beautiful, chest. A gold diamond encrusted architecture emblem hung around his neck, glistening under the recessed lights. He was so handsome. It was hard to believe that just that morning they were on the verge of disaster. Yes, he was a beautiful man, with what Nina had found out to be a heart of gold.

She smiled at him, but he never returned it. He gave her a focused serious stare. "Come here," He motioned for her.

Wearing nothing but lavender French cut lace panties and a matching bra, she walked over to him smiling generously. He put his arms around her waist and ran his strong hands down her lower back. He softly kissed her lips, sending a shock of electric waves over her as the taste of wine on her lips mixed with beer and the richness of Cuban cigar on his. He finally pulled away and stared at her with a smug smile on his face.

"I like your friends", she said breaking the awkwardness.

"I knew you would. They are very likable people. They like you a lot too. Especially Kyle, I do believe he has a little crush on you."

Nina laughed.

"He told me that he would play me a game of b-ball for you. At least he's got good taste in women. I taught him well."

Nina smiled, "He thinks a lot of you."

"Yeah, I've got to start spending more time with him. He actually has me looking forward to having one of my own."

Nina ran her hand over his hair playfully, hearing him, but not really listening to him.

"So what do you think about that", he asked her; trying to get her attention?

Nina stopped playing with his hair, "About what?"

"Having a baby."

Nina stilled and stared at him in shock, "Who? Us?"

"Yeah, you and I."

"Jeff stop playing.'

"I'm not playing. Let's have a baby."

"Jeff, we're not even married."

"I do know that that is an important step also, so marry me." He was looking at her with the most serious look in his eyes.

Nina laughed and backed away a little. She knew he was a spare of the moment, demanding businessman, but this was crazy. "Okay, you know what, I think you had a whole lot more than I did to drink. You are really drunk."

"I'm not drunk Nina", he said seriously.

"Babe, you're making my buzz go away. I don't want to talk about this. While I'm feeling good, there are a number of things I want to do to you." She was kissing his neck.

He wasn't responding. He didn't understand why she was blocking again. Any indication of a conversation turning toward talk of marriage, commitment or a future, always built up this wall in front of her. It was obvious when that wall went up in her eyes. He thought after the episode with Alicia, she would be ready to move into new territory with their relationship. Yeah a baby was a big jump, but what about a future together? He knew that she was accustomed to handling things on her own. She was use to being alone, and independent, but something was going on with her, and one way or another she was going to have to trust him and talk to him about it soon.

He sat there a moment lost in his thought. It just didn't feel right. The mention of marriage from him to any other woman would have had them bouncing off the walls. His happy feeling was about gone, and why Nina didn't trust him was confusing him. He pulled his arms from away from her waist and ran his hands over his head.

"Sweetie, is there something wrong", Nina asked concerned?

He wanted to talk about it, but changed his mind. Now wasn't the time. "No, I didn't get much sleep last night, and I'm starting to feel it. I'm just going to go to bed." He stood up and moved around Nina like she wasn't really there and undressed and got into bed.

Nina stood there stunned a moment. Just because she didn't want to discuss something as serious as marriage at a time like this made him angry enough not to even want her. He was so unpredictable. She got into bed herself hoping he would come over and just hold her, but he remained distant on his side of the bed.

And on his side of the bed, Jeff closed his eyes as well as tried to also close his heart to the aching pain Nina was beginning too cause him. He loved her so much it was near controlling. It was making him crazy.

---

Nina kissed Jeff a few more times.

"Sweetie, I've got to go", she said again, trying to pull away from him for the second time.

They had returned from David and Kim's around noon. Kim with the help of Nina prepared a big breakfast and they sat around a while after, exchanging numbers and making future plans to get together. When they arrived back to Jeff's, they had taken a long bath together, and lounged around with all the snacks they could find in Jeff's kitchen, watching Sunday afternoon movies.

It was now 6:30 in the evening, and Nina knew she needed to get home. It had been a busy weekend and she had some things to do to prepare for her children's event at the hospital that next day. Jeff ran his hands up her back as she moved over of him, trying to get up.

"Why?"

"Jeff, I've got a presentation in the morning. You know the one that the Board, which your father sits on, proposed I organize. I've got some last minute adjustments to make." She was moving slowly away.

"I don't understand why you won't just bring your things here to stay, so you're not leaving at all times of night. We're already pressed trying to fit each other into already hectic schedules. I mean Nina we had hit-and-run sex in my office last week, because I was working late and you had to turn in early that night. I'm tired of all that. I want more time with you. I want you in my bed at night, all night; every night."

She had her shirt and skirt on now. In her mind she replayed the evening that hit-and-run sex had taken place. She had called Jeff on the way home from the Center to see what his evening looked like? She had wanted to see him, before she had to turn in early. The Center was sponsoring a huge field trip the next day and the bus was arriving at 5:30am, so she, being the single one with no kids or a husband, had volunteered to be there to organize, giving the others time to get their families off for the morning. Jeff had said he would be at the office for the majority of the evening along with some of his techs. After establishing that they wouldn't see each other later, Jeff talked her into stopping by the office before she went home. When she had gotten there, with some take-out she had stopped to pick up, the security guard Steve told her where she could find Jeff. She let Steve know that she had brought extra dinner and he could come up any time to have some, before she set out to find Jeff. He along with two younger black guys, that looked like they were fresh out of college were in the conference room mulling over blue prints and designs. Nina dropped off the extra bag of food she had for them and Jeff told the guys he'd be back with them in a little while. They thanked Nina with nods and smiles, and went back to working.

Jeff took the remaining heaping bags of soul food that Nina had picked up from Pam's, and rummaged through the bag as he led the way to his office. The building was quite and not many people were left, just those who never knew when to quit. They had munched on fried chicken, pasta salad, baked beans, greens, and skillet cornbread, while Jeff talked non-stop and explained details of the new building he was working on. Nina listened attentively, letting him talk, because she knew how excited buildings and designs made him.

While showing her some sketches of some ideas he had done at his drafting table, he stood behind her as they looked at the designs before them. Jeff pulled her back against his body, nuzzling her ear with his lips as Nina thumbed through the sketches. Nina had felt the heat from him engulfing her as he grew hard and stiff against her bottom, and she had the sudden need to feel him inside of her. He obviously felt the same need. Before she had known how, they were tugging at each other clothes, and hungrily kissing and devouring each other. She never knew that a drafting table had that kind of strength to hold up two hot bodies. It was wild, and it was so good.

She blinked to bring her mind back to the present and the issue at hand.

Jeff pulled her between his legs to where he sat on the side of the bed, and ran his hands up her thighs under her skirt. After the way they had ended the night before after the mention of a wedding and baby, it had been on his mind to try a different approach with Nina. "Why don't you bring some things over to keep here?"

Nina knew where this was going, and she didn't like it. She thought she had avoided the subject the night before at Kim and David's when he brought up that whole marriage thing. What had gotten into him all of a sudden? She placed her hands on his shoulders and pushed him away, forcefully. The whole idea scared her. Moving in with another man was not going to happen after all she had been through with Quinton. She had let her guard down and fallen in love with Jeff, but living with him was one guard she wasn't letting down. Not again. She was trying to better herself both mentally and spiritually. This whole sex thing was bad enough. Her plan was to eliminate sins, not pick them back up.

"Because I pay damn good money every month for a mortgage for my own place."

Jeff widened is eyes. He detected the anger and tension in her actions and as well as her tone. "Are you trying to answer my question of moving in with me, before I ask you?"

Nina rolled her eyes, let out a sigh, and tried to move away. Jeff was quicker and grabbed her hand.

"Dammit Jeff, just let me go."

"No. I've let you go too many times before when we talk about anything like this."

"Jeff I'm trying to spiritually get myself together. I don't want to make the same mistakes I made in the past."

"Nina, I asked you to marry me, because I love you. I don't intend on you just moving in with me and living like that forever. I want you in my life. Now, look at me and tell me do you love me?"

Her head was suddenly pounding. It was getting hot and her throat was dreadfully dry. Anxiety was taking over. She didn't know where or how to start. *How could she tell him the thing she had been trying to keep him from finding out all this time? The one thing that she was sure would drive him away; the same way it had taken every man she seemed to love away. It had first taken away not only her father, but also her mother at the same time. A father that had been her world to her. It then drove Quinton away, and no matter how much she had tried to keep it from Jeff, he was now forcing her to tell him and she was sure he'd be gone soon too. It was all happening so fast.*

Nina lifted her now shaking hands up to head and massaged her temples. She took in a few breaths, trying to calm herself the way the doctor had advised her to do at times like these. After a moment of Jeff watching her; she felt she could speak again. She began to speak slowly.

"Jeff, please…I can't do this right now." Her throat felt like sandpaper as she whispered the words.

"Are you okay?" he asked calmly recognizing something wasn't right.

"Yeah, I just need time."

"Time for what; I just want to know do you love me?" A little both annoyed and confused as what was going on before his eyes.

She closed her eyes and sighed. Boy the night can change from happy to disaster in a matter of minutes. "Jeff, of course I love you. It's just that there is something I need to tell you, and I need time to get myself together. I can't tell you right now."

"You drop something like this on me and then tell me you can't tell me now?"

"Would you rather I say, let's cut our ties right now?"

She was staring fear in the eyes now; meeting his gaze with her own strong one.

"Nina, are you in trouble? Is it something I can do?"

"Jeff no. It's just something I need time to deal with before I tell you."

He rubbed his hands over his head and face.

Nina reached out to him gently now; more calmer.

"Babe, please just give me some time. I promise."

*Why, what, and how* is all he could think? He finally settled for what he could deal with. "Fine."

Nina kissed him softly on the cheek. Promised she'd call him later, and bailed before he could stop her. She had to be free of this house, and even Jeff, before she went into another attack and the walls closed in on her.

*Nina swerved for the third time, to avoid a fallen branch. She was hunched over the wheel and sitting up straight to focus through the debris and rain. A pillar of lightening dashed through the black sky overhead, and Nina jerked with fear. This was insane. She had to hurry, and this storm was not the friendliest weather to travel in when you're rushing. Her heart was beating out of her chest and she was sure if it wasn't for the tormenting winds swaying the car and the pounding rain on the roof of the car, she would be able to hear each beat of her heart.*

*The scenery outside her windshield was dark, rainy, windy, and eerie. Her focus was off and she kept pressing her brakes but there was nothing there in the darkness. Then before she could stop, she saw them. She felt the hit before she actually saw the bodies ascend through the air. As the car screeched across the highway, and impacted with a tree, Nina's vision blurrily left her, and total blackness engulfed her senses, as she slipped into unconsciousness, but the last thing that she remembered was the two faces of the couple she had hit. Her mother and father.*

# CHAPTER XV

## AND IN THE MORNING
## WHEN THE SUN RISES

NINA SLIPPED IN AND OUT of a sleep of nightmares. Reliving the night her parents died. She remembered the telephone conversation. Her mother had called from their vacation in the mountains to check on her. Nina had been reluctant to tell her about her doctor's appointment & the diagnosis she had been given. It hadn't been as if she could hide it from them. They knew she was going to the doctor, hoping to find out why she had been in pain for so long. It had taken everything she could come up with to convince them she could handle the doctor on her own, that they didn't have to cancel their trip. She wasn't as lucky at keeping them from cutting their trip short. Nina had tried to hold back how upset she was, while telling her mother what the doctor had said. Her mother and father had insisted on coming home a day early to be there for her. Her plan of convincing them to stay, had been unsuccessful, and they were planning to come back.

That's when the nightmare began. The closer it got to night the worse the weather had gotten. There was a terrible tropical storm on its way. A storm that was coming with intentions to claim lives. Never would Nina have thought it would have been the lives of her parents.

Just as the phone rung for the police to tell her there was an accident, and for her to report to the hospital emergency room as soon as she could get there, Nina's alarm clock went off. She bolted up straight in the bed. Her heart was racing. Her first thought was, yeah it was just a bad dream. But looking over at the portrait of her parents by her window, and realizing she wasn't in her old room at her parent's house, let her know it wasn't a dream; it was her reliving that whole night again.

Jeff hung the phone up and turned his chair so that he could look out at the view from his office window. He was beyond annoyed and pissed off. He couldn't get any work done, because he couldn't focus because Nina was the only thing on his mind. He had been calling/texting Nina's cell all day and she hadn't yet answered or returned any messages. Neither had she responded to any of the messages he had left at the Hospital or the Center.

It had been two days since her little outburst at his place. He had tried to call her the day before, but figured whatever was going on with her, was still fresh. He wasn't going to push her too much. After the way she had bailed from his house that night, he knew she needed time. But now it was going on day two, he still hadn't heard from her, and he was getting a bit concerned.

He couldn't for the life of him figure out what was going on with her. One minute he's asking her to stay the night, the next she looks like she's on the verge of passing out. Nina was strong and very independent, but the fear and look he saw in her eyes that night, scared the hell out of him.

*And what was all that business about cutting ties?* Could whatever this was bothering her be so bad that she thought he wouldn't want to be with her anymore? She knew he loved her, and if she didn't know how much, he couldn't find the words to describe it exactly.

His intercom beeped. "Jeff, there is a Janette on line 3. She said she's returning your call."

Jeff spunned around hurriedly to answer, almost toppling his chair over. He had called Janette earlier hoping to get some info about Nina.

"Thanks, I got it." He grabbed the phone up and in one quick breath answered.

"Hello, Janette. I hope I'm not inconveniencing you."

"Of course not." Janette was happy to be talking to Jeff. A conversation with him would be a welcome from the morning she was having with State Personnel at the Center. "I got your message, and noticed it sounded kind of urgent. Is everything okay?"

"Well Janette I was hoping I could talk to you about Nina. Is there anyway you could meet for lunch?

Janette hesitated. She knew Nina was having a hard time the past couple of days. She had called and said she would be working overtime at the Hospital and would take some of the Center's work home. She didn't have any tutoring or conferences, until later in the week, so she figured she wouldn't be inconveniencing anyone with covering for her. Net assured her they'd be fine. It didn't take much for Net to realize that when Nina drowned herself in her work and wanted to stay secluded away, she was dealing with something. When Nina did that, she was trying to ward off any anxiety attacks and trying to keep her mind off of her issues. Net didn't pry, but just let her friend know she was there when she was ready to talk. Nina was best at letting herself work through things alone first.

But now her man wanted info, she was sure, and she couldn't tell something that Nina hadn't told him herself.

"Jeff, I don't know."

Jeff could detect the being-in-the-middle hesitation coming from Janette. "Look Jeannette, I wouldn't ask you to do this if she didn't mean so much to me. I'm afraid, something is really wrong I can't just sit around worrying about her. Please, just meet me for lunch."

Janette could hear the concern in his tone. And her friend had been happier lately than she had been in a long time. She knew that Jeff was good for her. She couldn't let her lose him.

She let out a deep sigh, "Okay. Meet me at 518 at one o'clock."

"Sure, and thanks Janette."

An hour later, Janette noticed that the usually polished and distinguished Jeff, was not the man sitting across from her. The man that sat across from her, sipping on Evian water, wore a suit, but well rested and his usual demeanor, was far from Jeff's weary eyes and 5'oclock shadowed face right now. He was tired and his every action showed it.

Janette considered how to answer the question he had just asked her. "What was going on with Nina?" The last thing she wanted to do was talk too much. What if Nina was holding out from him for a reason?

"Janette, is she in trouble. Is she sick? What is it? I mean, I've noticed how she pulls away from me anytime I mention a future or marriage to her. Did her ex hurt her that bad?"

Janette took a deep breath, and told herself this was for her friend's best; before she plunged in headfirst.

"Jeff, the past few years or so, Nina has been through hell, on a revolving roller coaster. I'm telling you this because I believe you'll do the right thing because I can tell you love her. I don't really know where to start, but I'll do my best."

She began to tell Jeff of the 5 years prior to his meeting Nina; her diagnoses, the lost of her parents, the therapy, the anxiety, the bad relationship and everything that went wrong in it. Janette was sure Nina had never given Jeff all the details. It was just last year when Nina had shared them with her. Jeff listened tentatively.

"So about two months after her parents passed, Nina had pretty much isolated herself from everyone. The only family she had was her Aunt and Uncle. By now the doctors had told her that the cancer wasn't threatening and they were treating her with meds only. When she had no friends, and wasn't looking for any, she met Quinton. What started as a friendship turned into a relationship, and since Quinton's past had not been all squeaky clean, and he ran a nightclub, when Nina shared her plan to move in with Q, her Auntie and uncle weren't very happy. Nina's relationship with her Auntie and Uncle dwindled and she depended on Quinton for her overall happiness.

"In the beginning all he talked about was marriage and starting a family. But Quinton was a ladies man, who wasn't a stranger to entertaining the flirtations and teasing of women at his club, while Nina waited for him at home.

"After a year went by, the doctors told Nina they thought that they should operate because they saw some irregularities in her yearly exams. They also told her it would be a 25% chance that she wouldn't be able to have children after. When Quinton found out he started making excuses as to not coming home, working overtime at the club, meetings, out of town trips, whatever. He wasn't even there for her surgery. It was like he wanted her around for birthing him an offspring, but when he found out about her chances of not being able to carry, he started losing interest.

"Well, Nina constantly questioned him about their relationship, but he promised things were fine. Out of quilt, he would spend an actual evening with her once a week. Well Nina got pregnant as a result of one of those evenings. And for a while, things got better in their relationship. Quinton was excited about fatherhood, he started talking about getting married again, he was coming home every night, and there was nothing more important to him than his pregnant Nina and his unborn baby.

"Well, at three months, Nina miscarried. The doctor blamed it on the trauma the cancer had on her ovaries. Well of course the talk of marriage stopped and Quinton reverted to his old ways. Ten months later, Quinton's 2-month old baby boy, and the mother of his child showed up and told Nina, what Quinton hadn't told her? Nina packed her bags and left for good that time.

"After all the pain she felt because of the way he hurt her, all she could say was, her sickness had ran away everyone she ever loved. First her parents, because they were trying to come back to support her, and then Quinton because she couldn't give him the baby he wanted. She still holds herself at blame."

Jeff sat back in his chair, rubbing his hands back and forth across his face. "I'm an ass."

Janette looked confused. "What are you talking about?"

"I took her to see some friends of mine. I kept talking about their marriage and family. Then I kept pushing the issue of her moving in with me, getting married and us starting a family."

"Well Jeff, you didn't know. You were having conversations with her that anyone happy in their relationship would normally have at this point. Nina is a very strong willed person. She's dealt with depression, anxiety attacks, and at times she feels guilty for having an emotional moment because everyone expects her to be strong all the time, but I tell her all the time she's not weak. She's human. It just hurts to see someone with a heart like Nina who would do anything for anybody else, hurt."

Janette felt tears welling as puddles in her eyes. "I love her like she's my own sister and I hate to see her suffer. And what hurts the most is to not know how to tell my best friend about one of the most important moments in my own life. How do I tell her that I'm pregnant, without hurting her, or making her re-live any of her pain."

Jeff took the handkerchief from his coat pocket and handed it to Janette, as he looked around the restaurant, to make sure they didn't have an audience. He placed a consoling hand on top of hers.

"Let's get out of here. People are going to think I'm the one making you cry." He patted her hand and signaled for the waiter to bring the check.

Nina pushed her reading glasses up on her nose, and sighed as she heard her doorbell ring. She dragged her house slippered feet to the door. It was probably Net checking on her. When she opened the door, she saw Jeff. She had been avoiding him the last two days, and knew it wouldn't last much longer. She took the pencil she was biting on in her mouth, and stuck it in the mess of hair on top of her head.

"Hi."

Jeff smiled, "Hey sweetie. May I come in?"

"Sure."

He stepped in, kissed her cheek and handed her a beautiful arrangement of peach colored tulips. Nina felt her eyes welling with tears. She had acted like a petty wench the other night, and he was bringing her flowers.

"You look like you're busy." Jeff looked over at her laptop, and mess of papers set up on her ottoman.

"Just trying to catch up on some work." The truth was, she was working on work that wasn't due for another 3-4 weeks. She waited a beat then decided she should break the awkwardness she was feeling. "Look Jeff, I owe you an apology…"

"I didn't come here for that. You asked for time, you got it." He had sworn to Janette that he wouldn't speak of their lunch conversation or her news to Nina, but after lunch, he had to see Nina for himself to make sure she was okay. "I came to share some news; good news."

Nina was confused as to why he wasn't the least bit concerned with her actions from the previous night. But she was not going to push the issue. "I need good news, what's up?"

"Yours truly, has been chosen as Businessman of the year, and there is a banquet in my honor two weeks from Thursday. I want the most beautiful woman in my life to be there at my side to share it with me."

Nina was shocked that he was standing here in her living room like nothing had happened. But she really wasn't in the mood right now to discuss it either.

"So, you will be there, right", he asked after she stayed silent?

She raised her hands palms out, and shrugged her shoulders, "Of course, I will be there. Congratulations!"

He took her into his arms, and hugged her. He had missed touching her the last couple of days. He missed having the softness of her skin under his touch; squeezing her in the middle of the night to make sure she was really there.

Nina had missed being in his arms. She had been on an emotional roller coaster the last few days; isolating herself from everything except work, and on the brink of depression, because she didn't know how to handle all the truths she had to tell Jeff; not knowing how she'd handle him leaving her…alone; a word that haunted her in every corner of her life. But this right now, in his arms, seemed to erase all the torment she'd been putting her self through the past few days. His arms seemed to be more than any other comfort that she could need right now.

"What do you say to us going to grab a bite to eat? From the looks of your yoo-hoo and mini-powder doughnuts, I think you could use it."

He was still holding her. Nina didn't want to go anywhere that involved her leaving his arms. He was holding her tight, and Nina couldn't think about anything but him. The tears she was trying to hold back, where now streaming down her face. She sniffed and pulled away to wipe at them furiously.

"I'm sorry, I just… I don't know." She raised her shaking hands to wipe her eyes. Jeff took her by the arm and wrapped his arms around her again. He rubbed her back and calmed her hard sobs. But he didn't let go.

He rubbed his cheek against her hair. "I love you, and Nina you can always trust me."

Nina knew what he was saying; she could read between the lines. She couldn't keep hiding the truth from him forever; he wanted answers. But it was easy for him to say she could trust him, when he didn't know the facts that would destroy any future that they could ever have together.

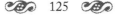

Nina bolted upright in the bed. It took her what seemed like several minutes, to realize where she was, and the realization relieved her. She was in her own bed, her own room, her own house, and though she was gasping for breath, and her gown was soaking wet with sweat that was all that was left from the nightmare she had just descended from. But it was still very fresh in her mind.

Nina looked over at the handsome man lying beside her. She could hear a faint snore come from him, and it brought a smile to her lips. She was glad the turmoil she'd just encountered in her nightmare, didn't bring her loud screams over into reality, waking him up. It was all she'd need on top of everything else for her screaming tyrants to make him think she was crazy, after the way she behaved the other night.

After they had went to dinner, (or better to say, Jeff used his persuasive business negotiations to make her go to dinner), Nina hesitated about him staying the night, since they really hadn't resolved anything from her panic attack at his place. She loved Jeff more than anything, but all this drama that was going on with her right now was sure to run him off. She already had to tell him about why she freaked out the other night, and she knew that since then it had been on her mind constantly, making her return to her anxiety attacks, nightmares and night sweats. She knew she wasn't crazy; besides the months of counseling after her parent's death had confirmed that, but the images of her nightmares, seemed to follow her even in the day. And this one was too vivid.

*There had been two, still born babies that she held in her arms, whose faces quickly turned to adult faces, in that quick transforming way that dreams do. The faces of her parents. And no matter how hard she shook, they wouldn't awake. Then suddenly she's sitting in the funeral parlor surrounded by everyone who knew her parents, waiting for the eulogy, but when the preacher gets up to speak, he doesn't mention her parents, instead he's pointing at Nina, and accusing her of being a disgrace to woman. She was no use to any man. When it was time for the procession and Nina followed the crowd, the horror of seeing her bloody uterus lying inside the casket was horrid. And that is when Nina let out a loud scream and bolted upright in the bed.*

Now she was sitting here soaking wet, from fighting the people who where trying to calm her in the dream, and trembling from the images of the dream that were still so vivid in her mind. No she wasn't crazy, but she was damn sure that she had issues.

She slipped from the bed gently, trying not to wake Jeff, and went into her bathroom and changed into another nightshirt. She then looked at herself in the mirror. *Why now? When things seemed to be on the upbeat for her. She had a man who treated her like a queen and loved her adoringly. He was honest so real.* She had finally made herself comfortable with the fact that working at the Center with kids and at the Hospital in the Pediatrics was the closest she would ever get to have her own kids, but now all that was being tossed out the window, as she contemplated how she would destroy her own happiness.

---

Jeff propped his head up on his hand, and stared at the still asleep Nina. The last thing he wanted to do was wake her. She had tossed and turned all night, jerking and twisting like she was fighting in her sleep. He had wanted to wake her, hold her and tell her it was alright, but after the way she had held him at a distance during dinner, and then the way she was hesitant about him staying over, he figured he should let her be and not pry before she was ready to talk.

He kissed her bare shoulder softly, and then slide from the bed to get dressed for work. He was sure that no matter what it was that was haunting her or tormenting her, he wasn't going to leave her.

# TEACH A CHILD IN THE WAY
# THEY SHOULD GO

Nina ran through her house one last time, from room to room, making sure everything was in place, dust free, and the air smelled of freshness and flowers.

She had spent a majority of the night before cleaning. When Jeannette had called and asked what she was doing and Nina told her cleaning, Net burst into a fit of laughter, and then asked her what was she cleaning? Anyone who knew Nina knew that everything always stayed in its place at her house. And Nina knew there wasn't much to do, but she just wanted everything to be extra clean and neat for her Auntie Laurie and Uncle George's visit.

Nina hadn't seen her Uncle and Auntie in about 18 months now. The last time she saw them was after she had left Q, and she had went to St Louis to get away and recoup. She truly did miss them. And though she was a little nervous about how they would like her new place, she didn't in the least bit feel nervous about them meeting Jeff.

They were supposed to have dinner at Jeff's house that night, and though he was handling all the arrangements, Nina didn't feel the need to tell him how to do it. In most situations, a woman would be full of questions as to whether her family would like the new guy in her life. She didn't feel the need to tell him how to act, what to do, say, or prepare, like she would have with Q. She was so sure that Jeff could handle this alone. He had told her how happy he was about them coming, but he was of course calm and collect about it.

Nina on the other hand was giddy with excitement. As she stood in her archway looking over her living room one last time before she was off to the airport. At first she thought her Auntie and Uncle wouldn't like the idea of her being in yet, another serious relationship, so soon, but they were actually glad she was moving on, and she had to admit it, she was too.

Nina laid on her bed, propped her head in her hand, and looked up at her Auntie Laurie as she stood in front of Nina's vanity, combing her shoulder length curls, before pinning them up and tying a satin scarf around her head. This before-bed-routine reminded Nina so much of her mother. Her Auntie Laurie and her mother were so much a like. Nina knew her Auntie missed her sister, as much as she missed her mom. They had been the only two of her Grandma Sarah and Grandpa Grant children, and now Auntie Laurie was the only one left.

Auntie Laurie looked over at the beautiful replica of her older sister and smiled at Nina.

"Every since we got back here, you've been quite. What's on your mind, girl?"

Nina smiled at the southern dialect shining through her Auntie's St Louis dialect. "I'm just happy you and Uncle George are here."

She laid her brush down, and walked to the bed and sat beside Nina. "Girl if I could be here all the time, I would be. We hate you being here alone. I think about all the opportunities you could have in St Louis. There are a lot of Youth Centers and-."

Nina gave her a scolding look. They had had this conversation too many times before. "Auntie Laurie, don't."

"Honey, you've got family there."

"I know and I always know how to get on a plane and where to find them. I also have 2 jobs here that I'm responsible for."

Her Auntie patted her hand, and pierced her lips and nodded; yet another gesture that reminded Nina of Ruth Jackson. "You're right. And you have that fine Jefferson here too. He's so delicious."

Nina fell over on the bed laughing. Her Auntie was in girlfriend mode now. Auntie Laurie was only in her early sixties and beautiful. A beauty that was so striking; it wasn't flashy or boisterous, but it made her glow; giving off a brightness that made you feel calm. A soft look; round face, full lips, her Grandpa Grant's nose, and big full eyes that Nina had inherited from both her and her mother.

"You laugh, but I know you are no saint, and though I'm only a few years older than you." She placed her hand on her chest and cleared her throat dignifiedly. "I know what two consenting adults of opposite sex do when they get together. And the boy is gorgeous and extremely attractive."

Nina was giggling hysterically and shaking her head while holding her chest. When she could catch her breath and looked at her Auntie;

she could see that her eyes where wide with amazement and she wore seriousness on her face, but Nina could see the smile in them as well. She swiped at the laughter tears that had escaped from the corners of her eyes. "Auntie Laurie?"

"What? Don't try to make it seem like if we weren't here, you two wouldn't be together right this minute. I can tell how the man stares at you that he's in love. He could barely take his eyes off of you; following your every move, smiling and winking at you when he thought no one was looking. That little horn ball is sprung. You've been putting something on him."

Nina dropped her mouth open at her Auntie.

"Honey, I know you think that all that makes the relationship, and things have changed since your mother and I were younger. By your age we were married and trying to support husbands, but today, young women are independent and they want to have a relationship with a man and work on their career as well. Marriage can wait, but the sexual desires you seem to have, you 'all don't wait so much on."

Nina was looking at her Auntie, listening to her every word now.

"I just hope you're being careful. You went through so much with that other guy, I never want to see you hurt again, or see someone else treat you the way he did. But I don't see that in this Jefferson. I see love in his eyes. You must have waited a while before you gave in to him."

Nina smiled faintly and waited. She knew what her Auntie was getting at.

"You love him, don't you?"

"You know me Auntie Laurie. Loving someone isn't the problem. It's getting the love in return, that's the problem."

"I wouldn't say that Q guy didn't love you, but I do know he wasn't ready for a real monogamous relationship. He wanted to be a crutch for you more than anything. He didn't understand the full potential of the independent, strong, woman that you are." She waited a beat, watching Nina nod her head. "Do you plan on moving in with Jefferson?"

BINGO! Nina knew that was the one major thing that was bothering her Auntie. "Auntie Laurie, I do have some morals left in me despite some of the paths I chose to take in my past, and I've learned my lesson. I'm not going to move in with Jeff, or any other man, for that matter."

Her Auntie looked relieved. "And for your info, if you must know, I was dating Jeff over 3 months before I ever slept with him. I know that doesn't make it right, but I do love him very much. And when he asked me to marry him the first time, I thought about saying yes."

Her Auntie jerked back and widened her already huge eyes. "He asked you to marry him? And you never said anything about this? What did you say?"

Nina regretted she had mentioned it. She was just so much into proving to her Auntie that things were different than they were with Q. "Auntie Laurie, it wasn't the right time okay? That is beside the point right now. Just trust me okay. I'm not going to make the same mistakes again. I'm my mother's daughter."

Her Auntie pierced her lips again, and then smiled. "That you are right about, and baby I trust you more than you think I do." She leaned over and kissed her niece on the forehead. "So why don't you invite Jeff to church Sunday, and I'll cook us a big dinner after."

"Auntie Laurie you know how I feel about those people at church; a bunch of phonies, and I don't want to be a part of something unless I am doing it right; unlike the rest of those hypocrites there. I'm trying to get myself together but I've got a ways to go."

Her Auntie took a stern look at her. "Nina Larisa Jackson, it is not the people you go to church for, it is the God. No one in church is perfect, nor will they ever be because they are human, and they will always have problems and issues. When people are in Christ, they die daily to be more like him. And I do believe you just shared with me that you haven't been a saint yourself. At least those people are in the right place. If they stay there long enough, something will come through one day and deliver their old, tired, crazy selves. Church is a symbol; sort of like a shelter or haven for the sick. While it isn't the only place to seek him, it is a start. It's God you should go to glorify not the people. And if you would stop trying to do it yourself and let God do it for you, it will be a lot easier."

"I do glorify him every morning Auntie Laurie when I thank him for waking me up another day."

"Well this Sunday, you're going to do it in church." She said matter-of-factly and got up.

Nina sighed and fell back on the bed looking at the ceiling. The idea sent an eerie feeling through her. She hadn't stepped foot in her family church but once since her parents death. At first she felt guilty, but as time went by it felt natural. She hadn't ceased in sending her donations, support, or anything else she could help with in the community, to church with Jeannette at least once a month, (that was a must), but making personal appearance on a regular basis, even at Net's church wasn't something she did either.

"Nina, I know you have been through some stormy days since Ruth and Paul passed, but you can't blame God. And I know you have questioned his real existence, since you have hurt so much in the past but his miracles are too evident in your life to not believe in him, honey. You have got to keep the faith girl. You have life, wealth, love, and a healed body. You need to build on all that he has blessed you with and bless his name for what you have. Build a relationship with him. Talk to him when there seems to be no one else around. Because though sometimes you may be lonely and down, you owe him so much more than pity for yourself. Everything you have been through has served a purpose in his plan for your life. Honey times are too hard not to believe in him. You need to learn to depend on him, and let everyone else fall in line as HE sees fit."

Nina remained on her back, staring at the ceiling as a tear slide out of the corner of her eye. She had never openly questioned God, or said out loud that she deeply blamed him for taking her parents, but her Auntie Laurie knew. The woman had a way of making her laugh and cry within seconds; from tears of joy, to tears of pain. She sniffled, and wiped at tears, as she turned on her side away from her Auntie and reached to her nightstand for a Kleenex. She remained that way, staring at the window.

"Aunt Laurie, I don't think God is too keen on hearing me. I'm sleeping with a man I'm not married to. I'm not actually walking the path to be worthy of him."

"Neither is anyone else." Her Auntie said as she placed a warm hand on her back and rubbed it. "Sweetie, I'm not preaching to you, and telling you to jump on a religion bandwagon. I already know you believe in him, if you didn't we wouldn't be having this conversation. I'm just telling you to be thankful for all you have; talk to God, and build a relationship with him; because you have so much to be thankful for. The rest is between you and God, on your time, or rather his time. Let him do things for you. Give your every concern to him. You can't do it alone, and you can't expect people on this earth to do it for you. Because me and your Uncle, we're going to love you regardless no matter what, but the Father and the Son loves you so much more than we could ever."

Nina sat up, faced her Auntie, and threw her arms around her neck. "I love you' all too, Auntie Laurie." They held each other a moment, both sniffling, then let go.

Auntie Laurie looked at the clock. "I'm going to get your Uncle; it's time for us to get some beauty sleep. It's almost 12am; I can hang because I'm still young, but not your uncle."

Nina smiled, as she got up from the bed, and went into the guest bathroom to make sure they had every thing they needed, as she heard her Auntie and Uncle in the living room teasing each other. Her Auntie was right, she had so much that she took for granted, including those two beautiful angels he'd placed in her life for so many reasons.

Nina slipped under her covers and picked up her cell from her nightstand. She dialed Jeff's number and waited to hear his sleepy voice answer. He picked up on the first ring.

"I was beginning to think they had turned you against me."

Nina smiled, "No. Did I wake you?"

"Are you kidding? I can't sleep without you beside me."

"You sleep many nights without me beside you."

"Not easily, and not when I've spent 3 hours prior looking at you and not being able to touch you the way I would like to."

"Oh, is that what you were doing? Auntie Laurie thought you were just horny."

"Well I'm always that when it comes to you." He laughed. "Is that the first impression I made?"

"She actually had lots of great things to say about you. Trust me if she didn't she would have let me know, very boldly."

They both laughed.

Nina took a deep breath before she said what was next, and prepared herself for his response. "She wants us to go to church with her Sunday."

"Okay."

"Okay?"

"Yeah, okay. I'm not a complete heathen. I go to church with Kay often."

Nina was shocked a moment. She didn't know what was more bizarre, him going to church or him going with Kay. "You never asked me before."

"I don't know, you never really opened up a door. I'm sorry. I never really thought about it."

They were silent a moment.

"Well, I'm going to get some sleep. Auntie Laurie wants to go shopping early in the morning, while you and Uncle George play golf. Then it's a day full of catching up with old friends. So you have a good night. I love you."

"I love you too."

Jeff held the phone a few moments after she had hung up. "More than anything", he said to the dial tone.

Nina cut her lamp off, and smiled at the giggling coming from the hall, as her Auntie & uncle passed by. And then she drifted off to sleep.

## A Soul that Won't Rest

Nina slipped out of her sliding door to her deck, hoping that her Auntie Laurie and Jeff would be so deep into their teasing and conversation to notice her.

It had been an overwhelming and emotional day. They had finished dinner, a feast in which her Auntie Laurie put her foot-in. Afterwards, her Auntie refused to let her clean the kitchen and instead had asked Jeff to help her. It was her turn to talk to Jeff alone, since Uncle George had done so the day before. Uncle George had retreated to the living room, where he sat watching a football game, so Nina thought it to be a perfect opportunity to spend some time alone, and try to regroup from the emotional tailspin she had been on that day.

The service itself had been beautiful. There had been many new faces from what Nina had remembered at Faith Victory. The Church itself had expanded tremendously, with a few additions, and the flock was steady growing. Of those faces that were familiar to Nina, it was nice to see again, but at the same time it was also troublesome. She had spent the majority of the service in tears; from the opening song to the end of the benediction. It wasn't just the memories of her parents that filled the church, but there was something else that was pulling at her.

Nina had felt like a basket case, sitting there crying. People probably thinking she was crazy. She felt bad, because though her Auntie and Uncle knew the real reason behind her tears, Jeff didn't know what was going on. But he never asked, he just kept holding her hand throughout the service, from where he sat beside her. Her Auntie Laurie was on her other side, patting her knee softly, and her Uncle gently rubbed her shoulder, from where his hand rested on the pew behind her Auntie.

After the service, her Uncle had swept her up in a big bear hug and just held her. He never said anything just held her, and that was more than any words he could have spoken. On the way home, no one spoke of her emotional state, and over dinner she had been silent most of the time, during the time which, Jeff and Uncle George and Auntie Laurie had talked like old friends.

Now, Nina thought as she looked in at her Auntie and Jeff, he was charming her of course and her Auntie was laughing and hitting him playfully with the dish towel. She turned away, and stared off into the moonlit darkness; nothing but peace and the sound of night. It was a clear night, and the sky was a deep royal blue. As she stared at the speckled, blue spread overhead, she thought about how at that moment she was sharing that same sky with many others around the world she had never met, even if they didn't share the same problems, they shared this one moment.

Jeff looked at the beautiful woman that stood beside him and thought of the best way to answer the question she had just asked him. He didn't know what answer she was looking for but he could only give her how he felt, and the truth.

When she saw his hesitation, she repeated the question. "Now honey, it doesn't take that long for you to figure it out, does it? I know you love her; it's obvious in the mere way you look at her. I just want to know what makes you love her. I mean it's no secret that you are a handsome, intelligent, wealthy young man. Those traits alone put you on the market as what every young woman wants. I also know that you could have any high maintenance little female that you would like, but my niece isn't that. Oh, I know she's beautiful, intelligent, and has a heart of gold, but she's also strong-willed and stubborn. And high maintenance isn't in her vocabulary. Most men miss how beautiful she is on the inside as well as the outside, because they fail to see past her efforts to keep them at a distance. But you love her still, and I know from what she's been through, my Nina has not made getting close to her, or loving her easy to do."

He gave her a smug smile. Yeah she definitely had summed up what was there between him and Nina. "I do love Nina dearly; in a way I've never loved any other woman. And at times it scares me that I could feel this way for someone, but at the same times it scares me that she pushes me away and may not love me the same." He couldn't believe he was saying these things to this woman that he just met. He was sharing with her what he had been afraid of admitting to himself, but the look on her face made him comfortable, and felt the need to say it out loud.

"It just seems like sometimes she's never going to trust me, ever. And all I want to do is be here for her. Give her everything she wants; yet all she does is push me away."

Auntie Laurie smiled. She walked over to the stove, poured hot water over the herbal tea bags and honey she had put into the two mugs, then walked over to Jeff and handed them to him. She patted his arm softly after he had taken them and looked up into the most beautiful grey eyes; honest eyes. It was about time her niece had someone like this in her life.

When she spoke, it was softly and sweet, "Baby, give her time. That's all you can do. I promise you, she'll come around. And when she does, you'll understand that what she tells you, is the reason behind her distance. Now take that tea out to her, she looks like she could use some company.

He smiled at her as he turned to go toward the sliding doors, but

turned back to her, and placed a soft kiss on her cheek. "Thank you." He said before he turned to leave again.

Laurie raised her hand to where he had kissed her; smiled and then lifted her eyes upward and mumbled, "Thank You God, it's about time she got a good one."

Jeff pulled the door closed, while balancing the two mugs. Nina didn't turn around because she knew it was him by the smell of his cologne mixing with the night air. He lowered the mug of tea to her. Shw took it into her hand then looked up to say thanks.

"Do you mind some company?"

She slide over on the top step for him to sit. "Sure."

He sat very close to her; heat from his body touching her but no actual contact. They sat silent for a moment, Jeff looking into the darkness where her gaze was set.

Then she spoke softly, still staring into the darkness. "Jeff, I didn't mean to be so distant today, it's just the whole day has been very emotional."

He remained quiet, waiting for her to go ahead, but she didn't. Seconds passed in silence then a soft chuckle came from her before she spoke again.

"When I was about 14; that age where parents and teenager don't get along because the teenagers don't want to be associated with parents, and parents can't get through to the teenager; my parents, I know probably wanted to disown me. My dad use to tell my mom that she would have to deal with me because he gave up on trying to talk to me.

Well one night I was fuming about something and I went pouting onto the porch to sit. Well there sits my father, like he did every night, watching the moonlight and the stars. We sat out there quite, listening to the night hours. Before that moment I never saw what he got out of being out there, but that night it meant something to me too. We didn't say any words to each other, but we somehow seem to communicate by being in each other's presences. From then on, we did that at least once a week, just sitting in each other's presence.

When I went to college, I'd call home homesick those first couple of months, and my dad would tell me how much he missed our weekly night talks." She gave a little laugh. "We never said anything, but we were talking. Sometimes I sit out here like this wishing he was still here, because now I miss those night talks too."

Jeff looked over at her, and saw big tears sitting at the brim of her eyes. He didn't know what exactly would be the right thing to say right now. So he sat his mug down on the steps between his legs and pulled Nina into his arms. She melted up against him.

"Jeff give me some more time. Please don't leave me. I just need more time."

"As long as you need." As she snuggled closer to him, Jeff knew what the beautiful woman in Nina's kitchen was talking about now. There was no way he could leave her for keeping him at a distance. Keeping him at a distance was nothing, compared to what he knew Nina had been through, and what more he was sure he'd find out about in the future.

---

Laurie sat down on the sofa, next to where her husband sat.

"George, I want to talk to you about Nina."

For the first time since she had entered the room, he took his gaze from the T.V., and looked at his wife with concern. "Is she alright?"

"I think for a change, she's more than alright."

George let out a little sigh of relief. He had grown very attached to his niece, and when his sister-n-law and brother-n-law, passed he felt an even bigger obligation to protect his niece like one of his own children. Though some of the choices she had made in the past, didn't agree with him too well, he'd learned to let her be the smart young lady he knew she was, because she would figure it out for herself. Life had definitely dealt her some lemons, but she'd managed to make the sweetest lemonade out of each one.

"I think Jeff is good for her."

"He definitely has her best interest at heart." George had learned the previous day how much in love with his niece the man was.

"Do you know he's asked her to marry him?"

"How do you know that?"

"She told me. She also told me the time wasn't right."

"Well good for her." He liked Jeff, but after that Q fella, he didn't want his niece getting into any situations with Jeff like she had with him.

"George, I think she's still afraid. There are a lot of things she still hasn't told him."

"Well Lo, can you blame her", he asked calling her by her nickname?

"No, I just wish she wasn't so stubborn like Ruth; always hiding her feelings. I wish she'd talk to us more about her feelings. I worry about her so much being here alone."

"Now woman, don't start. She's proven over and over she can take care of herself. And now she has him, and I'm not the least worried about him mistreating her. I feel like our Nina has learned a lot from her past experiences, and no one else will be getting over on her that way again." He snickered, "You know the fella is so intelligent, but he doesn't even know how much of a God fearing man he is. I didn't tell him because I didn't want to damage his ego, but it's there."

"Yeah, I know." She leaned back on the couch and prayed things would keep going well for Nina.

# CHAPTER XVI
## A DAY LATE, AND A FEW DOLLARS SHORT

NINA SHUFFLED PAPERS AROUND HER desk searching for her keys. She was supposed to be on her way back to the Hospital. School was back in, so other than tutoring classes in the evening, there wasn't much she had to do at the Center. So she thought she'd use the time to work on some presentations for the Board at the Hospital, but she couldn't find her freaking keys so she could get there.

There was a knock on her door, but she was too into her searching to look up, "Entre."

"Hey ma ma."

Nina looked up into the face of Quinton. She hadn't seen him since the night he had left her house. "Hey, you."

"You look like you are in a mood."

Nina smiled, she could imagine how she looked. She was standing with her hands on her hips and she was frantically searching for something that was pissing her off because she couldn't find.

"I have been searching for my keys for the last 15 minutes, and I'm a bit pissed off about it."

Quinton stepped toward the chair in front of her desk. "Could these be it?" He was holding her key ring up.

Nina sighed and laughed. "Maybe, I am going crazy. Thanks. What may I ask, did I do to deserve this visit?"

"Well, I was wondering if you could steal a minute away to join me for lunch. There is something I need to talk to you about."

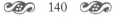

He must have detected her hesitation that she was sure she was trying to keep from showing in her facial expression.

"I promise, I really need to talk to you about something important. Really important."

She knew from the seriousness on Quinton's face that this had to be important.

"Okay, just let me get my things together."

They decided on a quaint little deli, a couple blocks away, where Nina was sure that they wouldn't run into Jeff, or any of his associates.

After they were settled in at their booth, and the waiter had taken their drink orders, Quinton began to talk.

"So I see the boyfriend is being good to you, in more ways than one, these days."

"What does that mean?"

"The bright smile on your face, as well as the sparkling diamonds on your wrist".

Nina ran her finger in and out of the tennis bracelet that Jeff had brought back from a trip to California. He had insisted on her taking it when she tried to refuse it; much the way she did all the gifts he brought her.

"It was a gift." She wanted to change the subject quickly. "Someone's been taking care of you."

"Baby girl, this is all self-help. Me, myself, and I."

They both laughed, but Nina noticed Quinton didn't laugh long. He went back to stirring his tea, with his straw. It was obvious something was on his mind.

"What's bothering you?"

"Is it that obvious?"

"I know when you're troubled and something is definitely bothering you. You're not yourself."

"Nah, actually things have never been as good as they are now. The club is doing great, everybody is on the street, no body locked down, no beef. Everything's cool."

"But-?"

He smiled, "You do know me." He paused. "But I want out; I'm for real this time. I've never wanted to get out of this the way I do now. It's just I feel I've outgrown all this hustling and club stuff. I want to just let Dee and Charles take over; I'll take the lost. I need to offer my son something more; more quality time, and a more stable home where I can put him to bed each night and be there when he wakes up.

Nina smiled, she knew this topic of conversation had been one that had erupted in several arguments when she and Quinton had been together. She was always begging him to trade in the fast lifestyle of clubs and hustling for an honest career in real estate. He already had the business, it just wasn't making the money as fast as he wanted. So now he was ready to make the change for the sake of his child.

"I think that's great."

"I figured you would. There isn't anyone else I could talk to about this, and they won't try to talk me out of it. It's just taken so long. If I had made the change a long time ago, I probably would still have you." He smiled at her. "Thanks for being here for me."

"Always, I owe you that much", Nina said.

As they dug into their food that the waiter sat before them, Nina assured herself she would always be a friend there for Q, because despite everything bad that they shared, the good was their friendship.

Being late was the one thing that Nina never allowed herself to be. But today, it seemed as though everything was standing in her way to make her late, she thought as she rushed down the Center's hallway. She had 30 minutes before she had to be in court. One of her kids, 11-year old Marty, was in the middle of a custody battle between his parents, and she had to go testify, from the sociological perspective, as to whether or not him being with his father was beneficial to his educational and behavioral attitude at the Center and overall academics; another one of her social worker duties. She had to get Marty's file that she had absent-mindedly left the day before, because she had too much other stuff going on.

It was 7:45am; the Center was pretty empty, a few of the workers, who didn't have kids of their own to get to school, were there. Nina had seen Janette's SUV in the parking lot on the way in, but there was no sign of her. Nina knew that since she had taken her little hiatus after her last episode with Jeff that she and Janette hadn't spent much time talking lately. Nina wanted to find her so she could make a date to take Janette to lunch, just to sort of catch up with her on things.

After she grabbed the file and rushed the corner to Janette's office, she decided to stop in the restroom. As soon as she opened the door, she heard the sounds of a soft moan, followed by coughing coming from one of the stalls. Nina looked at the designer heels facing the toilet in the stall the sounds were coming from, and realized that it was Janette.

"Net, is that you?" She knocked on the stall door softly.

She cleared her throat, and then answered softly, "Yeah, it's me."

Nina suddenly felt lightheaded herself, mostly from fear. "Are you okay?"

The door slowly opened, and Nina descended, wearing a forced smile.

"Yeah, I think I've just got a little upset stomach. Nothing to worry about." Janette could see the worry forming on Nina's face.

Nina knew, despite her friend's efforts to throw her off, there was something else going on; way more than a little upset stomach. She hadn't really looked at her friend closely the past few days, but something was different. She looked tired, but at the same time there was a newness about her, a sort of glow, and Nina didn't know exactly what it was.

"Janette, be real with me, what's going on? There's something more than an upset stomach, what is it?"

Nina watched as her friend's face, lit into a real smile that she tried to hide and suppress a little.

"I'm 6 weeks pregnant."

Nina's eyes suddenly welled with tears, as the same smile her friend was trying to suppress, came across her own face. Nina extended her arms for her friend, pulling her into a tight hug.

After they stood there crying tears of joy for a few minutes and hugging, Nina pulled away. "Wait a minute, you said you are 6 weeks pregnant, how come I'm just finding out about this?'

"Ne, you've had so much going on lately, and I really didn't know how to tell you, I didn't want to hurt you, or make you feel-".

Nina cut her off, "Janette Antoinette Taylor, how dare you keep something as important as this away from me. Don't you ever think that you have to keep something from me to spare my feelings. Janette you are the closest thing I've ever had to a sister, I am nothing but happy for you and Warren. I'm going to be an Auntie." She rubbed Janette's stomach softly, as she smiled at the imaginary mound.

They hugged again, and Nina felt as happy as she would have if it was herself. Her friend deserved this.

# CHAPTER XVII

"**N**INA, WHY ARE YOU DOING this?" Janette asked accusingly. Nina looked over at Janette in amazement where she sat across from her at the table. They were taking a break from shopping while sitting in the mall's Cup O Joe diner. They had spent the majority of the Saturday morning looking for Nina a dress to wear to Jeff's Award Ceremony, as well as spending great amounts of time in several baby departments.

Now they were sitting at a table, sipping on herbal tea and scones, and Nina had just told, what she had hoped would be good news to Janette, about Quinton. But when she told her friend she had went to lunch with Quinton, to discuss his future plans, Janette's expression and whole mood had turned cloudy.

"Doing what?" Nina was confused. Janette was acting like she had just told her she was thinking of robbing a bank.

"Why are you f-ing around with Q again? I mean that is the stupidest thing you could do right now after the problems he caused you. Jeff is the best thing that has happened to you, and you're jeopardizing that by still messing around with Q?"

Nina was stunned. She didn't know if this outburst from Net was some type of hormonal thing going on with her or what? She just thought she could share what Q had told her.

"Jeanette, so first of all, could we tone it down on the language? Secondly, I'm not messing around with Q. We can still be friends can't we? I thought you would think it was good news to hear that he had decided to dedicate himself to the real estate business. Damn, all I did was have lunch with him."

Nina was suddenly glad she hadn't told Net about having Q over, to talk to. From the way she was behaving now, she would have fainted if she had known Nina had let him come over and had almost slept with him again.

Net just sat there staring at her a moment. Nina felt like her mother was scolding her. Net had never been this opinionated about her relationship. Even when Nina use to go to her crying about something Q had done, she would always listened and ask Nina what she wanted, and to do what made her happy. But now it was almost like she thought her friend was ready to spit fire at her.

After staring at her for what seemed like minutes, Net finally shook her head and looked down at her tea. "Nina, how many times has Q said he was going to quit?" She paused, but not long enough to give Nina a chance to say anything. "When it comes to Q, you have this vulnerable spot, and his mere existence seems to feed at that spot. I just don't want to see you falling into some lies he's feeding you and getting hurt again. I don't want to see you messing up things with Jeff."

Nina was stunned. "Net, you make it sound like I'm some naive teenager, who can't determined what is best for myself. I know what I have with Jeff."

"Well you couldn't before. His dick obviously had you in such awe."

Nina was almost knocked out of her seat, at that blow. This pregnancy was definitely having an affect on her friend, already.

"Net-?" Nina tried to get a word in, but was cut off.

Just when Nina thought Net had stuck the knife in her to cause her enough of pain, Net decided to turn it with invigorating force.

"I mean Nina, you're acting like these young girls who come into the Center, wasting their lives because they keep letting a no good Negro mess up any remote possibility of having something great for themselves."

Nina sat back in her chair, and took a long look at the person who looked like her friend but didn't sound like her. The silence was thick between them, as they just looked at one another. They hadn't been talking loud, but even people who passed by, looked twice, because of the awkward looks they held on each other.

In a very faint, soft voice, Nina broke the silence as she sat on the edge of her chair. "Jeanette, I in no way intend to go back to Q. Though the mistakes that I made in the past with him seem to be very fresh in your memory, I have learned a lesson from them. And though I know I won't go back to a relationship with Q, he's still my friend. We were that before we were anything else. I do appreciate you being concerned for me, but I do know that what I have right now with Jeff is the best thing for me. I'm sorry I upset you so, I just thought you would like to know the news about Q."

Janette lifted her gaze to Nina. She saw pure love in her friend's eyes at that moment. Nina just mentioning Q's name had her so upset, and she suddenly felt bad about the way she had went off on her.

She shook her head, "Nina honey I love you, and I just don't want to see you where you were a year ago. I apologize for the way I came at you, it's just lately my emotions seem to get the best of me, and I'm running my mouth before I think."

Nina smiled, "Could it be you're pregnant?"

Net gave a chuckle, "Just a little." She reached across the table and patted her friend's hand. "Nina, I'm really sorry. I can't go on like this for the next 7 1/2 months."

"Hey I only have to deal with you for a few hours a day, Warren is the one I feel sorry for." They both laughed, then quite. "Thanks for caring so much, Net, really."

Nina didn't know why Net had been so upset with her, but it felt nice to have a friend who at least cared about her and her feelings.

# CHAPTER XVIII

*C*RAP!

It was 6:45pm and Nina had exactly 15 minutes to get through downtown Charlotte, and to the banquet before they started. And she knew that wasn't remotely possible.

She had promised Jeff that she would meet him there, on time, instead of him sending a car for her. She had so much going on at the Hospital and the Center that she was putting in overtime to make sure everything went as it should. And on top of that, she had taken on teaching a single parents class communication class that helped single parents relate to their teenagers. She knew she could be a perfectionist sometimes when it came to her programs and presentations, but she insisted on putting her best into whatever she was doing, especially when it was for others.

She had brought her dress to change into with her. The dress that she had searched inevitably for with Janette the previous weekend. The satin bronze dress was back less, with a full skirt was and pockets. There was a hidden side slit on the left thigh. It was elegant but simple. When she tried this one on, after the other twenty she had tried on that day, Net told her it was the one.

Jeff had wanted to know what the dress looked like. He had never made that much of a fuss of what she wore when they went out, except for those times he had sent her some new dress by delivery, for an event. She was beginning to think he was a shame of what she may wear on his big night and didn't trust her fashion sense, but then when a delivery guy with a box from Harry and Winston all the way from a jewelry store in NY, showed up at the Hospital. Nina was shocked at how the diamond and pearl choker seem like it was especially made for her dress. He had been at his gift shopping schemes again.

She was gathering up her things and rushing to leave, when Quinton peaked his head into her office door. Other than the last tutoring session for the teens at the other end of the building, the Center was empty, so it kind of startled her when he ducked his head into the door.

"Hi, Nina", he said dryly.

'Hey". Nina could see disturbance and pain written all over Quinton's face.

"You look nice."

"Thanks", she paused, "Q, what's wrong?"

He didn't speak, but slowly moved around the chair in front of her desk and took a seat, as if he was barley able to stand. She hadn't talked to him much lately but has heard he had sold the club to his cousins Dee and Charles. He was strictly running his real estate properties. Nina had only received a text from him a couple days before where he told her, he was so happy

But now in front of Nina sat a very disturbed Q. He shook his head several times, as though he was trying to clear something from it. Tormenting in his own head, some mental argument he was having with himself. He sat forward and rubbed his hands over his face and his head, before clearing his throat and speaking, in a low voice.

"They got, Dee."

Nina was motionless for a moment. One thing she had learned in her years with Quinton is that less talk was more, when it came to the business. But right now it was hard for her to figure out just what he was talking about. She assumed that whoever they, were had to be the police.

"Well, how long do you think they will keep him?"

Quinton looked up, confused at her. "You don't understand, it's not the police that has him. Nina, Dee is dead."

Nina's breath caught in her throat. She felt her way to her own chair and collapsed in it. Suddenly she felt she was back in the hospital, 4 years earlier, and they were telling her of her parent's death. She was not hearing this right. He did not just say that Dee was dead. Dee was Quinton's younger cousin, and they were closer than his own brother had been. Dee was also the one that Nina had told countless times, the right one she let get away. He had been nothing but a dear friend to Nina. He was always there to lend a listening ear, even when it was about Quinton. Now Quinton was here saying he was dead; this couldn't be.

She stood up and started to pace; her gown sweeping across the floor and wedging her between the small space of her desk and chair. She was so caught up in her own thoughts, she had forgot about Q. She looked over at him. He wasn't crying, but his eyes wore a glassy and red. He was staring into the wall over her desk.

"Quinton, how, when, I mean what happened?"

"Same stupid, shit that's been happening for years. Someone sees something that someone else has, gets envious and makes it an issue to get at that person. You know Dee, he doesn't even take notice to stuff like that. Well around 5 this afternoon, this idiot, who was jealous of Dee was at the same place Dee was, and ran up on him with a gun. Dee took two bullets in the back, one piercing his spine. He was dead when I got there."

Nina watched from what she believed to be an out of body experience. All this was not real. She felt she was watching a movie. Right before her eyes, she watched Q, in a way she had never seen him before. He was wringing his hands, and sweating like he was in trouble.

"Dee would have never even acted on some hating shit coming from that cat, and then he didn't even have the guts to step to him face to face, and shoots him in the back." Q dropped his head again. There was anger, and rage in his face now.

Nina stepped around her desk, and stood in front of Q. She didn't quite know what to say, but at the same thing, she couldn't find her voice to speak. Instead of speaking, she placed her hand at the base of his neck, and gave him a consoling rub. After a moment of silence, Q sat up straight, catching Nina hand in his own. He gently squeezed it, then lifted it to his lips then softly kissed it. A kiss so soft, if Nina hadn't seen him do it, she would have never known.

Nina finally spoke, "Are you okay?"

"No." He let her hand go, sat back in the chair, stretched out his long legs, and looked up at the ceiling. "I feel like this is my fault. If I hadn't turned all of this over, Dee wouldn't be dead and Charles wouldn't be plotting to go out and get revenge."

"Quinton, this isn't your fault. You said so yourself that this guy has been after Dee for a while now. He's probably been plotting for the right moment. Don't feel guilty because you wanted a new start for your son. None of this is your fault."

Quinton shifted his gaze from the ceiling to the floor. Nina's cell phone started ringing. She glanced at the wall clock. It was twenty after seven. She was very late, and she knew it had to be Jeff. She reached over and got it out of her purse.

"Hello." She was right it was Jeff, with a lot of background noise.

"Sweetheart, where are you? You were supposed to be here over 20 minutes ago. They are getting ready to serve the dinner soon and start the ceremony."

"Jeff, I'm sorry okay. Something came up I had to take care of."

"Are you okay?"

"Yeah, I'll be there shortly."

He sighed. Nina could hear the annoyance in his voice. "Alright, just hurry."

Nina laid the phone down on her desk, a bit annoyed herself.

"You got a big date with the boyfriend?" Quinton asked.

"No it's an Awards Dinner."

They both fell silent for a moment. Nina knew she had to go. She moved to go back around the desk, but Quinton intercepted her move and stood in front of her; heat from his body, hitting up against her own. He had his hand gripped on her arm and his eyes were just as sad now as they were before.

"Nina, I need you tonight. I can't turn to anyone else. I just need you to hold me down." His eyes were now pleading.

She knew that his statement wasn't sexual; it was what a friend needed from another friend. A friend that had been there for her so many times before. And now he was asking her to return the favor as a friend. She let out a sigh. She knew she had to do the right thing and be there for Quinton, but this was a big night for Jeff. "Quinton, I have to go to this dinner. It's a big night for Jeff, and I promised."

Quinton shook his head and gave a half hearty chuckle. "Ain't this

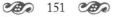

something? My fam just got killed and you, the person who said you'd always be there for me, rather go run off and play rich girl with your rich boyfriend."

"Q, that's not true, I promised Jeff–"

"Ummm, you promised Jeff". He was nodding his head as if he had just got the picture. "Well you promised me too. You promised you'd be there for me, like I was there for you, remember; but he wins hands down every time, right?"

"Quinton, don't make more out of this than it is. I just–"

He cut her off. "Don't worry about it. I'll deal with this by myself." He slammed her door open and was on his way up the hall.

Nina was afraid of what he might do. "Quinton, please, wait." She tried to catch up with him in her clanking heels that were obviously not made for running and the swaying of her long dress.

"What?" He turned to her.

She struggled for what to do or to say. "Look, give me a couple of hours, then I'll call you. I promise. Just let me go show my face at this dinner. " He just stared at her. "I don't want to break my promise to him or you."

Quinton waited then answered. "Alright. Call me when you're done."

Nina sighed as he left. She looked at her watch. "Crap!" She was now 35 minutes late, but better late than never at all.

When she rushed into the lobby of the Wellington Hotel where the ceremony was being held, she could see Jeff pacing in front of the entrance to the banquet room, with his cell phone glued to his ear. There were people everywhere. Maybe that could be used in her favor; Jeff would never make a scene in front of this many people, so it would save her a cussing out, at least for the moment.

She could see the suppressed anger on his face and in his eyes as she approached. She took a few breaths to calm herself and to get ready for whatever anger he had, as well as to prepare for the smile she would have to display for his mother and sister. When he saw her coming toward him, he lowered his phone, and took long, quick strides to meet her halfway.

"Where the hell have you been? You're an hour late, dinner is over, and I had to persuade them to hold off the ceremony until you got here. I've been calling your cell and you wouldn't pick up, and then when I couldn't get you at the office, I was sure something had happened to you."

Nina had kicked her self on the way for forgetting her phone. She had been in such a rush to leave; she left it on her desk. She had to calm him down. "Jeff, sweetie, I left my phone on my desk, in the rush. I'm sorry, it just took longer than I planned and time got away from me."

He looked at her a moment, then sighed. She was beautiful. He leaned forward, and kissed her cheek. It was that small gesture that let her know that he was pissed, this conversation would continue later, but right now he was glad she was there safely. "I'm just glad you're here. Come on, let's get you something to eat." He led the way to their table, letting the waiter know on the way to bring her dinner, and signaling the host at the same time.

When they reached the table up front, where Mr. & Mrs. Smith sat, along with his sister, Karen and her date, Nina could feel the tension in the air.

"Hello, everyone." Nina said uneasily as Jeff pulled out her chair for her.

"Good to see you made it." Mrs. Smith said sarcastically.

Nina gave an awkward smile, "I got held up at work."

Mrs. Smith and Karen exchanged looks sheepishly and turned back to their dinner. Nina was not in the mood for this right now.

"Nina, you look lovely", Mr. Smith said.

"Thanks, Mr. Smith."

"I told you to call me Edward."

She just smiled. He always said that, and she never did.

She looked over at Jeff. He was still looking at her, but with less anger now. She nibbled her bottom lip as the waiter brought her, a dinner plate. Needless to say the ongoing drama had her too uptight to eat.

Nina sat the bags, with Jeff's gift she had brought in on his living room sofa. She had planned to go straight home, but Jeff took for granted she was coming over and asked her to bring some of the things from the ceremony with her. It was 10:30, it had been a little over 2 hrs and Nina knew Quinton was probably calling her phone, thinking she was ignoring him, since she wasn't answering it. She hated she had left it on her desk.

She turned to Jeff to kiss him goodnight. "Sweetheart, I got to be going." She stood on her tiptoes to kiss his lips softly and quickly. He grabbed her around her waist into his arms.

"Not so fast, where do you think you're running off to?"

"Sweetie, I've got that big presentation tomorrow afternoon, and I still have a lot of things I need to work out."

"Come on, you have been over that presentation over and over again, you know it's perfect. Besides you have to let me show you my appreciation for how wonderful you look in this dress, and you have to give me my proper congrats."

"Jeff, I really need this grant for the Center, and I want everything to go perfect, so I need to work on the final details. I'm really nervous about it." Nina felt herself rambling now.

"Well let me help you relax." He began to kiss on her neck and nibble at her ear, while whispering, "I'm not letting you go anywhere. The man of the year needs some serious attention on his big night."

Nina couldn't believe this. She felt so guilty, but all she could think about was Quinton. She started pushing him away gently. "Jeff, sweetie I really need to go."

Jeff dropped his arms from her waist, and looked confused. "Nina, what's up?"

"Nothing, I told you, I just really need to get some last minute work done." She looked at her watch unknowingly again.

"Alright Nina you've been looking at your damn watch all night like you have somewhere to be. You haven't even paid much attention to anything that has been said; you've been somewhere else mentally, and on top of that you were over an hour late for something you knew was important to me, and your only explanation was you got caught up at work. What the hell is going on?"

The anger he had been bottling up was at the surface now. Nina started fidgeting. "Jeff, I told you its work, that's not an excuse. You of all people should understand that since you're always working late."

"Nina you're playing with me, aren't you?"

"Jeff, I'm serious!"

"Don't lie to me."

"Jeff, I'm not."

He sighed and shook his head as he moved to the sofa. He didn't like getting upset like this, especially not with Nina, but his own emotions at the present moment were so distraught that he was letting them take control, instead of handling this in a calm manner. The last thing he wanted to do was send her into an anxiety attach, but there was something up with her behavior.

He looked tired now. He had loosened his tie and he was rolling his shirtsleeves up. Nina walked over to him and put her arms around his waist from behind, placing her hands on his chest, and her face in the center of his back. "Baby I'll make this up to you, I promise. Just understand how important to me this is, the same way tonight was important to you."

He pulled her around him, and kissed her on the head. "You know I love you, right?"

"Yes I know that, and I love you even more."

He continued as if not to hear her, "Sometimes so damn much, it's crazy, but it's because I worry about losing you."

"Be real Jeff, you're the one who I thought I would lose in the swarm of women tonight. They were killing themselves trying to get at you." She laughed, trying to make light of the situation, but when he didn't laugh along with her, she knew he was serious and she was almost mad at herself for the joke.

"Call me when you get home, and don't make a habit of leaving your damn phone."

"Okay", she said now more serious, then paused for a moment. "I Love you."

He kissed her cheek softly and nuzzled in close to her face, breathing in the remnants of her Lost Cherry perfume before letting her go, "You too."

Nina controlled her speed till she pulled into her drive then rushed inside to call Quinton.

"Can I come over", he asked?

Nina hesitated, what the hell, he needed a friend? "Sure."

"Alright, I'll be there in about 20 minutes.

Nina hung up, and said a little pray. Lord forgive me for all the lies I've told tonight."

Nina promised Jeff they'd make-up for tonight, told him goodnight, and hung up the phone. She felt a twinge of guilt in the bottom of her stomach, but she wasn't doing anything but being there to console a friend. A friend who she had more scar wounds from, than victories. But she couldn't turn her back on Q, not when he had been there for her, through so many storms in her life. Their relationship hadn't worked but they had a friendship that would last a lifetime.

She changed out of the heavy gown and into a t-shirt and a pair of sweats then went back to her living room to find Quinton, lying stretched out on her sofa. He was staring at the TV, but not really watching it.

"You want a drink?"

"No, I've done too much of that already. I thought it would help clear my mind; but no luck"

"I can make some coffee."

He turned to her and looked in her eyes for the first time, since he had got there. "No, I'm okay." He took her hand, "Come here; sit down." He patted the couch beside him.

She sat instead on the sofa closer to the other end. They talked for what seemed for hours, reminiscing about Dee, laughing, trying to keep from shedding tears. It was just like old times.

"I'm going to miss him so much."

"I am too."

They fell on a silent moment, both of them thinking about a better time, when their friend was still there. Not wanting to believe the reality that was staring in their faces. Then Quinton spoke.

"What more could go wrong?"

Nina knew from experience how grief hit you like a ton of bricks, drained you, and left you feeling like nothing would ever be better. And that was just the first phase.

"Ni, I do want to thank you for listening and helping remember the good times with Dee. It's really what I needed tonight and I knew you would understand before anyone else would. It would mean a lot if you could be there with me at the funeral also.

"What about your son's mother."

"You know there is no us. I take care of my son, that's it. She wasn't fond of Dee, and you know he thought you were the only one for me."

Nina smiled, Q went on "I knew too, it's just took me too long to realize."

Nina and Quinton watched Jeff come toward the house with two bags. As he approached Nina took a deep breath. *This was not going to be pretty.* She had let Quinton crash on her sofa, and she was just walking him out, when Jeff, happened to be coming up at the same time. She had brought this on her self. There was no running inside the house, and hiding, leaving them both on her front step to introduce themselves. No, she was going to have to face the music herself.

"Good morning, babe", Jeff said kissing her cheek.

Q gave Nina an annoyed, disgusted look.

"Good morning, sweetie, this is Quinton."

Nina watched as the two shook hands firmly.

"You can call me Q."

"Nice to meet you." He turned to Nina, "Babe, I'm going to take this in before it gets cold."

When he was out of earshot, Quinton leaned over to Nina, "This is craaazy: he's not even concerned with why a Negro is coming out of his woman's house at this time of the morning?

Nina raised her eyebrow in confusion, she was curious as to what Jeff was thinking as well, "At least for the moment. Look call me with details about the funeral."

"Alright, and thanks again."

Nina took short, deep breaths, as she went in to deal with Jeff's wrath and anger that she knew awaited her.

"Jeff, I know I need to explain-"

He was smiling at her and licking cream cheese off his fingers. "About what?"

"About Quinton." He was really beginning to scare her with his lack of concern.

"What is there to explain? An old friend stopped by to chat; is there something more?"

"Ah, no." she said slowly.

"Then there's nothing to explain. Come here, I got your favorite crème rolls, some fresh strawberries, some scrambled eggs, with cheese, the way you like them, and some turkey sausage. I'm going to make up some mimosas. I thought you needed a special breakfast before your big presentation."

Nina didn't know what had happened, but some alien had sucked up Jeff's personality, and had left her with this man, who had not a care in the world.

She walked over to him, as he put a finger topped with crème cheese to her lips. She took the finger in her mouth, and smiled at him, as she slowly and sensually let it descend from her lips. She had to admit, she had missed having him next to her last night.

"You do that so sexy", he said putting his arms around her waist and kissing her. "What do you say to a quickie before you are off to your meeting?"

"I thought we were eating breakfast?"

"No, breakfast is for you to eat, I personally just want to eat you. So, how about it? We could go right her on your kitchen counter, if that's quicker."

"Aren't you in a good mood this morning?"

He lifted her up to sit on the counter, and kissed her. "I realized I needed to enjoy you more than I do."

Nina smiled and was relieved as Jeff teased her with kisses. She didn't need any more drama right now.

Nina stood in the foyer of the house she use to live in. Nothing had changed; Q had kept everything the way she had left it. The last time she was there was the night she left, now she was returning on another sad note, Dee's funeral.

People mulled around with plates of food chattering and speaking and then whispering as they walked away. Nina expected it; she knew things would be awkward when she first walked in before the funeral, where Dee's family and Quinton's mom waited the family car. Nina had spoke and ignored the snide looks. As for the rest of the old gang, they were happy to see her there. Quinton didn't want her out of his sight. It felt a little weird, but Nina told herself, this was acceptable, and she told herself that Dee was her friend too.

The funeral had been very sad, as to be expected. Nina tried to be strong and consoling for Q, as well as some of the others like Charles, who had no support there. She had sat between the two of them, both dressed in dark suits and wearing shades to hide their eyes, as well as any emotions that may escape from them.

She was leaning in the archway leading to the front door, watching people chatter about unrelated things that had nothing to do with the deceased, the way that people do, to get along with their lives. She watched Q walk toward her with a smile on his face.

"I want you to come upstairs with me, there is someone I want you to meet?"

"Who?"

"My son", he said.

Nina didn't know if she was ready for a face to face with the link that broke her past. But then again she couldn't be angry with the baby, and considering she had moved on with her own life, she should be able to handle this.

"Okay."

She followed Q down the hall, (that he hadn't changed any of the pictures she had hung), past the master bedroom, (that they use to spend countless nights making love), to the one of the guest room, (that they had done the same act in), but that had now been turned into a baby boy nursery.

Nina stopped in the doorway, looking at the precious and soft look of the room, as Quinton moved over to the crib. He turned the volume of the monitor on the table down, and Nina watched him stare down into the crib with a warm smile upon his face. Nina came closer to stand beside Quinton, and looked down into the crib also.

Her own wall of tough protection crumbled at the sight of the precious blessing that lay there before them. He was the cutest thing lying peacefully, asleep on his back. She looked up at Quinton, and he was beaming. It was obvious without a blood test, that this baby was 100% his. Nina had to smile herself.

"He looks just like you."

"You think so", Quinton said playfully?

Nina laughed.

"Nina, I can't tell you how much I still love you, and I know I messed up the chance of a lifetime with you, but I'm glad we can still be friends like this. I only hope the best for you."

Quinton pulled her into a bear hug, and as they stood there holding each other a moment, Nina couldn't help but think of how it would have been if it had worked between them, and the baby that lay before them, was theirs.

After Nina used her code to disarm Jeff's alarm, she dropped her purse and garment bag on the hook, in his hallway. The sweet aroma of chocolate drifted to the foyer to meet her. She was tired from meeting, greeting, and then helping to clean up after all those greedy folks. She just wanted to collapse into bed. She had told Jeff she would be back around 8:30, but it was now almost 10, but she had hated to leave Quinton with all of those dishes and that cleaning, plus the baby. His mom and sisters had left, without even offering to help; but she was sure that had more to do with her than them not wanting to help.

Before she left, Quinton had shared with her that he felt something more was stirring among his other cousins and Dee's friends. They wanted revenge for his death, and to a certain degree he too felt the same way, but he owed his son a life with his father and that meant a safe life, not one where he'd constantly be looking over his shoulder. To hear that, was music to Nina's ears.

Nina went into the kitchen that looked like a centerfold out of a Better Homes or Architecture Digest magazine. The in-kitchen table was set, candles were melting, there were pots and pans on the stove, and music was playing. Jeff was nowhere to be found. He wasn't in the dining room or his study. Nina was just about to check upstairs when she saw the patio doors, leading out to the pool, open.

"Jeff", she called as she stepped out. Jeff was stretched out in a lawn chair facing the pool, watching the moonshine across the blue water. He had a beer in one hand and a cigar in the other. He looked up at Nina, and then turned his head away, without answering.

Nina made her way down the stairs and across to where he sat. "Babe, what are you doing out here?"

"Thinking."

"About what?" The spaced out look he wore made Nina uneasy. She suddenly wished she had called, but the time had just gotten away from her, and she didn't think it was a big deal.

"About how you're the first person I have ever known, whose attended a damn 7 hour long funeral?"

This is not what she wanted to deal with. Nina bit back her anger, swallowed hard trying to keep her own temper in check.

"The funeral wasn't 7 hours long, I was catching up with old friends."

He stood up and turned to Nina just staring at her a moment. He then shook his head, and started smiling a conniving smile. "Old friends that I obviously have never f-ing met; now why is that Nina?" He was moving in closer to her.

"What do you mean?" She gulped some air, but dared not to look away from his burning eyes.

"What I mean is, how come the only family and friends of yours that I have met have been your Auntie and Uncle and some sneaky looking Negro who you use to live with, who obviously had no reason to be leaving your house at 8 o'clock in the damn morning?"

Nina knew it was too good to be true that he wasn't upset that morning.

"Jeff, I'm tired and you've been drinking, so let's just go to bed, and talk about this tomorrow."

"There you go again, pushing things to later, instead of dealing with them now."

Nina was getting frustrated. An argument isn't what she came here for. If this is what her night was going to be like, she could have went home and slept in her own bed. Her weariness was mixing with frustration and his anger was tipped off from his drinking.

"What the hell are you talking about? What the hell is wrong with you?"

"You want to know what is wrong. I thought we had plans to spend

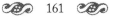

time together tonight. I went through the trouble of making dinner, and trying to plan a special evening for us since we hadn't been together lately, but what do you do? Not show up, and then once again you don't answer your damn cell. Where did you leave it this time?"

"Jeff, My phone died and finding a charger seemed to be more trouble than it was worth with everything that was going on. I'm sorry if I messed up your plans. I didn't know." Nina thought if she eased up on her anger they wouldn't have to end this night in a big argument, and they could still save the night; besides she could really use one of Jeff's foot rubs.

Jeff stared at her another moment, then walked past her. "Maybe you should be more considerate next time" he mumbled as he went, not even looking at her.

Nina followed. He went to the fridge to get another beer. Nina was on his heels. When he turned around with the cold beer in his hand, Nina grasped it and sat it on the counter. Then pushed her body into him. Feeling the heat from his body, as he tried to keep from putting his hands on her. She ran her own hands up the hardness of his chest.

"Jeff, babe I'm sorry, but can't we still save the night. Let's not fight. I'm just too tired. All I need and want is to be with you; maybe take a bubble bath, sip on some wine, and make a, whole, lot, of, love, until the morning." She said each of her words with a kiss to his chest, as she unbuttoned his shirt. She leaned in even closer and kept kissing him, as she rubbed her own body against his, causing sexual friction to run through his veins. She had to be sure he was going to go for this. Eventually he had to given into the urge and put his hands on her hips and kissed her back.

"You have a lot of making up to do to me, for dinner, being late, and anything else I can come up with", he said between kisses.

"The night is still young. How about you closing up and putting things away down here, and I'll go upstairs and run us a bath, and I'll be waiting for you."

"You're not going to eat first?"

"I don't have the patience. Besides afterwards, I'll be starving. So is it a deal?"

"Sure."

She kissed him once more passionately, then ran her hand down the growth in his pants, and then backed away smiling, letting her hand linger on his hardness. Jeff smiled also, that woman could drive him wild.

As Nina ran the water in the tub, and then lit her scented candles that Jeff kept around for her, she thought about how her body ached with weariness, but if she had to push herself a few more hours, to keep peace with Jeff, she'd just have to do that. She added some lavender petals to the bubbled water, dimmed the lights and hit play on the remote of the smart system. Maxwell started crooning from the speakers.

Jeff's house was a good 100yards form his nearest neighbors, so them seeing the two of them in the many windows he had, wasn't likely, so she left the drapes open, so that they could enjoy the star studded sky as a back drop.

Nina felt him rubbing up against her backside. She had taken her clothes off and was making sure the water wasn't too hot, by wadding her toe in it.

"Are you starting without me", he asked?

"Of course not." She finished undressing him, dropping his clothes where they landed. She took him by the hand and pulled him into the tub. Nina knew he was right, she did owe him and she wanted to make it up to him. They sat down in the bubbling cauldron and Nina threw her leg over him; straddling him. She normally like to relax in the warm bubbles, but tonight the water and the bubbles weren't important; just satisfying her Jeff.

She tilted her head just enough to meet the warm skin in the curve of his neck, and kissed there repeatedly: a trail up to his earlobes, where she nibbled, as he hands roamed over her body and he hardened beneath her. She lifted her lower body up, positioned herself on him and came down slowly.

A soft moan, erupted from deep within his chest.

"Umm, I like the way you make up to me."

She moved to his lips to kiss him, while her breast skimmed his chest. "It has only, just begun."

Later, after they had slipped into bed, he held her in his arms. Nina was propped up on his chest with her arms folded under her chin. She was glad they had managed to get beyond the argument earlier that almost had ruined this moment. But as she knew all good things must…

"Babe, are you still on the pill?"

*Where the hell was this coming from? One minute they are having an intimate moment, the next, he wants to discuss birth control. The answer was yes, why she didn't know? It was more for monthly regulation, more than it was for birth control. With her chances of getting pregnant, there was no concern in that department.*

"Of course I am, do you think I would be messing around with you if I wasn't", she kidded?

Jeff was glad she didn't blow up into one of her moods, from his question. The look of hesitation before she answered had him wondering if he shouldn't have even mentioned it. He hadn't tried to pursue any conversations concerning anything involving babies or future commitment since the night she flipped on him, but she had not made an effort to talk about what had happened either, and frankly he was tired of waiting.

He ran his hand through her disheveled hair and decided to push his luck a little. "So there has to be a timeline for stopping those in advance before you start trying to have a baby?"

Nina didn't like where this was going, but if she could keep herself calm, she could refrain from having an anxiety attack, as well as not have to have the conversation that she had been putting off for so long. The thing was, since that afternoon watching Quinton with his son, had her thinking so strongly about what if she could have a baby. It also had her reliving some dark moments when she had miscarried.

"Yeah, but I'm not planning on getting pregnant anytime soon."

"I know, I was just curious." He left it at that.

Nina rolled off of him and sat up to get a closer look into his eyes. She knew she should let this ride, but she was going to step out on a limb here. "Jeff, do you want me to stop taking my pills?"

"Yeah. No. I mean maybe you should go to the doctor to see. We need to have a plan and time line, right? After we get married of course. I don't want to rush things."

Nina smiled. She really loved him. She leaned over and kissed his soft lips. As much as this was scaring her, deep down inside she really wanted that.

The sound of John Legend bellowing out a melody from her purse caught her off guard. Jeff pulled away.

"Is that your phone?"

Nina looked confused, "Yeah."

"It's almost 1am, who the hell is calling you at this time?"

Nina got up uneasily, "It's probably the wrong number", she said as she was going to her purse. When she got to her phone intentionally late, it had stopped ringing. It was Q, she knew it was. "It said unknown, see". She held the phone up showing him. She was glad he knew not to let his number be traceable.

Jeff was still not content. "When I call, you never have your phone, but when I'm trying to be alone with you, it rings."

"Well it's off now." Nina said getting back into the bed. "Where were we", she said kissing him? She hoped nothing was wrong, whatever it was it would have to wait until morning. There was no way she was going to chance getting into another argument with Jeff.

Nina opened the door and stepped out of the shower to see Jeff standing there.

"Hey, babe, what's up?" She grabbed a towel and began to dry off.

He held up her cell phone. "It was ringing. I tried to get it to you, but it stopped ringing. Private number."

"Oh, okay." Nina said taking it and grabbing another towel on the way to the bedroom.

"I thought you turned your phone off last night", he asked following her.

"I did, but I called one of my clients this morning."

Nina busied herself finding a tee shirt and a pair of sweats in the drawers she had claimed to keep her things in. She knew if she looked at Jeff, he'd make her more nervous than she was now. She had gotten up, and while Jeff was downstairs in his office, she had called Q, at the house, and then on his cell to see what was up? He didn't answer either, so she left a message. He must have called, while she was in the shower.

"You couldn't use the house line?"

"Sweetie, the client I had to call lives with a boyfriend who isn't the easiest to get a long with. I didn't want to cause any problems, like what is happening here, by calling from here, and your number showing up on her caller ID."

"What do you, mean, 'like what is happening here'?"

"Jeff, you're getting upset with me over a phone call to my cell."

"No, don't get it twisted. How about a couple of calls to your cell? Your damn phone never rings that much when we're together, plus lately you've had a lot of other shit going on with this phone". He suddenly sounded like his black roots were coming through real strong; out the window went the sophistication of prep school and grammar classes. His eyes were blazing.

"Jeff you act as though I've been trying to hide something, or that I'm sneaking around."

"Well, are you?"

Nina got quite while just staring at him for a moment. Now she was pissed. "What the hell is this, you think I'm cheating on you?"

"A lot of things have been happening lately that are starting to point that way."

"I can't believe you."

"Well, explain why you're suddenly always late for appointments, you're acting suspicious when your damn phone rings; you're suddenly are so engrossed in work that you're staying later, and I tried to shake this, but your damn ex was leaving your house early in the morning. All of this, and the fact that you feel you can't trust me enough to talk to me. So, be honest with me Nina, what the hell is going on?"

Nina plopped down on his bed and fumbled with her hands. The words that Net had spoken to her a few weeks earlier came to her. *'A man is only going to deal with a problem but so long, before he snaps'*. She thought this had to be the so long mark for Jeff. She started with a loud sigh. "Jeff a lot has been going on lately. I told you about how Q was the only friend I had after my parents died, well I feel I owe him a lot still. He's been going through a lot lately, so I've been trying to be a friend and help him."

A moment passed before Jeff looked up from where he stood at bedroom window looking out and he calmly spoke. "Are you still f-ing him?"

"Jeff no!" she said looking at him in shock.

"Nina, it's not easy for me to just accept you spending time with this man, and not think you're not sleeping with him too."

*Was he really that jealous?* "Jeff I swear to you, I'm just helping a friend."

"You're returning to old ways, Nina; hanging out with an old crowd, how am I suppose to believe you're not turning tricks again also."

Nina could swear she smelled shit, because it had definitely just hit the fan. She was shocked, but hurt and anger were following close behind. Jeff had never referred to those things that she'd rather leave in the past, ever before. She was angry that he would even mention it now, under both the circumstance and in that manner.

"Jeff, first of all, I've done a lot of things that I'm not proud of, but I have never turned a damn trick for anyone. I am not a f-ing prostitute, and that I am not or have I ever been. I may have danced for money, but I didn't sleep with anyone for money. Second I'm hurt to know you even believe that you think I would go back to that. I thought you of all people could accept me for who I am, and not what mistakes I may have made in the past."

"How the hell can I do that if you're back to f-ing with your ex-boyfriend?"

"You know what, you're just like your damn mother and your sister? I don't know why I thought you were any different."

"I don't know either, maybe I just wanted to know what it was like f-ing around with someone like you for once so I took a chance!" Jeff was sorry for the words even before he had finished them.

Nina was speechless. She tried to bite her lip to refrain from crying, but the tears had already started streaming down her face. She couldn't believe this; what had gotten into him? Through tears she tried to get words out, "Jeff, why are you doing this? Why are you saying these things to me?"

It was too late; and he was just as hurt as he was mad.

"Doing what to you Nina, telling the truth? I'm tired of trying to tame someone, who obviously doesn't want to be tamed when I could have anybody I choose? So why should I deal with this shit from you?

*She couldn't believe he was referring to her like she was some type of circus animal he had to make presentable to the public.* "What are you trying to say?"

"You can get your shit, and get the f-k out of my house."

Before Nina could try to say anything, he was gone. She wanted to do something, anything but cry the way she was doing. In the past she could have thought of a million ways to get revenge, but all those things weren't in her anymore. So she collapsed on the bed, slide to the floor, hugged her knees to her chest and cried. Cried trying to erase the last few minutes, as she heard Jeff's motorcycle roar down the road.

Jeff tried to control his speed as he rounded the curve. He was mad as hell, but he wasn't mad enough to kill his self on a machine, especially since it had been a while since he had rode. He let his self relax into the ride and the roar of the engine. Letting the wind attempt to blow away the confusion and anger. He loved Nina like he had loved no other women before. He had been busy with business, and in his past experience with women, that wasn't a problem. He'd shower them with some expensive gifts, and they would be fine. But she was not that type of woman.

But now she was going back to a man who treated her like dirt and had hurt her in the past. When all he wanted to do was love her, and give her everything she had been lacking, and she wasn't satisfied with that. She was going back to what had caused her so many problems in the past, and she had yet to trust him enough to discuss her insecurities about commitment and family. He was still going on what Janette had told him. Nina had not yet brought the situation up, and that pissed him off even more because he couldn't control any of this, which put him in the very place her ex was, hurting her by calling her names.

He hadn't meant the things he had said to her, but under the anger and stress that had been bottled up, he had let the words escape his lips. *What the hell can you do when all your life, everything you've even had the slightest yearning for, you got if you worked for it hard enough; but Nina was distant to him, no matter how hard he tried?*

It was something pulling at him lately; some strong unexplainable force. His life seemed so unorganized and uncontrolled, and he had never felt that way before. He didn't know what it was, but he felt empty. His spirit felt drained. Maybe all that talk about a relationship with God that Nina's Aunt Laurie mentioned, wasn't so crazy. It had been a while since he had even prayed. It was like as soon as he got what he had asked God for last, he stopped praying. At this point he had no other choices and knew of nowhere else to turn. What could he loose from a conversation with something he couldn't see; that is if that something would actually listen to him?

## FOR ALL THINGS THERE IS A SEASON; TIME TO SPEAK AND A TIME TO BE QUIET

Nina wiped at tears furiously, while trying to keep her focus on the road. She hoped she'd got all her stuff, so she didn't have to see that jackass again. She left his keys, and everything she had on her that he had given to her, and was planning to pack up the other things as soon as she got home to have waiting for him when he came to pick up his things.

She hated him. That is why she wanted so badly for him to call her and beg for her to come back, because she loved him so much. She knew she was being redundant, but he just didn't understand her. And she would never be able to make him.

Her cell phone rung, interrupting her thoughts. She fished it out of her purse and answered, not looking to see whom it was first. "Yeah?"

"Ne, what's wrong? Are you crying?" It was Quinton, and he could tell the tears were obvious in her voice.

"No", she lied through tears, as she began to sob lightly again.

"Ne, tell me what's going on?"

"I can't talk about it now."

"Where are you"?

"In the car."

"Where are you going?"

"Home", she sobbed.

"I'll meet you there, be careful."

The last thing she wanted right now was to talk to Quinton about this. She wasn't in the mood to deal with another man right now, but it was too late. Quinton knew something was wrong and there was no stopping him now.

When she pulled into her drive, she saw Quinton already leaning on the hood of his truck waiting on her. He met her at the car as she began to pull clothes and bags from her back seat. He tried to grab at garments and help her, but only caught her elbow in his side, as she snatched away, almost tumbling over dropped clothing, as she stomped away.

"What the hell is all this stuff?" he asked picking up items she left trailing behind her.

"My stuff."

Quinton was confused, "what are you doing?"

Nina was huffing and puffing. He had to take full strides to keep up with her short muscular legs. "He told me to get my stuff and leave." She was at the door now, fumbling with her keys in the lock.

"What?"

"He told me to leave him the f-k alone."

"Why?"

She stopped just inside the door and dropped everything, then turned sharply to look at him. "Why? Quinton you want to know why?" She really wasn't waiting for him to answer, as she went on, fire in her eyes. "Because of you. Because of your calling late at night and then again this morning; because I've been spending too much of my time with you. Because you are asking too much of me, while I'm trying to move on with my f-king life." She knew she was yelling, because her head was pounding now.

The vein in Quinton's temple was pulsating with anger. He smoothed his mustache with one hand, and just stared at her. He had never been an arguer. He hesitated before speaking in a very calm voice. "Have I ever told you, out of all the things we've been through, everything I've ever done for you in all these years, that you asked too much of me?' He didn't give her a chance to answer; he was the angry one now. "No, because I always tried to give you what you wanted, including the opportunity to be with him. Now I apologize for causing problems, but

I though you could help a friend in need while I was dealing with some stuff. And I called you last night to let you know that Charles and the guys retaliated on the dude that killed Dee, but not before Charles took two shots in his back. He's partially paralyzed; we don't know yet if it's just temporarily. I was at the hospital when you called this morning and couldn't pick up. It's a big mess. But I wanted to tell you thanks for keeping me away from all that, it could have been me, and I could have been dead. Just thought you'd want to know."

He turned to leave.

Nina felt like a petty idiot. Selfish too. She remembered when her mother use to tell her, to listen first, then talk.

"Q, wait, please."

He turned back, "What?"

"I'm sorry, don't leave unless you have to. Stay a moment, please."

Nina went into her living room and sat down staring at her hands. Q followed her. She wanted to ball up in the fetal position, but knew none of this would go away if she did. "Q, why do we love each other so much, we're the best of friends, but we can't keep a relationship going?"

"I think it's because we should have just stayed friends. And also for the past few weeks, I've seen a happiness in your eyes that I was never able to put there when we were together."

"I was happy with you."

"No, I don't mean the type of happy you were when I did things for you to make up for the wrong I had done previously. Nina I made you happy when I tried, or when I wasn't out partying and I came home, or when I bought you things, or when I wasn't causing you headaches wondering where I was. But with Jeff, you light up with just the mention of his name, he doesn't even have to be around. That's different. Given another opportunity now to make it up, I would give anything to make it work for us, but I could never make you happy the way he has."

Nina leaned over and laid her head on his shoulder. "What would I do without you?"

"What to ruin your life? You may be finding out sooner than you think."

"What do you mean?"

"I'm thinking about taking Naquin and moving to Charleston.

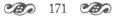

There's nothing here for either of us but trouble. I've got some leads on some real estate down there. I need to make a better life for us. And considering his mother is bored with motherhood, I have a responsibility to give him a real life."

Nina knew this is what she had been trying to show Q, for so long. But you can't change someone; they have to want to change for themselves. Q had finally reached that point. And she thought everything happened in due time. "I hate to see you go, but sometimes you have to make sacrifices, so I don't blame you. Just one thing."

"What?"

"Take me with you", she whined, grabbing his arm.

Quinton laughed a moment. "You have work here to complete, and there are a lot of kids depending on you, as well as a relationship you have to work on."

Nina pulled away. "That last parts isn't going to happen. Jeff said a lot of things that made it clear he didn't want me around anymore. Besides, we're just too different, from two different worlds."

Quinton laughed again. "You know you're repeating everything I've said before, and I was wrong. Bottled up anger makes you say things you don't mean, and that cat definitely was bottling up something when he saw me leaving here that morning. I knew he wasn't going to just let that ride, because if I was him, and I saw some cat leaving my woman's house at that time in the morning, it wouldn't have been so calm. Give him time."

"Yeah, that's all I seem to have."

"Well, I got to get back to the hospital, I'll check back in with you later."

"Tell Charlie, I'm praying for him, let me know if anything changes."

"Hopefully it will, I hope this incident makes him think about doing things differently. He's too smart for this." He leaned over and kissed her head. "I'll talk to you later."

Nina closed the door and leaned on it. Alone again. But she had managed life alone, and she would manage this alone, it was only a matter of time.

*Dear God,*

*I have been told that talking to you can make a difference. I've taken the whole thanking you for what you've done in my life, for granted by just saying it and not really meaning it. I have so much to sincerely thank you for, I don't know where to begin. There is so much I have to say, so many things I need your assistance with, even though I know I've always tried to fix it myself. I don't know where to start, but I'm sure you know it all already. So here I am. Me, my troubles, and my sins; I give it all to you. Could you help me fix my life? I am so confused. Please.*

Nina-

# CHAPTER XIX

NINA TUNED THE HUMMING SWEET voice, of her non-stop-talking Auntie Laurie out, as she padded across the plush of her siege green carpet, to her front door to see who was there. She loved talking to her Auntie, she had a voice that made the worse situation seemed better, but they had been on the phone for an hour now, and had talked about everything they could have talked about, except what was and had happened between she and Jeff. Nina wasn't ready to tell Auntie Laurie that they had had a fight; and especially not that it was concerning Q. That would really get her boiling; then that would involve telling her about why she hadn't yet told Jeff about her past. She was not in the mood for another headache at the moment.

But when she saw Jeff at her steps, she was pretty sure she'd have one anyway.

"Auntie Laurie I have to go, I'll call you later. Tell Uncle George I love him; love you too."

She hung up the phone and took one look at her very short, grey, sweat shorts, and tiny, yellow, midriff T-shirt. Her hair was pulled up in a messy ponytail. She was dressed for exactly what she was doing, a Sunday afternoon lounging around the house.

"Crap", she mumbled; for that is exactly what she looked like. The last thing she wanted was for him to think she was miserable, even though she was. But what should she care what she looked like, he's the one who made it clear how he felt? It had been 7 days, and 6 even longer lonely nights, since she had brought all of her stuff home. She had constantly fought the urge to call him and hear his voice, but she assured herself she had nothing to be sorry for. He's the one who had said things he should be sorry for.

She put her hand on the knob, took a deep breath, and then opened. He was beautiful. It was a lazy Sunday afternoon for her, but he was dressed as if he had just walked off of the cover of Ebony Men. He even smelled delicious.

*Crap! Crap! Crap!!* She could not let herself weaken from just the sight and smell of him. But his sexiness was shining through that smile of his. And Nina's head was winding down memory lane when he'd hold her, running his big warm hands across her skin, his moist lips on her every body part, and him satisfying her and every one of her bodily needs. She had to snap out of this.

"Hi, she said nonchalantly."

'Hi, I know I should have called, but I was just taking a chance on coming by to pick up my things."

The truth was he didn't call, because he knew she probably wouldn't answer and if she did, she would have told him to come when she wasn't home. And she had every right to. He had kept his self in torment for the last 7 days for saying the things he had said, but he hadn't know how to reprimand the situations in a way that Nina would accept. The woman was too stubborn and intelligent for any flowers and gifts with an "I'm sorry" scribbled by some florist.

Nina sighed, she would have told him to wait till she wasn't home; so she wouldn't have to deal with this feeling in the pit of her stomach that was shooting pains south to her womanhood. Why she had them, she didn't know?

"Well you're here now, come in." She stepped aside, leaving enough of space that he wouldn't touch her. He could see right through her efforts to be aloof. "Feel free to go get your things, you know where they are."

Jeff turned to face her, "Nina, I want to talk to you first." His face was soft, and his eyes were pleading.

Nina turned away, and started walking past him back to her sofa, so that she could remain firm. "Jeff, I believe you said all that you needed to say the other day. Unless there are some other names you would like to call me like tramp, or slut?"

He blinked at her words. That stung him. He could talk his way through million dollar business deals all day, but right now had trouble picking the right words to win over a billion dollar woman. He gulped some air and then began.

"Nina, I'm sorry. I said a lot of things that I didn't mean, it's just I was upset and you just keep-"

She cut him off as she whipped around to face him. "No, you will not throw this back on me Jefferson Edward Smith." *How dare he; yeah she may have been wrong for not being open and up front, but when she had told him, he had started accusing her of other stuff. Now he was trying to make it seem like she was the blame.*

She had one hand on her hip, the other in the air and was prepared to launch into a finger snapping, neck rolling rampage. She was mad with fury. But Jeff grabbed her by the shoulders so quick, it caught her off guard. It was one quick, strong action that he swooped her up off the floor a couple inches.

"Now would you listen to me for once? I love you. Yes, I said things the other day that brought out the jackass in me; I'm sorry, but that doesn't take away the fact that I love you like I have never loved any woman before. Lately I've been pouring myself into my work, because I couldn't take being around you, and you not trusting me enough to be open with me and tell me what is going on in your life. I've tried to give you time, but all it seems like you are doing is pulling away more and more. Then when this stuff started happening with your phone and your whereabouts were questionable, I got fed up, and I reached my breaking point."

He loosened up his grip and backed off a little. Now if you want to be friends with this Q, fine, just be honest with me. I need you Nina. I've never needed anyone the way I need you."

Tears were brimming at the edge of Nina's eyes. Her anger had simmered, and calmness had taken control, as she bit her bottom lip now.

"Babe I'm sorry, just forgive me please." The harshness had left his eyes, and were now soft, and pleading again. "The last few days I've done a lot of thinking and searching for the right way to come to you. I knew what I had to do, it was just hard to do it after the way I behaved. I wasn't even sure you'd take me back, but I had to come to you still, but didn't know how. But there are a few things that happened that gave me confirmation of what I had to do. Nina, baby, I just need you to forgive me please."

Nina blinked her eyes closed for a long moment, trying to make her head settle. He completely let her go. He was pleading her forgiveness, and asking her to just trust him, but yet she was still holding a secret from him. She opened her eyes to see him staring at her.

"Jeff, I love you." She sniffled.

He took her hand in his, and pulled her into his arms, holding her. After a moment, Nina chuckled.

He pulled away to look down at her. "What?"

"I'm glad you're not really picking up your things, because I destroyed a couple of your suits, and your shoes that I'll have to replace. Armani and Italian leather doesn't smell to well when it's burning.

"You're kidding right?"

She smiled again, and raised an eyebrow, "No."

He let out a short laugh, and then pulled her back in his arms.

Nina pulled away again. "What was the confirmation?"

Jeff laughed. "You're going to find this a shock."

He began to tell Nina how his father had came to his office earlier that week telling him about a young man who was moving and owned quite a few real estate properties in the area. Two of the properties were commercial warehouses. His father thought that they would make great investments for commercial building if not the buildings themselves, at least the land."

"So the day that I was suppose to meet this guy I had been through hell that night before, and I couldn't focus on anything because all I could do is think about you. Cint calls and tells me that, Mr. Morton is here". I tell her to let him in and who walks in, but Quintelus Morton."

Nina's mouth dropped open in shock.

Jeff smiled. "I was more than pissed, but after I got over being so upset, and we talked, he told me about him moving, what he wanted to do, and a few things about you. When he left, I wasn't so upset, and I had made a deal."

"You're kidding?"

"Nope".

Nina just stared at him. He took her in his arms again. "Nina, I realize that my life isn't as in tune as I thought it was. And there are a number of things I need to get right with myself, but I know it is a process. The first step is I've acknowledged it, and I'm working on it. Mr. Morton assured me, as if I didn't' already know, that getting you back was the most important thing I could do."

Nina was still stunned, but it had all worked out. It was amazing how one bad thing in your life could bring something good to you. She just hoped that love would help them survive the secret she would have to unfold to him soon.

# BODY, SOUL, LOVE, AND MIND

Nina nibbled on her pencil nervously while she eyed Jeff as he read. They were in her den, on the sofa. Her legs were thrown across Jeff's lap, and he softly rubbed one of his hands up and down it to steady her nervous bouncing, while he held in his other hand her a copy of her just finished proposal for the Center's new funding.

Nina watched Jeff's eyes closely as he read the papers; the widening and then squinting of his eyes, when he came to a point of understanding or confusion. She didn't know why she was so nervous about Jeff reading it; it wasn't like he approved proposals on a daily basis.

"Hmmm". Jeff knitted his eyebrows.

Nina jerked her pencil from her lips and sat up suddenly. "What? What do you mean by hmm? Is there something wrong with it?"

"No, it's good; really good."

Nina looked at him dead in his eyes and waited.

"What?" He looked up at her from the papers.

"But? I know it's coming, Jeff, so go ahead."

"I just think it would be more effective if you added some of the kids take on the Center, like their actual words, to show how important it is for them on a personal level instead of just putting in what the Center provides."

"So basically you think I should start over?" She snatched the papers from his hand and swung her legs around, to put her feet on the floor.

"No, I don't think you should start over, just add a couple more things, or get the kids just to come in at the meeting, like a testimonial. Actions in the presence makes things more effective to the eye, than just hearing to the ears."

Nina sighed and stood up. She walked over to where her laptop rested on the ottoman, threw the papers down, and then dragged her hands across her face and into her messy hair. Jeff watched how frustrated she looked. He got up, walked over to her, pulled her back into him, and then bent down to kissed the back of her neck.

"Babe, it's a quarter till 11; just stop for the night and you can finish up later. Let's go to bed." He kissed her neck softly again.

She pulled away, and went back to the couch and collapsed. "I wanted to finish tonight Jeff." Her tone was sharp and demanding.

He sighed. She was so stubborn, and he knew that her whining and frustration was only because she liked to finish way ahead of schedule. No one was making her do this. "Nina it's not due until next week. Take a break. You've got the majority done." He walked back to her again, and took her hands and pulled her up. He kissed her hands softly, and then lifted her chin so that she looked at him in his eyes. "I want you to go to bed now, and I'll take care of cutting everything off to turn in, okay."

Nina looked at him a moment. She was really tired, and though she had so much on her mind and knew she wouldn't fall asleep anytime soon, she still would welcome being able to lie down. She was sure she'd lie there for about 2 hours strategizing in her head about work, before she got to sleep. Her body and mind was beyond worn out, and she knew it was the reason she had been in such a bad mood all evening. It's a wonder Jeff was still there, from the way she had been behaving.

She sighed, "Okay."

Jeff watched as she slowly walked away, dragging her feet as she went. It was ridiculous how much you could see the stress sitting on her. But the thing was, she was doing it to herself

When Nina got to her bedroom, she wanted to just collapse in it, but she knew it had been at least a week since she and Jeff had been together, so she knew what he wanted tonight, and after the mood she had been in all evening, she did feel like he deserved it. So she pulled off the cotton grey shorts she was wearing and her tee shirt, and slid under the covers. She didn't bother to turn the T.V. on, but instead snuggled deeper into the softness of the sheets and her pillow, hugging it tight and closing her eyes to relax.

When she heard Jeff quietly enter the room, he turned the light off, and only the light coming from the lamp on the nightstand glowed over him as he peeled his clothes off. As Nina watched his body in the dim light, her body began to untense slowly. She enjoyed just the sight of him. Not just his physical beauty but also his whole being. She couldn't describe it but there was so much that radiated from him that had drawn her to him, that she didn't feel complete unless he was near. It was so unexplainable.

She kept her eyes on him, and he kept his on hers. Neither smiled at the other, or said a word, but the sexual tension built rapidly between them. He pulled the comforter back and saw her beautifully sprawled out before him. The curve of her arched back; the rich, dark chocolate of her skin, dipping in the center, tapering into a smaller waist and then expanding out into curvy hips; firm and round, that expanded into firm thighs meeting at the apex her sweet, and velvety softness. Physically her body was all volume and muscles; thick for pleasure, but smooth for the touch and kissing. A body so beautiful, it was intoxicating to look at.

Before, Nina would have grimaced for having Jeff stare at her naked for so long, but now that she knew how much he adored it and her, she soaked in the attention. He finally slide under the covers beside her. Nina felt the heat from his nakedness as he came so close to her, but never made contact between his skin to hers. But then she softly and slowly felt his moist lips meet her skin, as he left a hot, trail of butterfly-touched kisses along her spine, and the cold of the charm from his necklace grazed her tickling-ishly down her back. It was then that she eased her mind away from the work of the day. She wanted this. Her body was yearning for it.

He kissed every inch between her shoulders to the small of her back. Those mere gestures made Nina arch her back and almost purr out loud. He could feel her body loosen and relax under the touch of his lips. Jeff knew what he was about to do, most men wouldn't do, but there was something urging him; almost pushing him to do it. With Nina he just want to satisfy her, and the moan of satisfaction that came from her with each sigh, sent him into ecstasy mode of his own. Her body craved him as much as his did her at that moment, but he knew right then that what her mind and heart needed was more important. So he laid down beside her.

Nina felt her body becoming a feather. Floating. Serenity. Yeah this was Nirvana. She had slowly been drained of all of her stress. As Jeff rubbed her back, Nina felt tears well in her eyes. He then wrapped his arms around her waist and hugged her close to his hard chest; she could feel his love way before the words tumbled from his lips. He laid beside her; and they stared in each other's eyes. At that moment Nina felt the dept of Jeff's love, and she began to cry even more. She had thought she would never ever feel this type of love from anyone again. He wanted to make her happy, he wanted to give her comfort, and he wanted what was best for her. And he wasn't asking anything in return, not even sex. Jeff wiped away at the tears on her cheek. He didn't know why she was crying, but at the moment didn't want to destroy the moment, so he pulled her closer, against his chest, and held her, as he drifted off to sleep.

# CHAPTER XX

## THOSE THINGS THAT GO SILENTLY, WILL STORM AGAIN

NINA DOUBLED OVER IN LAUGHTER again at Nachelle. The girl was too much and didn't even know it most of the time. She fell back on her sofa, holding her stomach, and gasping for breath as Jeannette threw a pillow at her younger sister.

"You are a nut."

Nachelle looked nonchalantly at her older sister, as if not to see what she had said that was so funny to the two of them.

It was Friday night, Girls night at Nina's. Nina and Jeannette had left the Center and met Nachelle, Net's 24-year old little sister, at the mall to get in some retail therapy at the end of a long week and benefit from a lot of sales. It was normally just Net and Nina, but they didn't turn down the opportunity to invite Nachelle. Besides the girl always kept them in tyrants of laughter.

After leaving the mall weighed down with shopping bags, they stopped by Wegmans and picked up the ingredients for an indulgent dinner for themselves. Now they sat in Nina's living room, with empty pasta bowls, and half eaten cheesecake in front of them along with drained wine glasses, and Nachelle of course was entertaining them with her latest dating horror stories.

Nachelle was beautiful, just like her sister. She was a couple inches taller than Net, mocha complexion, with a honey blonde natural curly bob, that brought even more attention to her pretty features. Nina envied Net and Nachelle's relationship, because it was what Net would

have wanted, had she had a sister. But then from the way they argued sometimes, Nina was happy to be an only child.

"You two think I'm kidding. I thought by going to grad school early, I might meet an intelligent, older guy, that I might be on the same level with, but they are just as crazy as these guys my age. A mortgage and a 401k doesn't make a damn difference. You two just don't understand how it is being young, single and sexy these days." She smiled slyly and took the last sip of her wine and waited for them to blow.

"What?"

"Oh, no she didn't."

Nachelle was cracking up now.

"I have you to know, I may be married, but I am not old, you strumpet." Net threw her last pillow at Nachelle.

"And I am neither old nor married. I'm in the same boat as you, but a little sexier I must say" Nina smiled.

"I forget you're not that much older than I am, but you have an old soul, Nina"

Nina gave a slanted eye glare at her, and folded her arms across her chest.

"But that's a good thing." She said quickly clearing it up. "But Net has my fine ass brother-in-law Warren, and it is no secret from anyone in Charlotte that you are currently attached to that that fine and might I add rich, Jefferson Edward Smith III."

Nina's smile beamed. She wasn't happy about the attention she got when people realized who she was in association with Jeff, but it was fulfilling knowing that the association with Jeff is what made her happy.

"It's hard to refer to him without saying his whole damn name. Do you call him by his whole name in bed?" Nachelle laughed at herself this time.

This time, Nina threw the pillow.

"Maybe if you paid more attention to other characteristics besides a man in bed, you could find someone worth keeping." Net said.

"Here we go again." Nachelle rolled her eyes. "You mean to tell me, you didn't sleep with Warren before you two were married? And don't lie, because I know you have not always been the perfect little, church-going, hussy of a wife that you are now."

"No, but when I was dating, I didn't sleep with every guy I went out with either, and so quickly I might add."

Nina sat quietly, not wanting to get into sibling rivalry. She started collecting dishes, and tuning them out, until Nachelle brought her back into the conversation.

"Judgy a little, big sis? Nachelle, said making a face at Net and then turning to Nina. "Do you feel the same way, Nina?"

Nina stopped and turned to the young girl. Suddenly at that moment she felt like she was old. She knew what Nachelle had meant by old soul, but it was just because of what she had been through. She could see herself in Nachelle when she was about 22 years old. It seemed like more than a decade ago, but it had only been about 7 years. It's amazing how events in life could change your whole outlook. She wish she had the right words to say to her to let her know that sex wasn't the answer, or to make Nachelle realize that she should get to know herself first, and then let the guy know what she was about, rather than thinking they could only connect on a sexual level. That way was a whole lot better than sleeping with someone, falling in love, and then trying to work your way backwards to plant a foundation for your relationship to work.

"Nachelle, I think Net just wants you to be careful. There are a lot of things that you should be aware of and protect yourself from; actually there are a whole lot more things than it was just a couple of years ago. Each day that goes by, seems a lot harder than the day before. And she's not just talking about STD's here, but your feelings as well."

Net and Nachelle both looked at each other, and exchanged looks, then burst into laughter.

"You just went on a philosophical, social worker, trip. It is not that serious. When is Jeff coming back to rescue you, because I think you truly are going through some sexual deprivations right now." Net bellowed with laughter.

Nina smiled, "Even if he was here, there would be none of that going on."

Net and Nachelle both became quiet. "Nina what are you talking about?' Net asked.

"You mean to tell me you two don't have sex?" Nachelle asked amazed. Net threw another pillow at her. "What? Net you wanted to know too?" Nachelle whined.

"Lately it's been different. We haven't actually engaged in sexual activity in the last few weeks." Nina started toward her kitchen with the dirty dishes, and she heard Net and Nachelle rushing behind her.

"Wait Nina, what's going on? Are you sick? Is something going on wrong with you and Jeff?"

"No, Net; nothing like that. Everything is fine"

Net gave her a questionable look. "You two are always at it; what is it then?"

We just haven't had sex in the last few weeks. It's no big deal."

"And you are okay with that?" Nachelle asked surprised.

"Yes. Look you two; we're not having problems or anything. Nothing has changed between us; we still talk, and we are still very affectionate with each other. We just haven't engaged in the actual act of sex, that's all."

Net just looked at her friend, not because not having sex while they weren't married was a bad thing. It just seemed like when Nina was having sex, and she was in a relationship things were fine. When the sex stopped in her relationships, problems arose. Her relationship with Quinton had showed that.

"Let me get something straight. So you are affectionate and physical, with that fine-ass piece of man; you two haven't had sex in weeks, and you are okay with him in some other part of the United States right now, surrounded by God only knows what type and how many women; and you aren't the least concerned?"

Net nudged her younger sister to shut her mouth.

"I just mean Jeff is FINE! And women notice that. Some men too, if you want to be honest. I'm sure they all are going to throw themselves at him. Hell, if you won't my girl I probably would." Nachelle smiled as she pushed a wayward curl behind her ear.

Nina rolled her eyes at her. "Well I know that Jeff loves me very much, and just because he hasn't initiated sex lately, doesn't make me feel inadequate or think that he's cheating."

"Hold up now Nina. I don't want to be as much up in your business as Nachelle is, but you two didn't agree on this? I mean I think it's wonderful to have a relationship that's not based on only sex and that has so many other qualities, but you two were going pretty strong at it. And to just quit all of a sudden and not to have discussed it, is questionable."

"Well, look I'm thankful you two care so much, but I trust Jeff, and though we haven't discussed this little arrangement, I feel okay with it and I think it's good for us. This is a new step for both of us in a right direction. Case closed, alright?"

"Alright", both Net and Nachelle said together not fully convinced.

But Nina knew what she and Jeff had right now was amazing and special. And even Nachelle's thoughts of him being with someone else were not bothering her at all; or at least not too much.

Later around 12:30am, when all the cleaning had been done and they had laughed themselves into stomach aches; Nina saw them out, and picked up her cell to punch in the number to the Wellington Hotel in Kentucky, as she went through her house turning off lights and setting her alarm as she prepared to turn in. She had such a warm feeling inside. Nachelle and Net made her feel like she was a sister too.

As the phone rung for the third time, Nina glanced at her bedside clock. She knew it was late, but Jeff had called earlier, and told her to call when they were done, he'd still be up. Nina heard the rings switch and knew she was being forwarded to the Hotels answering system. Maybe he was really that tired that he had turned in early. She didn't want to wake him, but knew if she didn't he'd be questioning her the next morning as why she hadn't, so she pressed "0" for the operator when prompted to and listened to the greeting of the Clerk.

"Hello, this is Nina Jackson, could you tell me if Mr. Jefferson Smith is in?"

When the Clerk realized who she was, her southern tone took on less professionalism, and more perkiness. "Oh Ms. Jackson, how are you this morning?"

Nina realized she was exceptionally perky all of sudden for it to be almost 1am in the morning. She was sure this was due to again, to who Jeff was. "I'm fine. I was trying to reach Mr. Smith."

"Oh, Mr. Smith is out at the moment. Would you like me to give him a message when he returns?"

Nina paused in thought. She collected her thoughts. There was only a 1 hour time difference, so it was 12am there. Jeff hadn't said he was going out. And why hadn't he called to let her know, if he knew she would call? "Kirstine, do you know what time he left?" She didn't want this girl in her or Jeff's business, but was curious as to where Jeff could be?

She was hesitant for a moment. "Well I'm not suppose to give out that info, but I can assure it was at least an hour and half ago when they left."

'They?" She did not just hear her say *they*. "Thank you so much Kirstine."

"Did you still want to leave a message Ms. Jackson?"

"No thank you, I'll track him down."

"Okay", Kristine said slowly, as if she feared she had given too much information.

Nina hung up, then quickly dialed Jeff's cell. As it rung, her mind began to wonder. Where could he be? He hadn't mentioned having to go back out after he had called at 10. He had just come in from a dinner party then. She knew he had a planning meeting Saturday morning. When she heard his answering service pick up on the fourth ring, she just hung up in the young man's ear. She was not going to trip over this, or loose any sleep. She put the phone in its cradle, jerked the cover to her bed back and huffed, as she collapsed into the bed. She turned off her lamp, and winced at the pain the impact of her breast hitting the bed sent through her.

No she was not going to get upset about where he was, or who the other part of the 'they' was. But she knew when he told her he couldn't come home during the weekend that it sounded weird. When he had to be away for weeks at a time, he would come home in between. But he claimed he had other meetings to be in on during the weekend, so she hadn't been concerned about it. After all he was a grown ass man, and she was not going to be running after him. She had enough to deal with. She turned on her side, and hugged herself, trying to provide the protection of her upper arms to her now throbbing left breast. Wherever Mr. Jeff was, and who ever he was with, he'd better be have a damn good time, because good times would definitely be over when she was done with him.

Jeff balanced the phone between his shoulder and ear as he straightened his shirt in the mirror. He knew it was early, but Nina normally got up early, even on the weekends to run. Just before the 4th ring completed, he heard the phone being picked up.

"Hello", Nina answered sleepily.

Jeff smiled at himself as he peeked under covered servers of what room service had brought up for breakfast. He could imagine she looked just the way she did, when he woke up to see her lying beside him in the mornings; wrapped hair, hair, sleepy eyes, and full lips that he would love to kiss at the moment. "Good morning Sleeping Beauty."

Nina sat up to glance at the clock. It was so nice to wake up to such a sexy voice, that she had almost forgot she had barely slept; because even though she had told herself she wouldn't get mad, she had spent a majority of the night cursing him. "Morning", she said curt and short.

Jeff widened his eyes in amazement at her reply. "Well babe I know it's early, but I thought you'd be a little more excited to talk to me. What's wrong?"

Nina sat up on the side of her bed. He was acting as though nothing was wrong, or that he probably hadn't just walked into his own room a few minutes before calling her. She huffed out a small laugh. "Jeff, it's, 8am on a Saturday morning."

"I know but I was getting ready to go to my meeting, and wanted to call since I didn't talk to you last night."

"Well maybe if you weren't hanging out at 1am in the morning, you would have been in when I called." She growled sarcastically.

"Is that why you're being so short with me right now, because if it is, I apologize? It was close to 2 when I came back in, and I knew you were asleep and didn't want to wake you. So I decided to just call you this morning before I went to a meeting and then the golf course."

"So you playing around on the golf course is the reason you couldn't come home this weekend? What the hell does that have to do with work?"

Jeff sighed; he'd just about had it with her funky attitude now. "Nina, don't do this. Don't make this more than what it is."

"I don't actually know what it is Jeff, so tell me."

He hated when she did this, not because she was accusing him of

being with someone else, but because she actually didn't think as much of herself as he did, to know that there was no one more amazing then she was. It made him so damn mad at how she didn't value her own self.

"Nina, you act as though I wouldn't prefer to be there with you versus being on the golf course. I went out for a drink, with a friend whose also here for the Conference. Yes it was a woman that I went with, but considering she's old enough to be my mother, and we were discussing a business proposal that we started discussing at the dinner but didn't get around to finishing. She called me and asked would I meet her in the bar, because her flight was leaving early this morning. I was right back here in my room at 2am. Alone. If you can trust me that much, you should be able to handle that. So stop scheming up scenarios in your pretty head of what I'm here doing and whom I'm doing it with. It's all business. And FYI, there is a Charity golf tournament that is part of the Conference this afternoon."

Nina sat quietly, realizing she had over done the bad attitude and sarcasm too much. She didn't say anything.

In a calmer tone, he asked, "Nina, can we start this conversation over?"

She waited a beat, and then said, "Yeah."

"Now, as I was saying, "I called to hear your beautiful voice, how are you?"

Nina gritted her teeth and mentally kicked herself. "I'm fine." She listened tentatively as he told her of his plans for the two of them on his early return the following week. She had to let go of this mindset that he was doing what she was so accustomed to someone she was dating did.

When Nina hadn't said anything to any of his plans, he knew she was still fuming.

"Nina?"

"Yeah."

"Babe, you know I love you, right?"

She sighed, and ran her pink painted, pedicure toe over the design in her carpet. "I know Jeff, and I love you too."

"Well understand that I don't want to be with anyone but you. Baby, all this is what I have to do. It's strictly business. I guaranteed you that, okay?"

Nina remembered those words from her past. 'Strictly business.'

"Okay."

"I've got to get going, but I'll call you this afternoon. I love you."

"I love you too." She put the phone back in its cradle, and fell back on the bed.

# CHAPTER XXI

NINA SHOOK HER UMBRELLA OUT one last time before bringing it in and dropping it on the doormat. The umbrella still didn't do a good job of keeping her dry, as she looked down at her now dripping over coat. She shuddered from a chill. She hated being wet from the rain. She peeled the wet coat from her body then hung it on the coat rack, and went to the bathroom to get a towel to place on the floor, after removing her wet pumps as well.

After she had gotten up most of the water she began to undress. She should have watched the weather that morning, because wearing the grey, silk cargo pants and matching blazer was not a good idea for this type of weather. As she passed the table in her small hallway to her bedroom, she pressed the ancient machine that she still held on to because it use to belong to her parents, to listen to her messages while she changed. No one ever called during the day, because they always knew where to find her; at work. Most of the time there were messages from magazine companies or anyone else who was trying to sell something, but as soon as she heard the voice of the lady on the other end announced where she was calling from Nina's heart stopped.

Nina slowly moved to her bed and sat down while staring at the machinery on the table in her hallway, from which the voice came from. Her breaths became almost shallow, and as she listened to each word the woman spoke, Nina felt herself sinking. Sinking into a tunnel of little air. Sinking into 5 years prior when she had first heard that same voice reveal to her life changing news, in which from that moment, things in her life changed drastically.

As the message came to an end, Nina shook herself and suddenly remembered to breath. She opened her mouth and gasping almost for every bit of fresh oxygen the room held. She quickly rushed to her bathroom, and peering into the mirror saw that her face wore what she was feeling inside: FEAR. She fumbled, picked up a cup, and turned on the faucet to get some water. After she gulped it down, she felt a slight bit more relaxed.

*"Okay, get it together girl. You can deal with this, it's not like you haven't been through it before."* She told her reflection in the mirror. She gave a forced smile at the reflection that was immediately wiped away at a thought. Nina wanted to ask the reflection why? Why now? When she thought she had found happiness, peace, and stability; why at this moment? But she knew the reflection didn't have the answers to those questions, no more than she did.

Later that night, after dinner, she spent the majority of the evening on the phone with Jeff. He was doing the majority of the talking because all she could think about was the message on her answering machine. After promising Jeff nothing was wrong, she readied herself to go to bed with a book and the low sounds of the T.V. But before she did she had to hear the message one more time to be sure it was real. She pressed the replay button, and gulped while she waited on the voice to begin.

"Ms. Jackson, this is Dr. Patrick from the Regional Cancer Center. I need for you to give me a call as soon as possible to set up an appointment to come into the Center for some test. I know it's not time for your annual testing, but Dr. Davis called and forwarded your annual gynecological results and was a bit concerned. So please give me a call as soon as possible." She paused what seemed like a considerably, agonizing second, then added, "Nina, this is very important that you call me. Thank you."

As the lady who lived inside the phone, asked for Nina's next request, Nina thought back on her visit a couple days earlier to the gynecologist. Nina's annual visit had been scheduled at a time in which Nina had needed to see a doctor. She had been doing her regular breast self-examinations and had found no lumps, but yet her left breast was aching and tingling frequently. So her appointment was the perfect time to find out what was going on. She was sure it may have just been a side effect from her contraceptives; it was time to switch up anyway.

At the appointment Dr Davis had agreed with her that he felt no lumps, but was concerned that the pain may be a sign of fibro cyst, or calcium deposits around the tissue that was too small to detect by touch. He told her not to be alarmed, but he'd schedule her for a mammogram. But now she was receiving calls from her old Dr. at the Cancer Center, and Dr. Davis said she wasn't supposed to be alarmed?

She was suddenly brought from her thoughts as the woman inside the machine repeated the options again. She placed her finger on the erase button and held it firmly down, as if she could erase the message and the matter as well, and then went to bed.

# CHAPTER XXII
## THIS IS WHAT IT HAS COME TO

A s Nina walked into the conference room, she instantly felt the coldness and tension of the room envelope her. Even the comfort that her red power suit had given her when she had dressed that morning, was wearing off now in this environment. She could feel every one of the old, obnoxious, arrogant men eyes on her, but she still held her shoulders high, looking straight ahead until she reached her seat at the big mahogany conference table, next to Mr. Smith, and across from Jeff.

The events that had taken place in the last weeks were wearing down on her shoulders now and she was trying hard not to break. This meeting was another result of the turn of events. Just that Monday, the headlines on the Charlotte Tribune's front page read: *Local Community Center, has it's Own Run-in with Trouble.* The article started talking about how the Center was there as a refuge to keep kids out of trouble, but was now encountering its own brush with trouble. Then the mention of Nina and the Jamie incident was described from the papers point of view.

The article went into detail to embellish what happened with Jamie Clark. Nina's name had been mentioned quite often, along with the phrase, "girlfriend of prominent businessman, Jefferson Edward Smith III, this year's Businessman of the Year". That story started the domino effect of events.

State ordered a hearing, in which Nina was then happy for the statement she had prepared for Engle a couple months earlier. The

Hospital even wanted to call their own hearing. Jeff and Mr. Smith had been very supportive though. She had put her personal life and health on hold for the moment to deal with what was at hand. Though she seemed strong from the outside, she mentally felt like she would cave in.

She had made it through the State preliminaries and the hearing and the decision was made that since this was the first of complaints on Nina and no one was affected negatively, no disciplinary action would be taken, but she would be considered on the investigative list for any complaint whatsoever in the future and she had to be sure to adhere by State policies in dealing with future dilemmas as such. Which Nina knew meant, stick to the way the State wanted things ran because she would be watched very closely from here on out.

Now she had to deal with this. As she sat, Mr. Smith smiled and nodded, and Jeff winked at her, and gave her a slight smile from behind his raised tepee hands, which he held in front of his mouth as if he was deep in thought. He looked slightly disturbed himself. Before he had left her place that morning he assured her that this meeting was just a formality. There was nothing for her to fear, but now the look on his face made her wonder was there issues out of his and his father's control that had been discussed concerning her, before they had called her in.

Nina turned toward the other end of the table toward Peter Snyder, as he began to speak in his arrogant tone. He was your typical, anal, retentive white man. Snyder was old money walking. He owned major parts of Charlotte and parts of SC. Because he was old money, he felt the need to remind others frequently what his family had done, what they owned, and that his opinion should be taken very seriously. He was the main reason Nina hated meeting with the Board. The fact that Jeff and his father were the only blacks on the Hospital Board was because they were high percentage Stockholders of the private facility. There were no other women, and of course no other people of color; so Nina coming in with the education and experience she had, was still not suffice enough to prove her worthiness of thinking in Snyder's mind. She was just a woman, a black woman at that.

"Ms. Jackson, thank you for taking time out of your schedule to meet with us today."

Nina sat poised on the edge of her leather chair, legs crossed at the knees. Her hands rested on top of her legal pad, folded, shoulders straight, and waiting. She nodded in response.

"We don't want to keep you from your paper work, so we'll get right to the point."

Nina cringed at his remark; he thought that was all she did all day, just shuffle papers. Jeff watched as she tensed, but she stayed professional and firm. He smiled eternally. *That was his baby. Strong.*

"There have been allegations and rumors circulating in some of the newspapers concerning the Center you work for downtown. Up until now, no names were given, but a couple of days ago your name was mentioned and it is the Boards responsibility to ensure that the business of the Hospital is ran adequately and that the patients are well taken care of across the board."

Nina sighed. *Why didn't he just get to the point? He personally could care less about the patients in this hospital.*

"So we called this meeting today to stress to you what this issue could cause for your position here at the Hospital."

He waited. Nina was about to explode. *How dare this mofo threaten her position after all she had sacrificed for this place, all the extra work she'd taken on, and because of something he had read, and didn't even know the facts of, he wanted to make conclusions about her job.* Nina felt 10 sets of male eyes on her, all questioning different things of her.

"May I say a few things, Mr. Snyder?" Nina spoke calmly but firmly.

"Of course." He sat back in his seat as if to watch a movie.

"I would like to address these issues to the Board, and let you all know that I too have read the allegations and events that the newspapers are saying have taken place at the Center in which I am employed and much like each of you know, because you are successful businessmen in the community, that the papers stretch stories for ratings.

The situation that took place was one in which I used my judgment, and at the time that was the best choice available. The work and service that I have put into this Hospital should be proof enough that the so called allegations of not being able to maintain my job because of what happened at the Center are unquestionably false. So I forge the question to everyone on this Board, do you really feel my judgment has in the

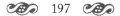

past, or will in the future put this Hospital or it's patients at risk, because of a so call inadequacy of me performing my job here?"

The room remained silent a moment. Jeff looked at Nina with a smile in his eyes. *She had them on the burner now.*

Snyder sat up in his chair, looking uncomfortable. "Ms. Jackson, it is not a question of what you have done for this Hospital because everyone here knows how valuable you are; but it's what our patients say and the way they feel about the stories in the papers. We have to take them into consideration."

Nina almost was startled when Mr. Smith spoke up. "Snyder you know as well as I do, that we hold the key to put this whole incident to rest. One call to the papers, and we can have them behind us instead of against us. You did not call this meeting for that. So what is it?"

"Well Smith if you must know, there are some other things that have surfaced because of this matter, that until now laid low."

"Such as", Nina and Mr. Smith spoke at the same time in unions?

"Like Ms. Jackson's involvement with your son and the favoritism that may have come from prior approval of program money in her favor."

Nina's mouth dropped open and Jeff was on the edge of his seat now ready to speak, but his father held his hand up to him.

"Just one minute Snyder. No money has been allocated to any programs that the Board hasn't voted on together, so favoritism did not play in any shape or form in those matters. Every cent of money that was allocated to her was used for programs that have benefited this Hospital. The evidence of every penny spent is right here surrounding you every time you walk into pediatrics or see employees that Ms. Jackson has made possible to keep on staff here. Furthermore, Ms. Jackson's and my son's relationship outside of this Hospital has nothing to do with policies and procedures of how this Hospital is ran."

Thomas Edwards, a man in his late 40's spoke up. He had been one of the gentlemen that were with Jeff the first day they had met. "What we all need to do right now is just try to find a solution to the issues at hand, instead of forming conclusions."

"That is what I thought we were doing. Look, I didn't come here to discuss my personal life. I came here today to explain the situations in the papers and to try to save the integrity of my job. I love what I do here, just as I love my other job. I put my whole heart into whatever I'm working on. I can say that I've never done anything that would cause inadequate behavior on the Hospital's behalf, but if you want to put me on probation from what I do, because of what you've read, I can't change that."

As she finished speaking, she sighed. Her insides were going crazy, for she didn't know if she had helped herself or hung herself. She waited silently with everyone else.

Snyder stood. "Well Ms. Jackson, we've heard how you feel. It is up to the Board now to vote on how we feel we should handle this. Thank you again for coming."

Nina forced a smile and stood. She didn't make any direct eye contact with anyone, because she feared she'd break down any moment. "Thank you for offering me the opportunity." She swiftly grabbed her briefcase and her things and walked to the door. When she was outside of the conference room she sighed and rushed to the elevator.

Once rushing past Carol without a word, and inside her office with the door closed, she collapsed at her desk with her head down.

***

Jeff knocked on the door and waited for Nina to answer. He heard nothing, but knew she was in, because Carol had told him so. He tried the knob, and pushed the door open slowly. He saw Nina leaning on the wall next to her window looking out.

She didn't turn around because she knew it was him, and she hadn't answered the door because she was sure he was there to tell her whatever the decision was. He walked around her desk and stood closely behind her. He placed his hands on her shoulders and could feel the tension as he rubbed them.

"So, did you choose the shortest straw, and have to come give me the verdict?"

"No, I didn't even get to vote. As long as my father is here, his vote is the only one that counts."

"Great, it will be 9 to 1", she said sarcastically. She turned around and went to her desk and flopped down in her seat. "You must think I behaved like an idiot in there?"

"No, I think you were wonderful in there. Considering the circumstances, none of this should even be going on right now, and I know that I would definitely have behaved terribly in your shoes." He came closer to her chair and pushed her hair away from her face slowly. "You know it's all going to work out, no matter what?"

She raised her big, brown, eyes to look at him. The fear they normally held was shallow, and accompanied with sadness.

"Jeff, I love this job. I don't want to lose it."

He knelt beside her and in a low, sincere voice began to speak. "I know baby, and I doubt that happens, but even if it did, you've got me. There's no problem with getting you somewhere else. And it's not like you really need the money."

"The money isn't the issue. I love what I do." She was getting upset, and was about to tell him about his tactics to save the world with his money and connections when her phone beeped. She reached over and pressed the button to answer, not taking her eyes off of Jeff.

"Yes?"

It was Carol. "Nina, Mr. Snyder called to ask could you come to the Conference room upstairs."

Nina widened her eyes and bite her bottom lip before answering. "Sure, thanks Carol." She stood up, and Jeff stood also. "I guess this is it"

He lifted his hand to touch her cheek softly with his fingers. He then leaned forward and kissed it. 'I'm right behind you."

She took a deep breath and walked toward her door. Toward her fate, whatever it was.

### And this too Shall Pass

# CHAPTER XXIII

NINA GRABBED HER BRIEFCASE AS she raced out of the door to her presentation meeting at the Hospital. Racing is what she seemed to do on a regular basis lately. She knew if she didn't speed she'd be late. She pulled her Pathfinder into the road, and tried to keep one eye on her rearview for blue lights, and her other eye on the road.

This would not have happened if she hadn't let Jeff talk her into staying last night. She knew the beige suit she was planning to wear wasn't at his place, so she'd have to get up early to come by home to change. It wouldn't have been a problem except Jeff woke up in the horniest mood, even though they had made love most of the night, (which had broken their whole sabbatical of not having sex). And that's why she was rushing so much now, not to mention, she was still a little sleepy. It use to be a problem to get to sleep; then it just seemed like there were too many hours in the night. She never had the ability to calm herself or relax. But since Jeff, there weren't enough hours to enjoy sleep.

Since Quinton had moved so many things had changed, both good and bad. Quinton had called to let her know that everything was well with he and Naquin, they were settled in Charleston. He had hooked up with a great deals on some real estate property and a new office.

As for she and Jeff things were calmer these days even though Jeff had been working out of town a lot lately. But she knew all good things would come to an end. Jeff wasn't moving slow at any expense. Just the night before he brought up the issue of her moving in again when she tried to leave.

Lying there in his arms, still trying to catch her breath; cuddling. What she really wanted to do right then was to scoot to her side of the king size bed, until she maintained normal temperature. She knew she

was being petty, but she had just been in a mood lately because of the way things were at the Center, her probation at the Hospital, and the way she had been feeling physically.

Jeff sighed, moaned her name and ran his hands up her back. He had noticed that she had been rather uptight the past few days, even now that they were over the issues with Q, and they had had that little spat when he was in Kentucky, and all the issues with the papers were over. He knew they hadn't been together intimately while all that was going on, but part of that was because he wanted more for them. Lately he was spiritually trying to get to a place where he could make the right decision as to how to make Nina believe in him and want to spend the rest of her life with him. But like a human man, his testosterone got the better of him and he was tired of just holding her. And all this torment he'd been putting himself through and nothing had changed with her. She had yet to discuss what Janette had already told him, and she seemed to be building up another wall.

He also noticed that she had been acting very timid when they made love or even when he merely touched her; she was fidgeting and jumping away, almost as if she didn't want him touching her at all. He swore, just when he thought he was getting somewhere with her, this damn woman was becoming more and more complicated than she was before. All the positive, spiritual building he had been trying to do for himself lately, was being wrecked, because she wouldn't cooperate. He had no choice but to push the issue himself, though he knew this might mean battle.

"So, have you given any more thought to moving in with me?"

Nina felt her whole sexual satisfaction cave in. Why did he have to fuddle up a nice moment? She sighed and pulled away, to sit on the side of the bed. Jeff sat up too, grabbing her elbow, before she had a chance to bail from the bed.

"Jeff, I wish you wouldn't do this. I told you before how I feel about moving in with you."

"No, you ran away from the conversation, the same way you did each time before that."

Nina knew her time was running out. She had managed to put that night, when she almost flipped in his bedroom after him asking her to move in with him, in the back closet of her mind and thought that

Jeff had forgot about it in a way that she wouldn't have to deal with it any time in the near future. Now the same issue that had caused all the anxiety previously was staring her in the face again, so now what? She knew if she told him now, they would be discussing this until lunchtime the next day, and she had to get showered and to work, and do her presentation. This was going to require some clever and quick to send this conversation in a positive direction.

"Jeff, we've talked about this. How can we spend more time together if you're going to be out of town on business all the time? I'll just be here alone, in this huge house, waiting for you."

"You know you're just using that as an excuse. I'm only gone maybe a couple of times a month, and even then, it's only one or two days. What's the real reason?"

*There went her idea, of diversion.*

She sighed, before turning to him and looking him in the eyes. "Jeff, when I moved in with Quinton, it was because I didn't want to be alone. I guess I felt if I was with someone else I wouldn't have to concentrate on my problems. I became very dependent on having someone with me all the time and I still was never more alone than I was then. Now on my own, I feel freedom, and I'm more independent than I've ever been before. I know you mean well sweetheart, but you spoil me tremendously, and I don't want to move in here and live off of you. Besides, I thought we were trying to be more positive in our relationship with each other as well as getting ourselves together."

"So, what are you going to do when we get married? Live independently then too."

'**Married**.' The word made her shutter. She would love to be his wife, but it was out of the question. There was no way she could marry him without telling him everything from her past. If she didn't, she would be living a lie from the start, and that isn't the way to start a marriage. She'd try to make light of the situation.

"How do I know you'll still marry me when you're getting your kicks for free, with no strings attached?" She teased him.

Jeff didn't see the need to laugh. "Why would I just live with the woman I love, without letting everyone know that she belongs to me and they can't have her? Babe I'm ready to settle down with one person, maybe start a family. And you are the one I want all that with. Now you're always making these damn lists, for everything to go as plan and the way you want it, but I don't see you being with me on any of those list for the future. So what?"

"Jeff I don't want to be with anyone but you, and if you don't know that, I'm telling you now."

"It looks like I'm going to have to make a believer out of you and prove to you that I'm going to marry you."

That sounded a little scary and it felt pressuring for her to finally tell him what was going on. Nina looked confused, "Just what do you have in mind?"

"Do you have to know everything? Just wait and see."

Even now though, Nina knew there were things that they had to talk about even if they were to make that step.

### After it Rains, Then It Pours

# CHAPTER XXIV

"COULD I GET A CRANBERRY juice seltzer?"

Nina smiled at the waiter as he went to get her drink. *Pauley's* was filled with a lot of Black good-looking men that night. It was funny how if and when she was seeking a man, they were rare to be found, but when she wasn't in the least bit interested, they were everywhere. But at the same time she pitied the women who were on the prowl, because there were just too many games, and questions in dating and having a relationship. That's why she was here now, confused, questioning her own relationship.

She smiled as the waiter handed her drink, and caught sight of Kim and Net coming into the dimly lit bar at the same time. They had somehow already introduced themselves and were talking like old friends.

She stood to greet them. "Well I don't have to do introductions now do I?"

They exchange hugs. "Any friend of Nina has to be cool with me." Kim said sliding into the booth; Net slide in on the other side of Nina. After placing a drink order, and the cute waiter left, Nina began.

"I'm glad you guys could take time out for me."

"I welcome the opportunity", Kim said.

"You sounded like you really needed us, so what's up, Net asked picking up Nina's glass sniffing, then taking a drink, hoping the bundle in her stomach, could handle cranberry juice?

Nina dropped her gaze to her hands on top of the table. "Lately I've been feeling the need to really talk to someone, something I rarely do when I have problems. And since Net you know more about me than

anyone, and Kim, you've been such a great friend since the day I met you, I felt you two were the ones I should seek for support."

Net looked at Nina seriously, fearing what her friend had to say, sure that it was bad.

Nina looked up at both of them; Kim was eager to know what was going on, but Net had tears forming in her eyes already. Nina knew what she was thinking. "Net, don't cry, please, it's not that bad." She reached across the table and patted Net's hand, then took her napkin and wiped the tear before it fell it's full path down her cheek. "Being pregnant really has you emotional these days", Nina smiled.

Kim looked confused.

Net took the napkin and chuckled. "Would you get to it then, I'm pregnant and I can't handle this suspense. Besides, I'll probably have to pee soon"

"With all the drama that has been going on lately, the one thing that I've been sure about is how madly in love with Jeff I am." She paused and looked at the two beautiful, smiling women.

"Ahhhh", they both joined in together!

Nina continued, "Unfortunately that is where the problem begins. Jeff has been constantly talking about marriage lately. He finds a way to work it into every conversation we have. But I can't marry him."

"Why not?!" Kim was alert and shocked on the edge of her seat. "Nina you two are wonderful together. Jeff has never had someone in his corner that has been so good for him like you are. And for him to actually pursue the topic of marriage constantly proves how much he has changed."

Net took Nina's hand from the table and held it in hers until her friend looked at her. She knew the pain and heartache that her friend was feeling. She had seen it all too many times in the last6 years.

Kim looked on in confusion. She knew something was happening, but couldn't find the words to ask what?

"You haven't told him have you" Net asked finally breaking the suspense in the air?

Nina kept her eyes on the table, and shook her head.

"Told him what?" Kim was getting more and more confused by the minute.

"Nina, you have to tell him. He loves you so much; everyone can see that."

"Net, I don't want to lose him."

"Nina, he loves you more than anything, he won't go anywhere."

"Q loved me too."

"Jeff isn't Q, Nina."

Kim was sitting with her arms crossed over her chest, looking disgruntle now. "Does anyone care to share with me what the hell is going on, or should I just leave?"

Nina looked at her and smiled softly, "Kim I'm sorry. There is a lot I should tell you." Nina took a deep breath and began to tell Kim of her life 4 years prior to Jeff.

When she was done, Kim sat with a look of awe on her face. They were quite, listening to the chatter of the background and restaurant music. Finally Kim found her voice to speak.

"Nina, all I can say is that you are as amazingly strong, as you are a beautiful, intelligent, giving woman, and I know that those are things that make Jeff love you, but honey you can't think that he's going to want nothing to do with you because of something that is out of your control."

Nina was shaking her head while Kim talked. "See, you don't understand. Jeff wants kids. As much as I want to be his wife, I can't promise him kids, just like I couldn't promise Q. It's not fair for him to be shorted on what he wants by being with me. He deserves better."

"Nina, he deserves you." Net said.

Nina bite her lip to hold back tears. "I often sit and wonder what I did, to deserve the crap life gives me?"

Kim looked across the table at Net. They both exchange looks, because neither knew what to answer to that.

Nina tried to pull away from Jeff subtly. He was truly in an aggressive mode. As soon as she had stepped across the threshold of her front door, he was on her. She hadn't even expected him to be there. Her plan had been to come home and think about the things Net and Kim had told her, and try to figure out a way to talk to him. But when she walked through her door, Jeff was standing there waiting for her. He had taken her into his arms and hugged her, but had never let go. His lips found hers, and from that point he pushed her up against the door, and ravenously tasted, and kissed her. He hadn't even given her a chance to put down her bag and purse.

He was playfully biting her neck, while pushing his hands up under her blouse. And what Nina wanted to do was ball up into a fetal position and cry. That's how much the shooting pain in her breast was hurting as he kneaded and grasped it.

"Babe"…Nina managed a moan over the pleasuring pain of his teeth raking across her neck and then him taking her earlobe in between his teeth. "Jeff", she moaned a second time.

"Humm?" He still didn't let up.

"Jeff, can I at least put my things down", she yelled?"

Jeff pulled back and looked at her. She sounded annoyed, but she also had a pained expression on her face. He raised his eyebrow, and stepped away from her. Maybe he had been a little aggressive. As she passed by him, he followed her to her bedroom.

"Sorry, did you have a good time with Kim and Net?"

"Yeah, I did." She started to undress as he watched from her bedroom door. When she stood in just a black, lace thong and bra, she looked up at Jeff where he stood. His face lit up. She smiled back and walked over to him slowly and seductively. When she stood in front of him, he put his arms around her waist and pulled her into him. She placed her hands on his arms and ran them up the length of his muscular biceps, and around his neck.

"So now can I get back to what I was doing?"

"Right here in my doorway", she smiled?

"I don't recall us ever doing it here before, so why not?"

Nina rose up on her tiptoes and began to take his lips into her mouth, sucking each one, while thinking about the fact that she was living a lie with him. Guilt was really beginning to tear at her insides, as the pain in her breast flared to remind her of what she needed to do. She kissed him passionately a moment, and then pulled away. Jeff tried to pull her back.

"Jeff there is something I want to talk to you about first."

He was kissing his way down her neck now, and tugging at the clasp on her bra. "Can't that wait till later, right now, I'm only interested in one thing", he mumbled between kissing.

Nina sighed; she knew if she didn't tell him now, she wouldn't have the nerve to later. But what he was doing right now, all over the spot he knew drove her crazy, was making her want him as much as he wanted her. She could tell him later. She promised she would. No ifs ands, or buts about it.

She closed her eyes as the sensation of him engulfing each one of her nipples into the warm and wetness of his mouth, making her enjoy the pleasure and ignoring the pain. Her back was pressed against the door opening, and his fingers were now roaming in her nectar, where he had pushed her panties aside and thrust them inside. After hearing her pant, and moan overhead, he kissed his way back to her lips. She took the hand that he has just used to thrust inside of her and lifted the still wet fingers to his mouth. He smiled, as she slowly let each finger connect with his warm tongue and then slide off of his lips.

She pulled him by the front of his shirt to her bed, then turned him, and pushed him into a sitting position.

"Who's being aggressive now?"

"Oh, you will enjoy it."

She pushed him back on the bed, and smiled as he watched her tug at his pants. When they rested on the floor in a pile, she dropped to her knees, and began to take the full length, and girth between her lips. She wanted to show him just how much she loved him, wanting him to connect with her. When he moaned her name to warn her of his forthcoming excitement, she let him remain in her mouth, taking in everything that flowed from him.

When she climbed on top of him, he welcomed her in his arms, and held her while he calmed himself. After moments passed, he broke the silence.

"You wanted to talk to me about something?"

Nina stiffened; there was no way she could tell him at this moment. She rose up and kissed his lips softly, "It can wait."

# WHAT FALLS OUTSIDE AND INSIDE THE CIRCLE IS MINE.... I WANT IT ALL

Nina sighed and flipped her cell shut. She had been trying to get in touch with Jeff all day and Cynthia kept saying he was still in meetings. She knew he had been putting in a lot of stressful hours with the projects they had turning up all over the place. Most of the time he was free, but when he was working, he was putting in the triple overtime. He had been working late the past few nights, and getting in at like 10 and 11:00, barely making it to the bed; just wanting to lie down and go to sleep. But she was having a selfish moment and wanted to whine about the Center. Her own day had been the worse. After starting her morning off with her appointment with Dr. Patrick that she had felt she had put off long enough, she had had to deal with the news they had given her, then she had went to the Center to deal with more bad news.

Due to budget cuts, the Center was being forced to close. State didn't believe that the Center was a necessity. She and Net had spent the majority of the morning going back and forth with State agents about the difference the Center made in the community, the neighborhood, and so many of the kids, who lacked guidance in other areas. No matter how much she and Janette tried to persuade them, it wasn't enough to keep the funding going. She damn sure would like to know what other progress they needed, besides the fact that they were saving lives and making a damn difference in the future black leaders of the world? The whole damn situation disgusted her.

It was 2:30, but she had to take a mental day before her head exploded. She left the Center, promising Net she would do her part of brainstorming to see what could be done. At this point a fundraiser to raise enough money to keep the Center open, as well as operating, would be a huge stretch. She really felt her little incident with Jamie had some type of influence on this whole closing deal, but Net assured her she shouldn't feel it was her fault. They weren't going to let the Center go without a fight. She hadn't told Net about her Dr appt, because she didn't want to add to her stress. It was bad enough, her being pregnant and dealing with the crap at the Center. Besides, Nina had told herself it wasn't anything to be alarmed by and she wasn't going to get upset at this early stage.

She decided to run some errands, pick up groceries and go home to do some cleaning; that always took her mind off of things. She realized without Jeff, and the time she spent at work, she would be a very dull person. It was as though her life was truly missing something. She had come accustomed to being without a lot of girlfriends, they were more trouble and drama than they was worth. She had Janette and Kim, but they had their own families, husbands, busy lives being wives and mothers, and having a single friend to whine to them about her every problem, was one thing she was sure they could do without.

It just seemed like lately she had this aching emptiness deep inside of her that she felt needed to be filled by someone who needed her, depended on her daily. She had been thinking more and about being a mother. Working with neglected kids at the Center, they had become a pride and joy to her, no matter how old they were. That's why they were more than a job to her. The money wasn't great, but at least she felt she was making a difference. Now she wanted to make a difference in her own life. She was 29, not getting younger, although she still had time. Until now, the self-battle that most women went through about finding a husband, and making a family weren't something she desired. But for some reason, she was beginning to think like Jeff. He was rubbing off on her. But the terror of being disappointed again like with her last pregnancy episode was too emotional to swallow again, especially after her appointment at the doctor earlier that morning. Then having Jeff leave her because she wasn't the women who could produce, was even more devastating.

Her cell ringing interrupted her thoughts. "Hello".

"Hey babe, what's up? Cint told me you've been trying to get me; is something wrong?"

Nina heard people asking him questions, and he was throwing answers out to them, in between talking to her. It was obvious he was still busy, and was trying to take a moment to just check in with her.

"Nothing, I just wanted to hear your voice. When do you think you'll be done tonight?" she asked, knowing the answer already.

"Baby, I don't know. I'm trying to get all this wrapped up this week. Thought we could fly down to St Thomas, or just go to a beach somewhere and spend some time together for a couple of days, when this is all over. Just you and I. I know we haven't had much time together lately."

Nina had told him that flying to exotic places and shopping sprees weren't something that she required. She wasn't a high maintenance woman, much like he was probably used to. Yeah she like manicures and pedicures, and shopping, and pretty clothes; but shopping sprees on Melrose, and birthday trips to Belize wasn't what she wanted from him. Aside from the few trips that they occasionally took to Miami and NY, she knew his leisure traveling lifestyle had changed dramatically with her. But she wanted him to understand that she was just an old fashion girl, who wanted his time more than expensive gifts and trips.

"Okay, I won't hold you. I know you got a lot going on. Call me when you get a chance. If you're too tired, go home and get some rest tonight; I'll understand."

"Thanks, babe, I'll call later. Love you."

"You too," Nina said, but he had already hung up before she got it out.

Well at least she could look forward to having her man to herself in a couple more days, even if she had to do without him until then.

# CHAPTER XXV

N INA PULLED INTO THE PARKING space beside Jeff's car. She pulled her sunglasses down slowly off her face to take a look at the now swollen bruise around her left eye in her mirror. With her complexion the area where she had been hit wasn't red, but she knew the sore swollen place would definitely have a darker tinted bruise by the morning.

She had had a day from hell, again, and now she was sure she'd be going into this restaurant and dealing with Jeff's constant questions and his usual speech of why she worked so hard at a job that only caused her stress and danger. She took a deep breath to ready herself for her battle; slide her shades back on and got out of the truck to go into Cenelli's. It was just months before, when she had came here with Jeff at its grand opening. That was the early stages of their relationship. The place was still a hot spot and vastly full. That first night she had entered nervous about being with the man at her side; giddy with excitement. Tonight she was returning hesitant about being with that same man, and tired from exhaustion. With the months, lots of things had changed.

She opened the door as the cute, Richard Grecio looking mat'urde, Phillip greeted her.

"Good evening, Ms. Jackson, Mr. Smith is at your usual table waiting for you."

"Thank you Phillip." She walked the distance through the crowded restaurant to where she and Jeff always sat, in a spacious secluded booth by the bar. She could see Jeff sitting, and waiting patiently; dressed in a smoky charcoal suit coat and a lime green dress shirt. She took a few deep breaths too calm her nerves.

Jeff stood and smiled as he watched every male eye in the restaurant, turn and watch, as some part of the designer, fuchsia suit Nina wore, hit every curve as she moved through the room. The suit stopped right above her knees, hugging her thighs and her hips, and she wore a pink halter and pink rose on her shoulder to accent the color. He leaned forward and kissed her lips softly as she approached and noticed that even behind the sunglasses she wore, he could tell her face was tight with tension. The day she had was showing tension and stress in her every body movement. He hated her wearing herself out, but had gotten into it with her many times before and thought he'd keep his mouth shut about it now.

"Hi, beautiful. How are you?"

"Hey sweetie, I'm here." She pursed her lips in what was supposed to be a smile, slide into the booth halfway and put her purse down beside her. The waitress, a tall light-skinned sister, with a pretty face asked her for her drink order, and Nina order a whisky sour.

Jeff widened his eyes. She normally had some pretty mixed drink or a glass of wine. "Another bad day", he asked? He knew she had been dealing with the State agents at the Center and she was also trying to train the new Administrator at the Hospital.

She didn't answer, but instead lowered her head to take her glasses off. Her hair fell over her left eye, hiding the bruise until she lifted her eyes to his. Jeff's eyes widen in shock. He lifted his hand to her chin and gently raised her face to the light so he could see her better.

"Nina, what the hell is this?"

Nina took a deep breath before answering. "I was trying to break up a fight between two of the kids today, and caught a left hook that was intended for the other kid. The worse part was I then had to meet with State Agents and explain the shiner I'm now wearing."

"Nina, I told you something like this would happen. Those kids can be dangerous and then you're placing yourself in the mist of danger every day you go down to that Center. Trying to stop a fight between those kids was not smart Nina, they could have hurt you in a much worse way than this."

Nina rolled her eyes. "Are you finished? For your information the fight took place at the Hospital; you know the private one in which your family seems to own part of. It was two kids in the Children's wing, who obviously feel better than the doctors' thinks they are. The Center had nothing to do with this. And I have told you over and over again I can take care of myself. It's just a little bruise. I had Michelle, the nurse, take a look at it; she put some ice on it and told me it would be sore for a couple days, but it would be fine."

Jeff sighed. She was stubborn as hell. Fussing with her was a waste of time. He slipped a hand behind her neck, resting it in her hair, and pulled her face close to his lips, gently kissing the bruise. "You sure you're okay?"

Nina placed one of her hands on his wrist, and gave him a faint smile. "Yes, I'm fine, well at least my eye is. State gave us a 30-day dead line today. They weren't going for anything I, Jeanette or the rest of the staff said to them. They kept bringing up the few negative things and overlooking all the advantages and positives of all our programs. Then if that wasn't enough, that wise-ass, jerk, Engle brings up the incident with Jamie. Telling me that we, especially me, don't know how to make wise decisions concerning youth in the Center anyway."

"I'll make some calls tomorrow, get Cynthia to do some research, and make them change their minds."

"Jeff, you can't."

"Baby all it takes is negotiations. And if that doesn't work, I'll just buy the building myself; hell we can just build another building, in another location."

Nina sighed and put her drink that she had been sipping on, down. "Jeff you don't get it, do you?"

He looked at her confused, "Get what?"

"Why do I expect you to get it? You're never been the one to need a place like the Community Center to shape your life, to give you normalcy. You've always had nannies, and play groups and money to buy you any thing you ever wanted. You're just like those damn people from the State. You don't see that this is the Community Center. It's a part of these kid's lives. Some of these kids have nothing stable or normal in their lives but the Center. It's the only thing they can depend on. For some of them it is the reason they get up everyday. In a world were some of their parents don't care for them, or they have no stability in their homes, and they face danger by just being outside in their neighborhood, the Center is a lifesaver. And then someone like you comes along and wants to move the building to another neighborhood, which would mean it would no longer be the Community Center, because these kids sure as hell couldn't go there. It would then be some Rec Center on the upper side of town. Then, like everything else, money would win, and the elite group would take that over too." She finished and took a deep breath. Her heart was pounding. She had just took the anger of the full day out on him and he sat there just staring at her.

Jeff finally looked down at his own drink. "I was trying to help Nina, that's all."

She was still fuming. "Well Jeff I don't need my rich boyfriend to reach into his deep pockets and try to buy the Center. I don't need you to flaunt some cash, which is how you solve all problems, and make people do a little dance for you, like puppets on a string to please you. Your damn people you can call have never been interested in anything on that side of town before, but when you make your damn calls, they suddenly take interest because of the green you flash them. We don't need that kind of f-ing help."

Jeff kept his eyes on his drink. He knew she was upset, but he wasn't the one who had made her have such a bad day. He was just trying to help. He sat back and stretched his long legs out under the table, twirling the glass on the table. He wanted to tell her she didn't know how far from the truth she was, but kept his mouth shut.

Nina suddenly felt bad for the way she had fired off at him. She lifted her hands to her head, and sighed as she tried to rub the frustration from her temples, without agitating her eye. She then lifted her gaze to Jeff, and placed a hand on his wrist. He was stiff and rigid under her touch.

"Baby, I'm sorry. I'm just really frustrated and everything is happening at once. Please forgive me okay."

He was quite a moment, as the previous words she had said still sunk in. So that's how she really felt about him? She thought he depended on his money for everything.

When he hadn't answered, she squeezed his wrist softly. "Baby, please forgive me."

He looked up, "Okay." His answer was curt, and Nina knew he wasn't fully receptive of her apology.

They ordered dinner, and ate mostly in silence. Nina could tell he was still a little upset, because he didn't speak much on anything she asked him. When they were done and where walking out, he turned to her.

"Are you coming over?"

"I thought... I mean I didn't think you wanted..."

"Nina, you're always welcome. I said I was okay with our conversation."

Nina hesitated, what she wanted to do was go home and sulk about the way she had talked to him, but reconsidered. "Okay."

He opened her door and made sure she was in, before he got into his own car. He would just keep her words in his memory, when it came to any future help he tried to give her.

When they arrived at his house, he opened the door and reset the alarm, as Nina walked in past him. She placed her keys on his foyer table, and then turned to go upstairs; the routine they always adhered to. As she descended up the stairs to his bedroom, she noticed Jeff wasn't behind her. He was still acting distant, and frankly she thought he had every right to. She had been really harsh and mean to him for no reason.

Jeff picked up the universal remote, setting the temperatures for the whole house, and turning the lights on upstairs before Nina got there. He could be crazy for wanting her with him, after the things she had said, but he guess that's what love did to you. He went into his study, dimmed the lights to almost dark, and started the music. Mellow jazz sounds seeped from the wall speakers.

He took off his coat, draped it across the sofa, unbuttoned his shirt, fixed himself a drink from the bar, and fell back on the sofa. He stared at the skylights and breath in deeply.

*What the hell was he doing?* He hadn't been in a serious relationship in 4 years, and after the way things were left after Alicia, that was a good thing. He knew he hadn't been in love with her, he loved being with her at times, but really in love with her, wasn't a matter. He had been the bachelor, dating, with no strings attached since then. Could have and had had any woman he wanted. Now he had gone and fell in love, with a woman he now was thinking about spending the rest of his life with. And despite the drama it seemed she was causing, it didn't matter, he loved her just the same.

So this is what unconditional love was. He was 35 years old and still trying to figure out his own emotions. The woman kept secrets from him, didn't trust him, and then called him a rich, arrogant, mofo to his face, in so many words, and yet he loved her just the same. He was hurt by what she had said, but the love was there all the same. All his life he had felt like he didn't fit into the rich lifestyle that his parents provided for him. Unlike the other kids he went to school with, he didn't feel elite like they did, and when he was a teenager he found out why.

And though Nina always told him, he didn't understand her job and the Center and the kids she worked with, he felt connected to them by those ties that bound him to where he really came from; the background that made up his past; the tie that he had recently found about himself. The tie that answered his childhood questions of why he felt he didn't belong. But all Nina saw was him being arrogant and flaunting his money.

He sat on the edge of the sofa, and dropped his head into his hands, massaging his temples. He sat there trying to clear his head, listening to Shade sing him into a place of calmness. Then he had the sudden feeling he wasn't alone. He lifted his head, and set his gaze on the silhouette of Nina in the doorway. The dim light picked up the soft purple, sheer, sheath that she wore. It hit mid-thigh, with slits on both sides, exposing the matching thong she wore as well as every thing bear from her waist, butt, and thighs. She stood with her weight on one leg, almost fidgeting. She looked a bit nervous, but still beautiful and loving in the dim light.

When she saw his eyes meet hers, she stepped further into the doorway. When she spoke her voice was so soft, he almost didn't hear her over the mellow music.

"Jeff, I need to talk to you."

He drained the rest of his drink and sat the glass on the floor beside him, and then started staring at his hands. He couldn't look at her anymore, at least not now when his mind was confused, and she was looking the way she was looking. "So, go ahead."

Nina bit her bottom lip nervously. He wasn't going to make this easy. "Jeff, I just wanted to say again I'm sorry for the things I said to you earlier. It's just the whole day was one big mess. There was the fight with the kids, then the mess at the Center, and all of this on the anniversary of my parent's accident."

She got quite and didn't speak for a moment, and when she started again, her voice was shaky. "It's just, my biggest problem is bottling things in until I can't handle any more. And by the time I got to the restaurant with you, I was about to break, but I had no reason to take it out on you. I'm sure you know now, that having people help me isn't one of my strong points either. I just want you to forgive me, please."

Jeff didn't say anything. He didn't look up, just stared down at his hands in front of him.

Nina sniffled back any tears that wanted to appear. She took in a deep gulp of air.

"Jeff baby, please talk to me."

He rubbed his hands up and down his face a couple of times before answering.

"Nina, do you love me?"

She was confused for a moment. "Jeff, you know I love you."

"No, I don't. Because for the last few months I have been trying to make myself believe you do. Despite all the signs you're giving me, I've been telling myself you do love me. Because you are the only woman I have ever loved the way I love you. You mean the world to me, and tonight I saw you unhappy, and all I wanted to do was make you happy. Make you feel better about everything, so I offered to help. But instead of gratitude, I was told I was a rich, arrogant mofo, who flaunted his money."

"Jeff, I didn't say that. I-"

"In so many words that's what you said." He looked up at her for the first time, before going on. "And for me that was the breaking point. You see Nina you have been pushing me away for so long. Every step I take closer to you, you take 3 away. You don't trust me, you don't talk to me, and you won't let me help you. If I had known about this being the actual anniversary date of your parent's death, I would have tried to help you get through this day. And until tonight, I didn't take any of this personal, but tonight Nina, it hurt."

She couldn't hold in the tears anymore "Jeff, I'm sorry. Baby, I didn't want to hurt you."

"But you did." He was just staring at her. He was tired of walking lightly around Nina to pacify her. His stare was making Nina feel even guiltier. She lifted her hands to her eyes, wiping her tears away, and then looked at Jeff forcefully.

"Come here." He reached a hand out to her.

Nina stared at his hand for a moment. She then took a few steps slowly to him, taking his hand into hers. He pulled her to him, between his legs, lifted his hands to her bare waist and pressed his head into her stomach, feeling her warmness, and feeling her heartbeat through every nerve of her body.

Nina was caught off guard and for a minute, just stood there with her arms and hands lifted above his head. She looked down to where he tenderly rubbed his cheek against the sheer material next to her stomach; and then she dropped her hands to his head and rubbed it slowly. Tears began to stream down her face again.

"Jeff, I love you so much. And I never meant to hurt you. I promise I'll get better about this all, Jeff just don't give up on me."

He lifted his head and his eyes to meet hers. "I love you too much for that. If those were my intentions, I would have done that before now."

For a few seconds they just looked into each other's eyes. The seconds seemed like hours. In the pool of tears in her eyes, Jeff saw love; love that she couldn't hide for him. He knew she loved him, but along with that love, he saw fear again. And he couldn't make her believe that she could trust him enough to help her with that fear.

He placed tender kisses on her stomach, where his head had just laid. Then he slowly slide his hands up the sides of the sheer material, lifting it as his warm hands tingled her skin, and then he brought his lips to meet her warm bare flesh; kissing first her stomach, then moving his kisses south to her pelvis, and around the band of her thongs. He then pushed those to the floor, and in a quick, smooth motion, he swooped her over and onto the sofa.

He gently kissed the bruise under her eye, running his fingers over it softly. He then passionately kissed her lips. From there he left a trail of kisses down her body, until he reached what separated women from man. Indulging himself in her womanhood; loving her orally, while she showed her satisfaction vocally; calling his name and moaning with each twist, until her body jolted in shock, from his devouring her; and then he came up to meet her eyes, pushing his way into her as they joined; becoming one as they made love like never before.

After, Jeff shed the remainder of his clothes, grabbed the two afghans off of a near-by chair and wrapped himself and Nina in them, while they held each other's body close; the music still playing. Jeff nibbled her ear. She had her back to him, spooning herself into his form; giving him herself to caress. He brought his lips to her ear and whispered softly, "Are you warm enough, or would you like to go upstairs?"

Nina didn't want to move or go anywhere. Aside from the tenderness she was feeling from her breast being crushed in his tight embrace, this was heaven. Besides the bruise around her eye had taken away the thoughts of her breast aching, while they had made love. "No, this is just fine."

Jeff cupped his arms around her waist a little tighter, Nina grimaced to herself.

"Nina, can I ask you one thing?"

She was about to drift off sleep. "Humm, what's that?"

"Would you agree to let me help with the Center? I mean I think what you, Janette, and the others have going on there is terrific. And it would be terrible, if it all went away because of the funding not being there. I also know with an independent sponsor, who has their own money that isn't detected by State policies, would have a whole new avenue of programs and funding would be at your disposal for those kids. And you all would have more say in what decisions are made."

Nina smiled to herself. This man had just finishing licking her up one side and down the other in the freakiest way, and now he was talking business while lying naked on his study sofa. "And you just came up with all this?"

"I've just been thinking. Besides, I know how happy the Center makes you. I remember the first day you were beaming with smiles, when you showed me around and introduced me to those kids like a proud parent.

"Sometimes I get so emotionally involved with them; their lives, their school, and their well being, that I feel like they are mine, but then

I have to realize that they belong to someone else, and I have to take a few steps back into reality."

"You'd make a wonderful mother."

Nina was silent. She didn't want to go there right now. At that ironic moment, his hand grazed her scar, and she jerked. "We should get some sleep. I love you, goodnight." She turned over and kissed his lips, then settled back in her position, without waiting for a response.

Jeff knew that quick change of conversation meant she was on the verge of telling him her past again. On the verge of tearing down a wall.

# CHAPTER XXVI

O N FRIDAY, JUST AS JEFF had promised, they were on their way to the Outer Banks of North Carolina. Nina was satisfied with just the beach; being at some exotic island wasn't necessary, as long as she got to spend some time with Jeff. But Jeff had spent more time on his cell than he had talking to Nina on the way down as he drove. She stared out the window, and tried to tell herself that at least he was getting away, and he had just closed a 20 million dollar project, so there was probably a lot of loose ends to gather. So instead of being pissed off, she let her mind revert to brainstorming for the Center.

Jeff must have detected her disappointment; he looked over and placed a hand on her knee. Nina looked over at him, and he gave her a smile, as he talked with Cynthia about some papers he needed signed. Nina placed her hand on his and just held it as she turned back to look out across the country green woods of North Carolina.

**It was September, right at the fall of the year when the weather changes, and the leaves become rainbows of colors; the da**ys are warm and mild and the nights were chilled just enough to cuddle up with a warm body. The season was changing and soon she'd be a year older. A trying year it had been, but alive she would be nevertheless.

Jeff took his earpiece out of his ear, and looked over at Nina. "Babe, I promise I won't spend the whole weekend working on the phone."

"Okay." She said calmly. She didn't even look at him.

"I do have to meet up with someone tomorrow, just to sign some papers, and then that's it."

Nina looked at him confusingly, with her finely arched brows knitted together, "Jeff you came down here to do business?"

"Sweetie, I didn't. I mean I do have a meeting, but I figured afterwards I'd just want to spend the rest of the time with you."

Nina sighed and rolled her eyes. "Fine. She let his hand go, and turned her back to him as she stared angrily out the window.

"There's this little jazz place I want to take you tonight. Just me and you."

"Okay" was all she said.

"David and Kim are suppose to be coming out tomorrow, maybe you two can go shopping or something while I'm meeting."

'That's fine" Nina said. She knew what a meeting was for him, would turn into the whole trip.

"Nina, Baby, I know that we haven't been together for a couple of weeks, but this is a really big deal; $24million to be exact, and it's the first one I've done totally alone without my father. I just want to make sure everything is legit, so that's why I wanted to come out here and check these sites out. It's just a few meetings, baby and then it's you and me."

"Okay." She said curtly.

"Is there something else wrong?" he asked

"I just got a lot on my mind." She couldn't tell him that she was actually thinking about moving forward with the marriage thing, because she was now ready to have a baby. But that meant she also had to tell him about all the other things that until now she had done so well at hiding from him; like the likely chances of her not being able to carry a baby full term, or not getting pregnant at all. And then there was the new health issues she had going on. Besides she was sure the last thing on his mind, right now was having a baby. This also wasn't the moment that she wanted to discuss the Center either.

"You want to talk about it?" he asked looking over at her, then back at the road.

"Maybe later", she said and reached over to turn up Lauyrn Hill. Now was definitely not the time.

"So girl, tell me, I know you two have not even left the beach house since you've been here." Kim said as they browsed through the aisle of shoes at Sack's.

They had spent the day at the spa and now were doing some shopping; getting much needed retail therapy in Nina's opinion. She was hoping it would relieve some of her frustrations.

"You got part of that right, I haven't left the house until now, and Jeff on the other hand has been in meetings non-stop. I'm so glad you came. Last night he took me to this little jazz place, it was really nice, until we ran into one of his business associates. Then for the rest of the night I had to pretend to be enthused by their Constructing and building talk. He said he was sorry, but the night was gone to hell then."

"Well, Jeff wanted David to come out to see some sites he may want him to do some engineer work for, and since Kaleen is away with family, we decided to come on. Of course David jumps at the opportunity of work."

"Have they always been this way?"

"David use to be worse, but since I've had Kaleen, he's better. He wants to do the family thing, and be around more. Girl these are just the consequences of having a black man who loves to work, and loves his job. Besides this is how Jeff and his Dad have become so successful. They know at all times what is going on in their business, because they are in there working too. Look at it this way the more they work, the more shoes we can buy." Nina laughed with Kim.

"Well tonight after dinner I plan to make him forget about work. That white nightly I just bought will definitely be used. So if we don't see you guys tomorrow, you'll understand we're making up for lost times." She laughed

"I do, I may have some time to make up of my own. I'm childless for the weekend".

Nina noticed the way Kim lit up when she so-called complained about something Kaleen had done. It was true communism; the behavior of a mommy who while she's fussing about the child's latest bad habit, she wouldn't have it any other way. Nina found herself envying that. She didn't know what the hell was going on with her lately. This sudden need to nourish something or someone with the maternal emotions she was having. Maybe she needed to get a dog.

They did a little more shopping and then separated, assuring that they'd see each other that night when they went out. When Nina got back to the beach house, she was surprised to see Jeff.

"Hey" he said from the sofa were he laid watching TV.

"Hey, I thought you'd still be in meetings. What are you doing here?"

"I can't come back to be with the most beautiful woman in the world? I told you I was doing the meeting thing and then the rest of the time was for you."

"What's the catch?" Nina asked putting her bags down and putting her hands on her hips to look down at him. She knew there had to be some sort of catch, or joke, maybe there was even a camera somewhere hidden to get this joke for TV.

He sat up and put a hand on both sides of her waist pulling her to him. "There isn't one. I'm done working, it's just me and you for the next two days; no more work. I promise". He kissed her stomach through the pink peasant shirt she wore. The delicate material of the shirt, felt like it wasn't even there, as his lips burnt heat through her skin.

Nina couldn't believe she actually had him to herself now. They may just have to cancel dinner with David and Kim when she was done with him. She placed her hands behind his neck and smiled as he tickled her navel with kisses and he moved his face under her shirt now. He moved his hands to her knees and ran them up under her skirt, exposing her thighs, as he rubbed. It felt soooooooooooooooo good! God she loved this man. For something that was so wrong just felt so good.

It had been over 2 weeks since they had actually taken their time with each other. Even the day before when they got there, neither were in the mood, because of the awkward ride in; and then last night, after the way dinner ended, they didn't really have makeup sex like normally, it was more of he was tired, and he had to be up early. She had really wanted to discuss the Center with him over dinner but after the way his client was really persistent about them joining him, there was no talk among themselves.

But now he was touching her the way he did when they were really taking their time making love. She let out a sigh as he pulled her panties down a little and kissed her just waxed pelvic area; the scent of flowers lingered in the air. He pushed her panties to the floor, then took her hand in his and pulled her on top of him.

"Did you just get that done for me, or is this just coincidence."

"Oh, it's definitely for you", she said leaning to kiss him while she wrapped her arms around his head and held him close. Her heat was rising while he ran his warm hands across her back. Then it happened. The same thing that had been happening non-stop for the past week. Nina had hated the sound so much, she didn't even want to hear her own. His cell phone was chirping away, but Nina was determined she wasn't letting him go. He finally got his lips free.

"Sweetie, my phone". He was struggling to get free.

"Jay you said no more work".

"Sweetie I know but this one is important", he said reaching behind her, to the coffee table to pick up his phone from the collection of electronic devices that kept him connected to the business world no matter where he was.

She sighed and rolled her eyes as he said hello. Yeah, they all seem to be more important than her lately. He patted her thigh to let him up, as he went to the kitchen talking. Nina glared at him, and collapsed back on the couch. *So much for the moment.* She flipped through the channels. *Might as well watch some TV at least it wouldn't get her excited then leave.*

———⬥⬥⬥———

Nina sat quietly playing with the sloping collar of the white dress she had bought that day. With its sexy, slits up both sides, and her bone color stiletto heel sandals, she had hopes it would make Jeff want her all during dinner. He said he loved her in white; her chocolate complexion in white, was so damn sexy to him. But all he had time to say was "you look nice", before they left to come meet David and Kim. The rest of the time he was back on his phone.

They were at this dim lighted Italian spot, and everyone was talking but her. How could she when she'd rather be on some horizontal surface with the man next to her, doing horizontal things, but he obviously didn't care? She was aching she wanted him so bad. *So what if she had some obsession with sex, at least it was only sex with a certain individual.*

"Nina, are you okay; you haven't said much", David asked?

"I'm okay. I just got a lot on my mind", Nina said looking at Kim. Kim gave her an I-feel-you-girl look, to let her know she knew what the problem was.

Jeff placed his fingers on her lower ching and rubbed her cheek with his finger."You sure you okay?" He whispered.

"I just have a little headache." She lied.

"Maybe you'll feel better, after we eat."

"Yeah", she said, 'Maybe."

Dinner came and Nina decided there was no need in being the party pooper any longer, and joined in the conversation. It wasn't David or Kim's fault. When they were almost done, the waiter came over to whisper to Jeff. Nina looked puzzled.

Jeff moved to get up. "I have a phone call." He said, mainly to Nina.

Nina was about feed up with this shit. "Jeff?' she said looking up at him questioningly.

"Sweetie it won't take but a minute", he said getting up and following the waiter.

Nina sighed, put her fork down and closed her eyes to maintain her temper, as she sat back in her chair. She had just forgot about this whole work thing and was trying to have fun, now they track him down at the restaurant. They couldn't even have dinner peacefully.

David detected her anger, from her body language. "Nina, he's a workaholic; a very busy man who loves his work."

Nina didn't want to make a scene in front of Kim and David. "I know", was all she said and tried to smile and retract her anger. A few minutes passed while they listened to the band, then the waiter came back with a bottle of champagne and a folded piece of paper.

"Ms. Jackson, Mr. Smith had to leave and wanted me to bring you and your friends this bottle of champagne and this note. He said to apologize, but something came up. If you'd like I could call for you a driver?"

Nina was pissed, and there was no hiding it now. She gasped, "I can't f-king believe this", she said snatching the note from the waiter.

David and Kim looked on in silenced. The waiter asked again if she needed a ride called.

David answered, because Nina was too upset and in shock. "Sir, we'll see that she makes it home; thank you."

After a minute, Nina was still shaking her head. "I can't believe him, he can't spend one f-king evening with me."

Nina maybe it was an emergency", Kim tried to fend for him

"And he couldn't even come to tell us that himself. I'm beginning to believe there is more to this than just work."

'Nina, I've known Jay for a long time. He is crazy about work; its just something he loves to do. It's been the cause for him having a lack of a social life, but I can guarantee you, he's even crazy about you, and there is nothing else or anyone that means more."

Nina sighed and tapped the corner of the note on the table. She had almost forgot she had it. She unfolded it and read:

*Sweetheart, I know by now you are tired of me and my consumption with work. It seems like work is more important than you are these past few days, but that is the farthersest thing from the truth. The truth is I'm a 33-years old man who, has everything that anyone could ever want, but I'm not happy and won't be until I have you fully to share it with. So what I need to know is...*

Nina stopped reading, she was confused; that was it. He stopped writing right there. She turned the paper over looking for more, as if the words had dropped off the paper somewhere. She was confused and puzzled.

"Nina, what's wrong?" Kim asked.

"He writes this note and didn't even finish it, where is that waiter?" she asked turning around and motioning for him to come over. "Sir was there more to this?' she asking holding up the note.

"Oh, Ms. Jackson, I am so sorry. I seem to be having a long night myself; here it is." He reached in his pocket and pulled out another piece of paper, and then he stood there waiting for her to read it.

Nina eyed the waiter a little meticulously, and then decided she wouldn't question him as to why he was still there, and instead she turned back to her note? It read, in bold capital letters: **"WILL YOU**

MARRY ME?" Then the waiter placed a ring box on the table, and Nina's hand went up to her mouth almost automatically. She looked over at David and Kim and they wore we-knew-it-all-along, grin. Nina opened the box, and there sat, the biggest diamond she had ever seen up close in her lifetime.

"OhmyYesgosh", followed by the well of tears that had collected in her eyes is all she could get out.

She didn't even realize that Jeff was standing behind the waiter, until he said, "So what's it going to be?"

Nina still had her hand up to her mouth. The last thing she wanted to do was to cry, but it was too late, the tears were already flowing. She bit her bottom lip, and took in a deep breath. "Yeah", she said through tears and stood to kiss him. Applause went up from the crowd, they had created as an audience.

When she had contained herself again and things settled down, she looked over at David and Kim. "You all have been plotting against me haven't you?"

"Man, you should have seen your face when that waiter said Jay had to leave, you were ready to spit fire." David laughed.

"And you, Kim?"

"Girl, you know if it had been anything bad, I would have never agreed, but it was for a good cause, besides I got to do some shopping out of the deal."

"You mean the whole trip was about this?" she asked Jeff.

"Baby, that deal was closed even before we left. All those phone calls were just to make sure your ring was going to be here in time and being sure that this plan was going to work. I knew you were pissed at me for working too much lately, so I had to play that up in order to not make you curious in any other way. I didn't plan to meet associates here, that was coincidental, but the only meeting I had, was meeting David at the golf course to play some holes, after we made plans for tonight."

Nina smiled, "You know you were on my list, right?" she said to Jeff.

"You don't know how hard it was for me to play this out. It is way too hard lying to you, because your eyes are like swords when you're mad; I was afraid you'd cut me in two."

"So are we forgiven, Nina?" Kim asked.

She smiled, "This time" and leaned over to kiss Jeff on the lips. "I Love You.'

"I love you too", he said kissing her back.

Kim and David both cleared their throats. "I think we should get these two out of here, before they turn the hose on us." David said.

Nina pulled away, and wiped lipstick off of Jeff's lips. "I am ready to get him alone." She said mischievously.

Jeff turned motioning for the check, "Please hurry man", he said across the room to the waiter.

They all laughed. Nina smiled again, she had found her knight and shining armor, if only her parents could be here to see him.

---

Jeff pulled Nina back. "Don't move yet, stay right there. I forgot how much I had been missing having you like this, the past few weeks."

She laid her head on his chest. He was right, she had missed this too. At the moment she felt like she was in some fairytale, especially since she had said yes to a proposal she couldn't possibly go through with. But she wanted to live in this fairytale a little longer, before telling him the truth and ending everything.

"Jeff, what does your parents have to say about this?"

"I told them, Dad was excited."

"And your mom?" she rose up and looked at him.

"She's mom. She can deal with it. Don't you worry about it? As for your Auntie and Uncle, I had to call them to let them know, and your Uncle had a little talk with me. Your Auntie said she couldn't stand keeping the secret, so the only way she could not tell you, was if she didn't talk to you until this weekend was over."

"No wonder she hasn't returned my calls." Nina laughed. A moment passed, "Jeff, what about the date?"

"Whenever, you're ready, it's up to you. I personally like the sooner the better. It would be nice if you'd move in now though. This late night and early morning leaving is too much. I want to see you when I close my eyes each night as well as when I open them the next morning. ."

"We'll talk about that later." She became quiet and rubbed his chest for a moment before speaking again. "I know big and fancy is something that you and your family want, but Jeff without my parents here, it brings a lot of feelings and emotions up and I just want something simple & small."

He stroked her hair, "Okay, whatever you want."

Nina wanted to show him just how much she loved him. Maybe morning would be the best time to tell him everything else, right now she wanted to continue making herself believe that all this could come true.

# WASH AWAY THESE STORMS OF PAST AND TEAR DOWN THESE WALLS OF PAIN

*Do not remember the former things, nor consider the things of old.*
*Behold, I will do a new thing, now it shall spring forth;*
*shall you not know it? I will even make a road in*
*the wilderness and rivers in the desert.*
*Isaiah 43:18,19*

Jeff slowly brought himself back to a conscience state from the deep sleep that had consumed him. Still groggy, he opened his eyes to the dark room that was dimly lit from the moonlight coming through the balcony door. The sound of the ocean lapping against the shore lulled the night away. And the rain sung a lullaby as it hit the roof and the balcony. This weather was the best time to be in bed, holding close the most beautiful woman that would soon be his wife.

He turned over on his side, extending his arms to take Nina into his warmth, but his hands meet only cold and emptiness where her warm body had laid before he feel asleep. He sat up looking around the room. He suddenly realized that it was odd that the balcony doors were opened. After Nina had taken a long hot bath she had been chilly so he had closed them.

Her whole spirits had changed from the way she was after they had came in from dinner. One minute she was talking about the wedding and was acting like the happiest woman in the world every time she looked at the ring. Next, she had just stopped talking, and completely closed up. When he had questioned her as to what was wrong she had said she was just tired from the excitement and needed to rest.

Jeff knew it was more. She had that same fear in her eyes that she got the night she slipped into that anxiety attack. He believed it was all coming real to her all of a sudden. He didn't want to force her to tell him, but he wanted her to talk to him about this, so he could assure her that he wanted nothing more than to be with her; the other issues were irrelevant. Just him spending the rest of his life with her was what was important. But she had to trust him.

He got out of the bed and pulled on a pair of pants from a near by chair, then padded across the cold tiled floor to the double French doors before going to find out where Nina had went. Just as he stepped out on the balcony into the cool air, the smell of sea and rain meet him, and in the corner of the balcony, just where the roof dropped off and gave way to the drizzling rain that fell, sat Nina. Half naked, on one of the loungers; hugging her knees to her chest, in a fetal position, rocking. Her hair was sticking to her face from where the rain had drenched it. Before he could think twice, he was kneeled beside her, getting soaked in the rain too.

"Nina, baby, you're getting soaked out here."

She just kept rocking and shaking her head. When he lifted her chin for her to look into his eyes, even the rain, couldn't hide her red, pain-filled eyes.

"Baby, what's wrong?" His own heart was beating fast now.

Between sobs, she tried to speak. "Jeff, I, I have to talk to you. I have to tell you."

"OK baby, but can't we do it inside? You're going to get sick out here. You're wet, and you have no clothes on."

She was still shaking her head. "I have to tell you now."

Jeff dropped his head in his hand a moment. He had to get her out of the rain. He quickly scooped her up in his arms and whisked her inside. He sat her in a chair by the door, closed the doors, and then went into the bathroom to retrieved towels. She was shaking and still rocking when he returned. He went about dabbing water off of her, and then grabbed the blanket from the bed to wrap around her. She was still sobbing.

He sat on the bed in front of her, and took her pruned, cold hands into his. "Baby, what arc you so upset about?"

She stopped staring at the floor and lifted her swollen eyes to look at him. As if her body had suddenly shifted, she stopped shivering and looked firmly at him.

"Jeff, I can't marry you."

Wrinkles creased his head in confusion. He wasn't quite sure if he had heard her correctly, or if this was all part of a dream.

"Nina, what are you talking about?"

She began to talk quickly. "Jeff, when you started asking me about our future and starting a family, I freaked out. When you mentioned to me about a commitment, I'd have anxiety attacks. You always said that every step you took toward me, I'd take three steps back, and that I was hiding behind a wall. Well, all those things you said were true, and until tonight, I secretly knew that we would never have a long-term future together. There would be no marriage, and no kids, because I wasn't the right person for you. No matter how many times you told me you loved me, and that I was the only person in this world you wanted to be with. And tonight, for a brief moment, I forgot all those promises I had secretly made to myself about us not having a future. Because when you asked me to marry you, I truly wanted to be your wife and start a family with you. For a moment, I was in this fairy tale, where I really was thinking about wedding plans.

"Then when we came back here and made love, and you went to sleep, it hit me. I had lost my damn mind. There is no way I could keep lying to you. I had to tell you what I had been hiding from you so long, because I knew it would be the end of us."

Jeff was so confused, but at the same time knew that the moment had finally come for Nina to tell him what he thought he knew all of. He kept quite. He was finally getting to see what had been going on behind her fear filled eyes all these months. And the pain he hadn't been able to reach, or take away from her.

"All I ever wanted to do was go to college, get a job helping people, meet a nice man to marry and start a family with; then live happily together like my parents; carefree, loving, and devoted to each other, no matter how much they fussed and got on each others nerves sometimes. Well I went to college, got a job with Child Protective Services, and I remember my first 3 months were so stressful, because I would get so emotionally involved with those kids. I'd bring all of their problems home with me and it was emotionally and physically draining me. I started getting sick, having these really bad cramps and pains. I tried to ignore them, but they got so painful, so I had to finally make an appointment to go to the doctor.

"Well the day that I went to the Dr. my parents had been on a trip to the Mountains. We were always close, so my parents of course called to know what the Dr said. I didn't want to tell them over the phone that I had been told that I had a tumor on my cervix, and even though I tried to play it down, they still got upset and insisted on coming home early. I kept begging them to stay, but they said they needed to be there with me. They called to let me know that they were leaving out, and would be home that evening around 8pm. There was a really bad hurricane coming so I decided to go over to their house, and await for their arrival. Being tired myself; I fell asleep, and was awakened by the phone. It was a State Trooper, telling me there had been an accident, and that I needed to get to the hospital as soon as possible.

"I remember the whole way there, I was thinking they are alright, because they wouldn't make me come all the way to the hospital if they were dead alreadyYe; they had to be okay."

Nina paused as she remembered the weight in the pit of her stomach when she had gotten to the Emergency room that night. Her hands began to shake and she started wringing them among each other to stay calm. Jeff watched her closely, and then put a calming hand on her knee.

"The storm had knocked two big trees across the highway, and my Dad had crashed into one. He was too close to stop and avoid it when he realized what it was. My mom had a lot of internal bleeding and died the next morning, my dad died two hours later. No one ever told him, but I think that he knew she had left, and being here without her wouldn't have been the same, even if he had to sacrifice being here with me. Nina took a deep breath."

"For me, I stop circulating in the real world. I started isolating myself. Dealing with my parents death, made me not even care about the tumor, and when I did, it was like more burdens being added. I started going to counseling and therapy, to help me deal with the lost, as well as some of the depression. As time went by, and after doing away with a lot of anti-depressant drugs they were trying to make me take, I got better. The medication for depression wasn't needed anymore and I was just on medication for what was going on in my body. Things were going a little better, since the doctor told me, they'd do their best to just treat me with meds for the tumor. So I decided to just bombard myself with work. I started volunteering at a lot of Community Centers, tutoring, anything that would keep me busy, and keep my mind off of feeling lonely. Auntie Laurie and Uncle George were helpful, but it wasn't enough."

"That's when I met Quinton. A breath of fresh air is what he seemed like then. We became just really good friends; he was a really good listener. At that moment, I couldn't talk to Janette. I needed someone who was a stranger to everything in my life. I needed someone who wouldn't be partial to being sympathetic and pitying me, and that was Q.

After months went by, we became more than just friends. After about 6 months, I was moving in with him, despite what Auntie Laurie thought. It was as if I was trying to do away with all the pain in my life and starting over new, doing things I would have never normally done. It really upset Auntie Laurie and Uncle George, but I was being selfish, falling into what I thought was best for me. All along I was just really running away from my loneliness."

"Things were perfect with Q in the beginning. He was such a gentleman, and all he talked about was marrying me, and wanting me to be the mother of his child. He was almost thirty with no kids that I knew of, and was very set about having one. The marriage part was something he wanted to do when things got settled the way he wanted them to with the club and his real estate business. Then I got sick again. This time the doctors wanted to do away with it all by surgery. At that moment things started changing with Q and I. It was like he slowly started losing interest in me. And then after the surgery, the doctor informed me that my chances of having a successful pregnancy were now slim, because of such a huge portion of my cervix being removed with the tumor. I think when Q found this out his behavior that had been slowly changing for the worse toward me, suddenly did a nosedive and he was being more obvious and bold about not coming home. He had lost interest in me and our relationship, because I couldn't 100% full proof provide him with the thing he wanted me for the most in the beginning; a baby."

"His preoccupation with other women started becoming an issue as these women boldly were calling the house, leaving threatening notes on my car, and making passes at him in front of me, as if they were sure I didn't care. Eventually, I didn't. He constantly told me there was no one else, he was always working, or with his boys when he wasn't with me."

"I think he started feeling guilty because he promised we'd work on our relationship. Well, I finally got him to at least spend one evening a week home with me. No work, no friends, no company, no telephones, just he and I. It was on one of these evenings that I got pregnant. He was so happy, he suddenly turned into the guy I first met, and fell in love with, again. He started coming home early every night, working at his club less, preparing for fatherhood. Then at 3 1/2 months, I miscarried. He never came out and said he was angry with me, but his actions showed that he blamed me for losing 'his' child. Needless to say, he slowly returned to his old ways.

"I was tired; so tired of being alone. So tired of being in the situation I was in. I finally got up the nerve to call my Auntie Laurie one day, after a year and half, and apologized. I missed them so much, they were all I had left of family, and I had abandoned them for a man.

"I wanted to leave Q, but I loved him, and even though I never had proof, deep down inside I knew he was with someone else. He still was cordial to me, and I felt like he still cared about me deeply. He provided everything I needed and he still respected me as his girlfriend when it came to the public. So even though he wasn't there all the time, I couldn't make myself leave.

"Then one day, all the proof to make me pack my bags and leave, showed up on our doorsteps. His 3 month old baby boy, and his baby's mother. The baby was beautiful, and the mother was very respectful, and she told me she just wanted me to know, because Q had been promising her he would tell me, and she knew he hadn't, and if she was I she would want to know. I thanked her and started packing. I didn't need a paternity test, because that baby she was holding was the spitting image of Q's baby pictures, and he had the same eyes that I had fell in love with.

"I was beyond hurt. Everything that I loved was being taken away from me because of a sickness my body had incumbent. I'd lost my parents and the one man I thought I'd ever love, because I couldn't provide him with the one thing he wanted: a baby."

She looked over into Jeff's eyes, "So see Jeff, when you started talking about the same things, I knew if I really loved you I had to hide my health issues from you if I didn't want to run you away too. I mean we were already from two different social levels, your family wasn't the fondest of me, and I came from something different from anything you've ever been involved with. The strip clubs, the street life, I know those are the things that you probably never even seen up close. I just wanted to enjoy being in love with the wonderful black man you are, for as long as I could. I was just being happy that I was able to fall in love again." Tears started forming in her eyes again. She pressed her fingers to her eyelids to push away at some of the pain leaking from her emotions. "So, I guess my time is up. The past 8 months have been the best moments of my life Jeff. I know that being in love happens more than once, and the second time around for me, was the best." She sniffled back some tears, and gave a little smile.

"So I can't marry you because I can't give you a son to carry on you and your father's name, or a daughter for you to marry off, so that she and her husband can carry on the family business, or the family that you want to carry on the traditions of the royal Smiths."

The tears that she had been managing to hold on to, exploded from her and her body began to shake with each sob again. Jeff sat staring at her in silence. He didn't move to touch her, but just watched as she wiped at tears with the still damp towel. She had told him mostly what Jeannette had already shared with him, but it was somehow different coming from her. He could see more of the pain she had been through. He now understood the reason she tried to hide so many scares both emotionally and physically, and he was glad he never pushed her too far to explain. The things that made her such a stubborn, strong, independent woman were so much more obvious now. He even understood now what her Auntie was talking about that day in her kitchen. He remembered her exact words had been, 'when you find out you will understand what makes her who she is". Well now he did; he saw it clearly.

He raised a hand to push the damp hair from her face, and then skimmed her cheek with his hand. She was calmer now, and eventually looked up at him. She held his stare in hers a moment then turned her eyes to the ring he had put on her finger just hours ago, which seemed like centuries. That solid piece of ice, sitting on a stage of platinum, was still unbelievable to her that she was wearing it. She started to take it off, but he stopped her. He knew what she was about to do.

He spoke for the first time. "You keep that."

Her voice was still shaky. "Jeff, I can't keep a ring like this. First of all I don't deserve it after the way I've strung you along for the last few months, and second this isn't a gift you let your ex keep. I know for a fact, this isn't even a friendship ring."

"But it is the ring that I want my wife to have, at least until one of those anniversaries down the road, where we get you something bigger." He was smiling that gorgeous smile.

Nina was shocked. *Something bigger, this damn ring was already weighing her hand down*, she thought. Besides that, he was talking crazy. "Jeff, did you hear any of what I said the last half hour to you?"

"Yes, and frankly I think that's a terrible cope out for reneging on a yes that you have already given to marry me." He stretched his long legs out, and sat back on his hands to look at her.

Nina dropped her mouth open. He had lost his damn mind. "Jeff, that wasn't a story, it was all the truth. I really can't promise you the family you want."

"No, but you can promise me that you can at least try at having one either. Your doctor said the chances were slim, they didn't say they were impossible. And if trying doesn't get it, we can always adopt; I'm a faithful believer in adoption. None of that is the issue right now; the issue right now is you. You are the best thing that has ever happened to me. I love you and I want to spend the rest of my life with you, until the day I leave this world, which I hope is one day before you, because I can't live without you."

Tears formed again in Nina's eyes. The man was unbelievable. With all her drama, her history, her issues and her mishaps, the man still wanted her in his life.

"So I'll ask this question again, will you marry me, Nina Jackson?"

She couldn't get any words out, so she just nodded her head.

He stood, pulled her body up to meet his, and kissed her. They stood there for what seemed like hours. The sun was peaking over the ocean when they let each other go. And all traces of rain were a memory. It was a new day. Nina was afraid to speak, because she was afraid she might wake up from the dream she was having.

"Baby, I don't think anything could make this anymore wonderful and perfect than it is right now." He whispered in her damp hair.

"I could think of one thing."

"What's that?"

"If your mother would accept and like me."

Jeff smiled and looked down at her sheepishly. That grin he got, when he knew something she didn't. "My mother has loved you from the moment she laid eyes on you."

Nina pulled away. "Jeff don't say things to make me feel better. Despite what you say, just because you are her only boy and she's protective of you, can't account for the way that woman loathes me."

"Some of that is true; she is overprotective of me, but I'm not talking about that. From the first time my mother saw you she loved the fact that I was with you."

Nina took her arms away from his waist, folded them across her chest, stuck her hip out, and pursed her lips. "I know you're not talking about the seminar her and her Women's organization came to, that was only because I wasn't in her son's circle then."

"No, I'm not talking about then."

"I would hardly call, her trying to hook you up with one of your old girlfriends at their summer party, liking me."

"No, not that either."

Nina was annoyed; she shook her head, and lifted her arms, palms out. "Then when Jeff?"

He smiled that charming smile again. "I believe she told me you were scared straight to see some one come through my backdoor, while you were standing in my refrigerator; ham, cheese, eggs in your arms and grapes hanging from your mouth. You were wearing a pair of bikini underwear and a T-shirt, and embarrassment on your face."

Nina smiled herself, as she thought back on the morning, of the weekend she had first spent over his house. That was many, many months ago, but his mother hadn't been there just-.

"Jeff, Kay was the only one there. Your mother wasn't there. Thank God, because I was embarrassed as it was for Kay to see me like that. Can you imagine what your mother would have thought if she had seen me dressed like that in your kitchen?"

"That you were a very beautiful, and smart young woman."

Nina raised her brow at him; she was getting more and more confused by the moment.

"Nina, there is something not many people know about. Actually no one knows besides my family. I think I've just told David a few years ago. When I was growing up I never quite fit into the elite social groups that I was forced to be a part of because of my family's money. The older I got, the more it bothered me that I was different; extremely different from Karen, because she was born to spend money and be a part of the elite society we were apart of. I think it bothered my mother more than it did me, because it hurt her to see her son not living up to the potential of his money he would one day inherit.

"So when I was 17, applying for a lot of ivy league colleges whose tuition cost more than small family homes in the South, I had to know why I was set so far apart from my family. I couldn't deal with the thoughts and confusion anymore. When I questioned my father this time, he looked upon me with a stern look, and told me it was time I knew. I was adopted. My real mother had been a woman who was single when she got pregnant. She couldn't afford to keep me alone, so she wanted to find a good home for her unborn baby to be raised in.

See my Mother and Dad didn't think they could have kids for a long time, so they wanted to adopt. Through some acquaintances they met Kay; who just wanted to do what was right by her unborn child. A few years after me, is when Karen surprisingly popped up. Anyway, my Dad assured me that my real mother did it for me, because she still lived here in North Carolina. So after I discussed it with them I had to find her; not because I felt she owed me anything, but mainly because I wanted to see the me I had been feeling all those years, and couldn't quite comprehend.

I found out she had a small business in catering. She had never married, and didn't have any other kids. When I found her, it was a relief. We got to know each other, but we didn't try to hold each other to a relationship. She had been keeping up with me through the media. That was almost 17 years ago; to this day we are very close. My parents are okay with it, because they and I know I love them, and they will always be my parents. But Kay is a part of my make-up, my background, my roots. She doesn't try to make me call her mom, she doesn't try to tell me how to live my life, and she doesn't try to be to me what she knows I already have, but she's important to me just the same. She enjoys doing for me little things like watching over the house, and being that woman that makes the house come together. She's never asked me for anything. And she's more of a friend than I could ever ask of anyone. Kay will always be my Kay. I know that's a weird relationship, but that's just the way it is."

Nina stood in awe for a moment. So many things were questionable; he looked and acted so much like his father? Kay was his mother? His real biological mother? That explained the relationship and the love she could feel when they were around each other. It also explained why Jeff was so different. The fact that he hadn't told her before now was understandable. But the fact that he chose now to tell her was important. He was really serious about their relationship, he entrusted something in her, that only his family knew.

"But Jeff, you and your father are so much alike. I mean you look so much like him and you have his name and-?"

Jeff smiled again. "You know that old saying about a dog and his owner starting to look alike as time goes by? I guess that came into play with us, and also the fact that I found out down the line of the family tree, my dad and Kay are somehow related distantly.

"So, you see that first time Kay saw you, she told me there was something special about you, and though she saw it too, I already knew. And despite what you think, my mother has to accept you for who you are, and I think she's a little threatened by you, because she knows how good you are for me, and knows that she can't keep me from spending the rest of my life with you. Baby you are stuck with me."

Nina smiled, because for once in her life she felt her true self and she had gained tremendously from being her true self. No more losing out on the happiness of life, because of what bad cards she had been dealt. Now, her walls had been torn down, she was free, and it was a new day.

Sahra Patterson

Dear God,

*My life has taken me on a journey of pain, filled with stormy, cloudy days.*
*But what didn't kill me, made me stronger, it just*
*took me a long time to realize that.*
*And if there is anything that I will never forget,*
*is when you take something away,*
*It doesn't necessarily mean you have forgotten me, but that*
*You have something bigger planned for my life.*
*So I take those things that once were,*
*As experience in preparation for what is next to come.*
*And I thank your for crumbled walls, peaceful*
*endings, and new beginnings.*
*And most of all, thank you for not giving up on*
*me. For the lost and lonely need love too.*
*In Jesus Name,*
*-Nina*

## AFTER THE WALLS CRUMBLE AND THE STORMS HAVE CEASED

*6 Months later*

As Nina laid in her husband's arms, she thought to herself that life was so good. God had made all her pain worthwhile, and had given her happiness to replace all her losses. Yeah she had scares now, both emotionally and physically, but they were her proof that she had made it through the struggles, and that she was a survivor. She was the wife to a wonderful man, the new Auntie/Godmother to a beautiful new baby, and Director of the newest Community Center in Charlotte that catered to kids that needed it most. But most of all she had a healed healthy body; cancer free. Yeah life was wonderful.

In the last six months so much had happened. In November she and Jeff had gotten married in a small ceremony in St Thomas, where just his parents, Jennifer, David, Kim, Kaleen, Warren, Jeanette, Kay and her Auntie and Uncle had attended. Though Mr. and Mrs. Smith agreed to the private ceremony, they could not give up the opportunity to give them a lavish and elegant reception when they had returned home.

The New Year, brought new life. In January she had a mastectomy that removed all lumps. On January 18th, Natalia Rayn Taylor entered the world at 7lbs, 5 oz. She was a beautiful combination of both of Net and Warren. Nina thought she was even more proud than they were. In the 4 months she had been in the world, Nina and Jeff had spoiled her ridiculously, and the little thing didn't even know who they were yet.

The State pulled out from the Center officially in November, but that wasn't before Jeff had bought the building, as well as some of the other properties in that area. With the New Year, the Center was renovated and operating in its new name, "Life's Survival Community Center", under the supervision of Nina as Director, and Net, upon her return from maternity leave, as Co-Director. The other property that Jeff had purchased around the neighborhood was under construction to become the home to a newly constructed apartment, townhouses, and strip mall. All of this opened opportunities for new programs, jobs, and prosperous growth for the whole community.

Nina had given up her job at the Hospital and had handled most of the new building preparations alone with the old staff and the new while Net helped as much as possible from home on the phone. Kim and David had even helped in the process. It was ironic but the same people, who had hated Nina, now were more cordial to her. Nina had even hired Tonya Clark as the Center's new receptionist.

With all the new development in town, as well as projects that Smith & Smith had on their plate, married life for Jeff and Nina wasn't all honeymoon since there was so much work to be done. They barely spent an awake moment in each other's presence. They sneaked any free moment they could with each other, whether it was during lunch or a quickie in the afternoon, or between meetings at one of their offices. And even those had been scarce since her mastectomy.

But right now, Nina was lying in her husband's arms, on a hammock in the quiet garden of their backyard on a sunny June Sunday afternoon. They had turned down dinner invitations from both friends and family for the day and after church had rushed home, sent anyone who wanted to stick around away, locked the doors and escaped to the privacy of their backyard to be alone. It was crazy how it was just the two of them in this huge house most of the time, but they were always occupied with everything else but each other. But this afternoon they promised it would only be each other they would be occupied with.

Jeff had wanted to just retreat to the bedroom and stay there until morning, but Nina had talked him into some quiet, quality time first; some time where they could talk to each other, or better yet, listen to each other. This was heaven to her.

"What are you smiling so hard about", Jeff asked?

She turned her head to look up at Jeff. "I'm happy that's all. I could feel this way forever."

"Good", he kissed her lips, "Can we go upstairs now?"

"Jeff, come on, just enjoy the moment okay"

"Alright, alright."

They both fell silent again, listening to the chirping of the birds above their heads and then the natural chirping started sounding electronic-like, and Jeff was reaching for his phone.

"Jeff we promised no phones."

"Baby, I know, but I was out here before I realized I had it on me and didn't want to go back in."

"Well you don't have to answer it."

"You're right." He said looking at it confusingly. It was his sister Karen, calling on his business line. That was weird.

Nina looked at his wrinkled creased brow. "What is it?"

"I think its Karen."

Nina was confused herself. Since she had become part of the Smith family, her new sister-n-law had done a 180. She had gone out of her way to make herself available and friendly to Nina. At first it frightened Nina, but when she was in the hospital after her surgery, she saw just how genuine Karen was being with her desire to be a supportive friend to Nina. It showed in the way she stopped by everyday, and called to see if it was anything she could do? Since then they had been spending girl time together pretty frequently. So Karen knew that Nina and Jeff hadn't been spending much quality time together lately, and their plan was to try to catch up today.

"I think I should answer it."

Nina sat up and watched Jeff's facial expressions changed as his sister talked hurriedly on the other end. She suddenly had a cold feeling. Something was going wrong. Right there in her backyard on the prettiest June Sunday afternoon; there was a storm brewing.

"Ok, we'll be right there."

Jeff lowered his phone and was on his feet before Nina could move. "Dad just had a heart attack."

Nina rushed behind him as he ran.

The sun was still shining on the outside, but the skies in their life had just clouded over.

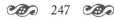

Printed in the United States
by Baker & Taylor Publisher Services